firefly wishes

FIREFLY COVE
BOOK 1

ASHLEY TEMPLIN

This book is dedicated to all the women who love the idea of red flags, but would go absolutely feral if a man researched a car seat buckle tutorial to keep their little one safe.

Ladies, meet Max Daniels.

prologue

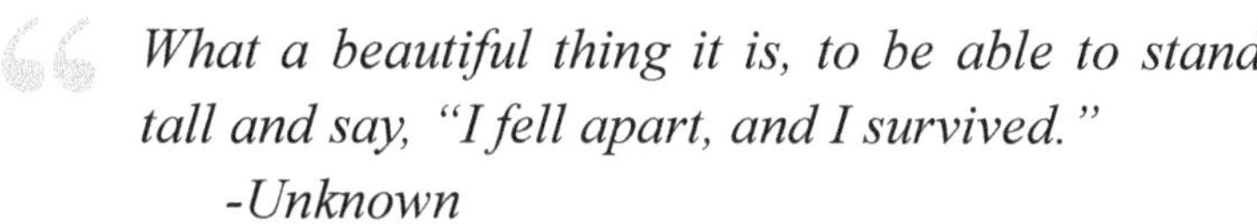 *What a beautiful thing it is, to be able to stand tall and say, "I fell apart, and I survived."*
-Unknown

THE SOUNDS OF SLAMMING DOORS, *frustrated shouts echoing through the hallway, and the occasional drunken stumble to the bedroom were a familiar soundtrack to my life. I'd grown accustomed to the sounds of impending doom. I never imagined I'd live to see thirty; it always seemed like just an illusion.*

Year after year, the same hollow promise repeated itself: "Just one more year," a mantra that numbed the ache of unending struggle. It became a relentless internal battle, first for a month, then a week, a day, an hour, and finally just another minute, each increment a struggle against the urge to give up. The inevitability of death felt like a familiar weight, a constant companion. With fervent hope, I pleaded to any higher power that might hear my prayers to grant me refuge.

See, when each day brings unbearable suffering and agony, death doesn't seem so bad. It seems almost peaceful.

For years, I tiptoed through life, each step measured and cautious, the silence heavy with unspoken tensions. I prayed every single day for it to end. With each passing day bringing no relief, the hope for divine intervention dwindled, the silence of the heavens a heavy weight on my soul. After all the years of unimaginable suffering, I craved escape; anything was preferable to this existence.

My only comfort was the subtle, persistent fluttering in my belly, a fragile, insistent beat of life. Each night, I whispered my hopes to it under the cover of darkness. I shared the daily beauty, whispering promises of a brighter tomorrow. All while silently praying for it all to end. Yet, this child was my salvation. Realistically, he couldn't hurt me if he knew, right? Dreams, like boundless oceans, hold vast, uncharted wishes.

ANOTHER DAY HAS PASSED, *the sun setting, casting long shadows, and I'm still here, breathing. The shift from living to merely surviving wasn't a sudden event, but rather a slow, creeping erosion of comfort and security. It probably started around the time that the drinking got heavier. His tongue grew looser, his morals faded from gold to grey, and his hits got harder. I've been counting myself lucky lately. Discovering my pregnancy seemed to sober him; an unexpected, tense quiet replaced the familiar sting of his blows. Until his verbal assaults escalated, a torrent of insults and accusations. But at least I knew those wouldn't kill me.*

I've grown accustomed to blocking out the insults. Whore,

slut, gold-digger, stupid, useless, worthless, hopeless, and pretty much every other word in the English language with the ending of 'less'. Yet, I didn't feel 'less'. I felt 'full'. Mainly, I felt hopeful. I hoped that one day I'd be free. I'd make it out. We would make it out. Together, this little one and I will shatter the bonds of this living nightmare and carve our destiny free from this hell.

I'll fight for improvement, sacrificing everything if necessary, for this child's sake. I'd taken to calling it Squish. Squish seemed fitting, seeing as how I'm having to squish into my jeans, it's squishing on my bladder, and everything was a new level of squishy. I know I shouldn't have given it a name. I don't even know how far along I am. He refuses to take me to the doctor. The simple act of giving it a name fills me with a quiet hope that everything will be alright, a small comfort in the face of uncertainty. This darkness hints at eventual light. I'm holding onto that light every single day.

TWENTY WEEKS. *Twenty entire weeks of Squish and I. Dean finally decided I needed to be seen by a doctor. He invented an excuse for the OB, saying we had just moved and hadn't yet transferred our medical records—the hushed tones of the clinic a stark contrast to the urgency in his voice. I'm not sure if they bought it; however, their lack of follow-up questions hinted at their acceptance.*

He could be awfully believable; his words were carefully chosen, and his expression was perfectly controlled. His heartfelt confession of love filled me with a sense of certainty, and in that moment, I was a believer. His words, raw and defi-

ant, that we didn't need my parents' approval, that it was just us against the world, convinced me. Convinced by his assurance of pulling out, I trusted him and opted not to use a condom.

Belief, I'm learning, is a dangerous thing. I had a sheltered childhood, fostering a belief in human goodness. Though I remained oblivious to others' shortcomings.

The doctor asked if we wanted to know the gender. Dean answered for me and said we did. Initially, I was hesitant to hear the baby's sex, but the doctor's announcement, "It's a girl," released a silent torrent of tears. I realized then, I had to do better. I needed to keep this little girl safe for all the times that I wasn't. My responsibility was to provide her with happiness, the comfort of security, and the steady ground of stability in her life. I needed to get out.

WE NAMED HER CHARLIE. *We settled on that name, though I'm still not sure why. If I were to ask Dean, he would likely give some philosophical justification for the name. I'm even more sure that it's a name he picked out at a strip joint with his buddies. I'm going to put on my rose-colored glasses and imagine him, country club blazer still on, sipping seltzer water after a game of golf, casually paging through a baby name book. His brow furrowed in concentration.*

Charlie is the sweetest and most perfect baby; her soft skin and tiny fingers are a constant delight. She took to feeding like a champ, thank goodness. Dean made it clear that formula was not an option. I'm sure it's because we can't afford it on his meager salary from the quarry. All the books I read said that breastfeeding was best for the baby, anyway. I'm not sure how we got so lucky, but she's a sound sleeper. The nightly yelling, slamming doors, and thrown objects from Dean likely taught her to make earplugs before she was even born. I don't blame her.

From my seat in the recliner, the silence pressed down on me, and my gaze fell on her, a heavy ache settling in my chest. I find myself constantly astounded at how tiny everything about her is. I run my fingers down her button nose and watch as her eyelashes flutter open. She's so alert. At two weeks old, her intense gaze feels like she can see straight into my soul, piercing through me with her innocent eyes. This must be the experience people describe: that breathtaking moment when you look into your child's eyes, the warmth of their gaze melting away all other thoughts and concerns. She's perfect and all mine. I resign myself to the harsh reality that it's us against the world, a lonely battle against insurmountable odds. This girl deserves a life filled with joy, laughter, and love, and I will make sure she has it.

stella

THE RHYTHMIC THUMP-THUMP-THUMP of tires against pavement, growing louder as the seconds ticked on, pulled me from my thoughts. I had been driving for what felt like days, the monotonous hum of the engine and the blurring landscape outside my window inducing a hypnotic state.

I blinked the sleepy haze from my eyes as I chanced a quick glance in the rear-view mirror at the little girl peacefully snoring in her car seat. With the softest of movements, her eyelashes brushed against her chubby cheeks, a picture of sweet and innocent youth.

I let loose the stagnant breath I hadn't realized I'd been holding. We were free. We were safe.

A glance at the dashboard clock showed it was well past midnight, making me wince. I'd been driving for over fifteen hours, only stopping when absolutely necessary. We had to get as far away from our past as I could manage. I wasn't taking any chances.

Lifting my eyes back to the road, I saw the neon sign of a motel ahead. We weren't close enough to any semblance of civilization to get picky with our accommodations. Honestly, I wasn't sure how much longer we'd have to keep driving or when we would come across another place to sleep.

The state of the lodging left much to be desired, with peeling paint on the building serving as a clear visual indicator of its poor condition, and the desolate emptiness of the parking lot further highlighting its unappealing nature. It didn't look Bate's Motel sketchy, but it most definitely had a high chance of bed bugs. At this point, I didn't have much of a choice.

I pulled into the parking lot of the dingy motel and cut the engine. Bracing my palms on the steering wheel. I dropped my head between my shoulders in resignation. With a tense back, a throbbing head, and a gnawing anxiety, I wondered how much longer our drive would last before the persistent unease finally subsided. I felt the lump in my throat tighten and I lifted my head to the roof of the car to blink back the tears from falling. I'd held it together this long, I could keep holding it together - I had to.

That sleeping little girl in the back seat relied on me to keep it together. She relied on me to keep her safe. We had nothing left except each other, this car, and the will to make a better life for ourselves.

I took some fortifying breaths, counting to ten to calm my racing heart. Once I felt the tightness of perpetual anxiety begin to fade, I took one last deep breath and unbuckled my seatbelt. Stepping out of the car, I rounded the hood to the passenger side.

As quietly as I could, I pulled open the rear passenger door and started unbuckling my sleeping baby from her car seat clips. Charlie stirred; her eyelashes fluttered open, revealing her large brown eyes that met mine with a sleepy curiosity. Her smile was instantaneous, causing a flutter of warmth to flow through my chest.

"Well, good morning sunshine," I cooed.

She made grabby hands at me, her eyes wide with expectation, insisting I pick her up. I slipped her arms from their straps and tenderly lifted her from the car seat, cradling her against my chest, soaking in the snuggles I knew wouldn't last forever.

"Did you have a good nap?"

Her response was a nonsensical string of baby babble that sounded far too animated for the current time and situation. Shifting her weight onto my hip, I pressed a tender kiss to her head as I grabbed our go bag of essentials.

A heavy sigh puffed past my lips as I tucked my phone in my pocket and hoisted the diaper bag over my shoulder. An hour into our drive, I had turned off my cell signal and didn't plan to turn it back on anytime soon.

I was terrified that if I switched it back on, that signal from my phone would lead *them* straight to us, so I kept it off. I wasn't sure if that's how they worked, but I wasn't chancing anything. The absence of waiting messages about my whereabouts hit home. A profound sense of isolation settled over me; we were truly alone. No one was wondering where we were.

I brushed the hair off of Charlie's forehead and gave her another quick peck right above her eyebrow.

The heavy thud of the car door couldn't muffle the ache in my chest, a dull reminder of the painful truth I couldn't face. It was just the two of us. We could do this; it may feel like everything was going to shit, but I'd figure it out. I had to figure our new life out…and fast.

max

"*FUCK*!" I shouted, slamming my hand down on the steering wheel of the hunk of scrap metal that my dad called a tractor. Hours bled into each other as I struggled with the machine, each attempt met with a sputtering groan and the irritating whir of the starter.

"Have you tried turning it off and back on again?" My brother Wade called from the barn doors behind me. The smile in his voice was evident in its cheerful, uplifting tone. His arrogant smirk, that self-satisfied expression, ignited within me an overwhelming urge to choke the life out of him.

I took a fortifying breath before responding. He knew just how to push my buttons - pretty sure he'd learned it in the womb.

Wade was my fraternal twin. Although people confused us for being identical because the differences were slight, we were one hundred percent fraternal.

"It's not a fucking computer, dick weasel." I grumped back in his general direction, not bothering to turn my head to see the wry grin that was plastered across his face. He'd been telling me for hours to give up on trying to get this tractor to run, but I was determined.

I lifted the ball cap off my head and grabbed the rag I'd draped over the throttle to wipe off the ever present sweat that was clouding my vision.

June in Georgia wasn't my idea of a good time. It was always oppressively hot and humid; the air was thick with the scent of damp earth and the incessant whine of unseen insects.

I threw the rag back onto its resting place, knowing I'd need it again in a couple minutes and placed my hat back on my mop of chestnut hair. A head of unruly, sandy-blonde hair popped up over the side of the rusty red tractor, his mocking grin still stuck smugly on his face.

Wade and my hair were only one of many ways that we couldn't be more different - I had our father's chestnut brown shade that I kept cropped short on the sides and a little longer on the top. I was constantly working outside and needed to keep my hair out of my face, especially in the months that felt hotter than Satan's ball sack.

Wade's hair was a couple shades lighter, bordering on light brown or a dark sandy blonde. He got that from our mother. He had always kept his hair longer, claiming that the ladies thought it made him look like Tarzan and that he was bound to find his Jane. I thought he just looked like a damn city boy, especially when he pulled it back in a "man-bun", as he liked to call it.

"It's almost quittin' time. You coming out to Jack's with us tonight or are you going to hole up in the house and watch reruns of Grey's Anatomy with your face mask and wine?" he teased.

He loved to give me shit about my quiet lifestyle. His jabs portrayed me as a lonely bachelor with nothing better to do. In reality, well… he wasn't wrong.

It's not that I didn't want to go out, it was that the thought of going out to Jack's, the lone bar in our little town, a dive bar at that, and being social, sounded like a fresh form of torture.

Wade thrived on being social. He was constantly the life of the party. He possessed an undeniable charisma; the moment he entered a room, people were drawn to his magnetic personality. Meanwhile, people skirted around me, their faces a mask of indifference.

I'd always been told that I was the grumpy brother - Wade was the sunshine, and I, the storm cloud.

"Not tonight. I'll probably hang out here and try to get this thing runnin'," I groused, slamming a hand down on the rust bucket I'd spent countless hours tinkering with.

"Dude, you've avoided coming out with me for weeks. Get out of this barn immediately, or I'll think you've suddenly turned into a horse."

"I get out." I retorted under my breath, knowing that the last time I'd gone out to the bar with Wade was months ago, and I'd left before even finishing my beer.

Wade's laugh was boisterous as he bent forward and pretended like what I said was the funniest thing he'd ever heard in his entire twenty-eight years of life. I didn't find it amusing and shot him a glare.

"Bro. Broski. Brother from the same mother. The grocery store, feed store, and your yearly visit to Doc Jericho for your physical don't count." he wheezed out "When is the last time you got your dick wet?"

I reached for the rag again and wiped my forehead, avoiding the topic.

It *had* been a while since I'd been with a woman. Shannon leaving me for my supposed "best friend" the night before our wedding turned me into an even grumpier recluse. I had avoided getting close to someone again, knowing that it often ended in heartache.

Town, a local girl, and their usual routine held absolutely no appeal. Anyone I'd met recently had been when I'd gone into the city, which in the last couple months hadn't been that frequent. Leaving the farm for a weekend in the city proved challenging following Pops' retirement. There was always something that needed to be done around the ranch.

I managed the daily operations of our small working ranch. Though the old man still lived on the property, having moved out to the bunkhouse shortly after Ma passed, he had turned over most of the responsibility of the ranch day-to-day business to me. When he moved out of the big house, Pa claimed he didn't need all the space, but we both knew it carried the oppressive memories of the love he had lost.

The ranch sang with the memories of Ma, her touches clear in each and every thing. Losing her had been one of the biggest hits to our family, and I don't think Pa would ever recover. I don't think any of us would ever fully recover.

"I'm good, Wade. Stop trying to play wingman for me. I can find my own chicks," I grumbled and threw the dirty rag directly at him. He sidestepped, narrowly avoiding it before it whacked him directly in the face.

"I'm not saying you can't. I'm saying you *won't*," he countered with a quirk of his brow.

I sighed. It *had* been a while since I'd been out with my

brother and our friends. I'd been so busy keeping the ranch running that I had taken no time for myself.

"Give me thirty minutes to shower, shit and shave, and I'll come out for a beer." I mumbled, reluctantly accepting his offer, hopping off the tractor to pick up the fallen rag, draping it back over the steering wheel of the tractor.

Twin senses tingling and before he could hoop and holler, I held up a hand to settle his excitement.

"One. Fucking. Beer," I emphasized.

THE BIG HOUSE'S front door clicked shut thirty minutes later; the earsplitting blare of Wade's truck horn immediately followed the purr of his engine. An immediate and profound wave of regret washed over me. What the hell had I gotten myself into?

I patted my pockets to make sure I had everything.

Wallet - *check.*

Cell phone - *check, even though I never used the damn thing.*

Keys - *check.*

I went to the passenger door and got in. The sound of new age country music was blaring through the speakers. I reached across the center console and turned the dial down, hoping to preserve my hearing. Immediately after I lowered my arm, Wade returned the radio to its offensive volume.

"Get in the mood, bro!" he shouted over the music before throwing the truck in reverse and cruising down the dirt road to the property line.

I watched out the window as we retreated away from the

dim lights of the ranch and out towards town. The ranch was my safe space, a quiet haven where the only sounds were the gentle breeze and the distant mooing of cows. Having grown up in Firefly Cove, we weren't strangers to small town living. The ranch offered a small slice of privacy from prying eyes and wagging tongues.

The city of Firefly Cove was small. Our route took us through the main downtown area, which included a large park, many locally owned shops, a small grocery store, a feed store, and finally, Jack's—the dive bar we were heading toward.

When we reached the edge of the town, the headlights of Wade's truck shone upon a small, dark-colored sedan that was stopped on the side of the road.

We didn't get many "out of towners" as we liked to call them here in the Cove and it wasn't a car I recognized. Hackles raised, I reached across the console to turn the music down again and Wade grumped with frustration.

"Slow down," I instructed, craning my neck to get a look at the car and who might occupy it. I couldn't see the driver, but the Missouri plates told me that it was more than likely not anyone from around here.

"Doesn't look like anyone I know," Wade surmised, echoing my thoughts.

"Pull over behind 'em," I instructed.

Wade slowly eased the truck onto the side of the road behind the car and cut the headlights so they wouldn't blind the occupants.

Unbuckling my seatbelt and throwing open the door, I stepped out into the muggy night air. "I'll be right back"

I walked up towards the car, keeping my eyes open and a hand on my belt where I always carried my handgun. Even small towns required vigilance. I always kept my .44 holstered on my hip tucked into the waistband of my jeans, just in case.

As I got closer to the car, I could make out a female occupying the driver's seat. Her forehead rested on the steering wheel; the car wasn't running. As I stepped closer, I could hear crying coming from the back seat. A quick glance revealed a small child in a car seat, their face barely visible but their crying audible even through the closed window.

Approaching the driver's side door carefully, I gently rapped my knuckles on the glass, doing my best to not scare the woman. Even so, she was startled. I could see her quickly wiping tears off her face as she reached for the button to roll the window down. With the window opening, the toddler's cries from the back seat intensified.

The woman looked up, surprising me. Her eyes were red rimmed and puffy. She had clearly been crying awhile. That wasn't what had me off kilter though, it was the color. A striking green, almost emerald in depth. Beyond the color, her eyes looked almost lifeless. She looked lost.

"Sorry, officer, I stopped for just a minute to give my eyes a rest. I won't be parking here or anything," she sputtered out, not bothering with so much as a glance in my direction.

I could tell she was flustered and wasn't thinking clearly, especially if she thought I was a cop. Nothing about me screamed 'police'. I was in a pair of lightly faded Wranglers, a grey tee shirt, and my cowboy boots. I had snagged my Stetson off the seat of the truck before exiting, and that was atop my head.

"Not a cop." I grumbled, although gently, to not spook her. "Everything okay?"

A sarcastic chuckle escaped her lips, her head drooping slightly as she answered.

"Yep, everything's *peachy*." She huffed. I could sense the sarcasm dripping thickly from her words.

A soft whimper replaced the backseat screaming; I peeked behind the driver to check it out. A little girl sat in a car seat with a light blanket over her lap. Her cheeks were flushed red and her eyes were heavy. She looked like she'd spent some time crying as well. She couldn't have been any older than one.

"You *sure* you're okay?" I asked again, knowing that the first answer she gave was bullshit and genuinely concerned for her and the child's wellbeing.

"If by okay, you mean stressed, lost, hungry, tired, and an absolute wreck, yep, all good here," she spat out with another one of those little breathy chuckles. "Sorry, that was rude. If you could kindly point me toward the nearest motel, that would be helpful."

She looked over her shoulder at the toddler in her car seat, and the ghost of a smile graced her face.

"Oh, *now* you're going to stop screaming? A handsome man walks over to the window, and you act like a perfect angel?" She huffed towards the little girl.

The toddler responded with incoherent babble and a whack of her pacifier that she held in her iron grip on the side of her car seat. I chuckled, dismissing the flattering remark. It was evident from her body language and facial expression that she wasn't interested in flirting, even though the thought may have briefly crossed my mind.

"There's a small inn about half a mile up the road right in the center of main street. They should have a room available for you two ladies." I said as I pointed towards the road, signaling that she was to head in the same direction she was going.

"Tell Connie at the front desk that Max sent you, and she will make sure you're taken care of. She owes me a favor or two," I added with a sly smile.

I saw her shoulders sag in relief. Was finding somewhere to sleep the reason she seemed more at ease, or was it the fact that someone was nice to her? Her emerald eyes meet mine in the darkness. I noticed a hint of pink on her cheeks as she gazed up at me, her nighttime savior. Giving her another rusty attempt at a smile, she straightened herself in her seat and looked ready to head off.

"Thank you, Max," she said breathily.

Hearing my name from her lips sent a zing to my senses. It had been so long since I'd been captivated by a woman, and something about her made me want to know more.

I watched as her shoulders pulled away from her ears and her hold on the steering wheel relaxed as the tension visibly released from her posture. I wondered what her story was.

Was she running from something or someone?

Was she in danger?

I dismissed the thoughts, reminding myself she was just a roadside stranger, not some damsel in distress that needing rescuing. She didn't need saving, and all she needed was to get herself and that little girl somewhere safe to sleep. She didn't need some random storm cloud cowboy throwing himself into the mix.

"It's no problem…" I trailed off, realizing that I'd never gotten her name.

"Stella," she finished for me with a gentle smile. "And the little traitor in the back seat is Charlie." she added as she hooked a thumb over her shoulder at the now content little girl sucking a pacifier and fighting the sleep that was threatening to overtake her.

"No problem at all, Stella." I reiterated with a wink, her name rolling from my tongue like warm honey.

Quietly tapping my hand on the windowsill, I started back towards Wade's truck. Walking backwards so I could keep an eye on them as they pulled away. I hesitated until I could see the taillights of Stella's car turn on and her blinker flash as she pulled back onto the roadway.

I waited by the passenger door as she eased the sedan onto the road. Gripping the handle of Wade's truck, I yanked the door open. I popped my booted foot up onto the running board and hoisted myself into the seat.

"Everything okay?" Wade asked without even glancing up from his phone.

"Yeah, just a woman who got lost and needed some directions to The Mayfair," I responded as I buckled my seat belt. Wade, after a subtle nod, turned the key in the ignition of his truck, and smoothly pulled onto the road.

Just the most beautiful woman I'd seen in ages and the cutest toddler in the back seat.

I shook the thoughts from my head. No use getting hung up on a woman that I'd never see again.

As he eased down into the main street, I found myself wondering if Stella made it to the inn okay. Did Charlie wake up and start crying again? Would she be around for a while or was this just a stop through for whatever she was leaving behind?

I was so lost in my thoughts that I didn't even realize Wade had pulled the truck into a space outside of Jack's. He slapped his hand on my shoulder and it jolted me back to reality and out of my day dreams of the way my name sounded from Stella's lips.

"Lets go get fucked up, brother," he said cheerily as he opened the door to head in.

So much for one fucking beer. I was going to need a couple of drinks to get those mesmerizing emerald eyes and the tortured look on Stella's face off my mind.

I was so fucked.

stella

SUNLIGHT PERMEATED the room's curtains, letting me know it was time to get up. I blinked away the grogginess of a good night's sleep, feeling more refreshed than I had in a long time.

Max was right, Connie had taken care of us when I'd pulled into The Mayfair, easily finding us a room for the night. She had happily doted on Charlie, making sure I had a portable crib for her to sleep in as well.

The Mayfair was a quaint little inn in the middle of the quiet downtown area. A faded brick facade showed the building's long history in this small town, its weathered edges softened with age. It stood tall amongst the small shops that lined the streets, a beacon of solace for my weary soul.

Walking in that evening, we were greeted by a small reception area and an even smaller woman sitting behind the check-in desk. She had looked up from the worn pages of a paperback novel that sported a scantily clad woman and a shirtless man in a lover's embrace on the front.

Sounds like my type of book.

The woman, Connie, had been kind when I'd mentioned Max and his offer of hospitality. I didn't miss the slight flicker of curiosity that had graced her face upon hearing his name. She hadn't asked many questions as she checked us in and I was beyond thankful, as I didn't know the answers to many of them myself. She *had* seemed shocked that Max had gone out of his way to be kind. To be honest, *I* wasn't even sure why he'd been so nice to me.

After all, I was just some random damsel in distress on the side of the highway with a screaming baby.

Pushing away the intrusive thoughts that the only reason he'd been kind was for pity, I rolled over to check on Charlie. Looking down into the portable crib, my heart fluttered with an overwhelming sense of love as I watched the gentle rise and fall of her chest.

Sensing my staring, her eyelids fluttered open. I brushed away the fine, downy baby hairs from her forehead, feeling the warmth of her skin beneath my touch. Her eyes met mine, and she greeted me with an irresistible, toothy grin.

There's something so innocent about toddlers that makes even the darkest of days seem bright. They have no reservations about life. They are just content being around those they love. I craved the quiet contentment that seemed to effortlessly emanate from Charlie; just a taste of it would be enough.

I had been an only child, often seeking the approval and praise of my parents. My parents, although nice people, worked often. Nannies, family friends, or child care centers took their place in their absence. Growing up, I craved affection, often finding it in places that weren't ideal. Hence, how I ended up tangled up in Dean's web.

Again, pushing the wayward thoughts of my past from my

mind and forcing myself to focus on the present, I leaned over into the portable crib, scooped Charlie's little body up into my arms, and plopped her on my lap.

"Good morning, sunshine," I cooed.

I woke Charlie with the same greeting every day. Starting your day with a smile, I theorized, was a good way to set a positive tone for your mood. I wanted to instill in her a positive outlook on life, even when the world seemed bleak. I wanted her to know that every single day, there was something worth smiling for - even if that something was as simple as getting up in the morning.

Her toothy grin spread so wide that her cheeks nearly squished her eyes closed. She reached out and grabbed hold of my tank top, trying to yank the neckline down to reach what she wanted.

Charlie had been exclusively breast fed for the last ten months. She'd taken to nursing like a champ and now that she was getting older, it was supplemental at best and a comfort item at worst. It felt like a double-edged sword, but I wasn't ready to let go yet; neither were my boobs, knowing our bonding time was ending soon.

I huffed a small laugh and tugged the tank top down, releasing my breast and positioning her to latch. She took right to eating, eyes wide as she looked around at our surroundings. I glanced at my phone as she ate - six in the morning.

We'd gotten a solid eight hours of sleep, which in the world of a parent, was unheard of. I let loose another small chuckle as I looked down at my girl.

"Got some good beauty rest, didn't you, love?" I asked, stroking a finger down between her eyes and over her button nose. She grinned around my nipple and reached for my finger, holding it in her tiny hand.

My heart swelled with joy as I watched my beautiful daughter cling to my hand. She was the only good thing to come out of Dean and I's relationship. I regretted many things in my life, but Charlie had never been one of them.

The experience of motherhood often showed you just how fragile life could be. You handled the wellbeing of another human, not just yourself. Often, it required you to sacrifice your own wellbeing for the safety and happiness of your child. Being a mother was a truly selfless act, and often one that was inherently thankless.

I'd never seen myself as someone who desperately wanted children. I'd always seen myself as someone who would be steadfast in a career, maybe something to do with design or fashion. Being a mom had been a foreign and terrifying concept.

Throughout my pregnancy with Charlie, I couldn't help but wonder about the kind of mother I would become. I hadn't grown up with the doting, unyielding, and motherly role model that most families are blessed with.

Many women claim to possess certain motherly instincts, but I certainly lacked them. I didn't get butterflies or bursting ovaries when someone had a newborn baby in my small friend group. I didn't offer to babysit when you needed a night out. Motherhood hadn't really been something I'd ever given much thought to.

But, Charlie was the light I didn't know I'd needed. We'd had a rough go of it in the first couple months of getting acquainted as I found myself doing everything alone, and once we had gotten a routine down, she'd become my tiny best friend. She'd become the one thing I couldn't live without and the one thing I continued to live for. I never intended to be a mother, but I was fiercely determined to provide my little girl with the best life I could.

A twinge of pain shot through my nipple and I let out a wince. Looking down, I saw Charlie had stopped nursing and was using my nipple as her personal teething toy. I lifted her upright and righted the neckline of my tank top, standing her on my lap so that we were eye to eye.

"Listen here, little lady. I don't want to give up nursing just yet, but you need to keep those little piranha teeth to yourself. No chomping on my nips," I gently scolded, not able to hide the small smile that was fighting to escape, as I watched her eyes crinkle in confusion.

"Ma.. ma.." Charlie cooed back.

"Yes, Mama. Mama's boobs are not teething toys," I said, bopping her on her tiny nose.

I walked her over to the portable crib and sat her down on the padded bottom, handing her one of her teething toys and a stuffed dog that made all kinds of obnoxious sounds when you pressed the buttons on its belly, hands, or feet. Charlie grabbed for the stuffed dog and started whacking away on it to get to her favorite sounds.

That would keep her occupied for a couple minutes so I could pop into the shower, rinse off the stench of 18 hours of driving, and get a good scrub of my hair in a shower that didn't reek of mold.

As I turned on the stream of water, I noted that there were toiletries already available on the ledges. Lifting the shampoo and conditioner to my nose, I popped the caps, taking a quick sniff. Lavender filled my senses, and I sighed. I loved the smell of lavender. Something about it was so calming.

I undressed quickly and stepped into the steaming spray of

the water. It had been almost two days since I'd had a proper shower. I felt grimy and needed a few minutes just to feel human.

I grabbed the body wash from the ledge and squirted a good amount into my palms, lathering it into rich bubbles. I let its earthy fragrance wash over me and act as a balm for my weary soul.

After scrubbing and rinsing, I repeated the motions to ensure that I had gotten myself sufficiently clean. I did the same thing to my hair, peeking outside the shower curtain into the main area of the room to check on Charlie. She was still babbling away at her stuffed dog and chewing on her teething toy.

Content that Charlie wouldn't start screaming anytime soon, I took an extra minute to let the conditioner sit in my hair and enjoy the hot water pulsing on my back. As I leaned back into the water, I closed my eyes and allowed the stream to drip down my face.

Despite leaning forward and wiping my face, it became wet again moments later. I let my tears mingle with the water of the shower.

I could take a minute just to feel. Charlie was busy. I didn't need to be strong right this second.

Leaning my head forward to rest on the tile wall of the shower, I gave myself a second to feel all the emotions swelling inside me. Anger surged through me like a tidal wave crashing against the shore of a forgotten beach. Followed by sadness, the gut churning realization that we were truly alone. Then more anger, a fire burning brightly, flames licking at the edges of my vision, and finally resolution and strength washed over me in a calmness I hadn't felt in far too long.

I let the direness of our situation flood my mind, threatening to drown me in the undertow. We needed to settle down somewhere, and fast. I couldn't keep moving from place to place with Charlie. It wasn't feasible or responsible, and the way to moving on wasn't to keep moving.

After my debilitating breakdown over our circumstances receded, a quiet sense of peace washed over me. There was something about this small town that felt… right. I couldn't put a finger on what it was about this sleepy little place that felt a little like home, but I didn't hate the idea that maybe we had found somewhere to start over.

Even though I'd only been from the side of the road to the local inn, there was an overwhelming sense of security here. I felt an intense pull to this quiet little town that I hadn't felt in any of the other places we'd stopped.

If anything, that fact that I could sleep for a solid eight hours said a lot. It said that I felt safe - which was a glaringly foreign concept in my life.

I shut my eyes for one more second as I relished in that feeling. It had been a long time since I'd had lived a life not riddled with a choking knot of anxiety threatening to constrict my throat.

I leaned into the calmness surrounding us, realizing that maybe we were destined to stop here. Maybe Firefly Cove wasn't just a stop over town. This could truly be our fresh start.

IT HAD TAKEN me another 30 minutes to get myself and Charlie up and dressed for the morning. Charlie had fought me tooth and nail to get clothes on. I was sure the child would prefer to be constantly naked if someone let her. She had alligator rolled around the bed as I attempted to shove her chunky arms and legs into shorts and a tank top.

Walking down the main stairway, my stomach growled incessantly as we reached the inn's lobby. I heard a chuckle from behind the counter as we walked past the front desk and headed for the front door. Startled, I paused.

"Well, I'd say you two look like you could use a substantial breakfast," Connie called from her chair behind the desk.

I let loose a shaky laugh, relieved that it was just Connie. She wasn't wrong. I had been surviving off of energy drinks and beef jerky for almost two days. Thankfully, Charlie wasn't used to eating much in the way of solid food, so she snacked light along the way.

It still felt a little foreign, laughter. It had been ages since I could relax and not be consumed by fear enough to laugh.

"Do you know somewhere around here I can get some coffee and maybe a bite to eat?" I questioned.

"Try down the block at The Grind. They've got decent coffee, but the pastries are to die for," she said with a sly grin.

Something about her gaze seemed meddlesome. I brushed it off as a figment of my imagination, reminding myself that small towns were full of little quirks and if we were going to stay here, I should get used to it.

My stomach growled again loudly as I nodded. I hiked Charlie up higher on my hip and turned towards the front door to leave.

"You know, dear, I'm not one to meddle.." I could sense the 'but' coming before she even opened her mouth.

Oh, here we go.

"But?"

"But small towns have a way of calling to wayward souls." She paused for emphasis. "Just thought that it might be worth mentioning."

I peered over the top of Charlie's head, back at the old woman behind the counter. Her eyes were kind. The surrounding crinkles formed from years of smiles and laughter. She gave me a quick wink, and I nodded in understanding and turned back towards the front door.

I wasn't so sure the small town vibe and I would get along. I disliked the idea of everyone knowing about my business, or at the very least, attempting to. Gossip wasn't something I generally dabbled in. I had perfected the art of walking in the shadows and keeping a low profile. I didn't know if I was ready to stand under a microscope of small town good intentions.

"Thanks for the advice," I responded, pushing the front door open with the hip Charlie wasn't perched on.

The stifling summer air hit me with a whoosh and I squinted my eyes against the offending sunlight. I wasn't used to this type of heat and humidity. It was nearly oppressive. Georgia during the summer was a cruel form of torture, but I guess I should get used to it.

I trekked my way down the quiet street, noticing how quaint and homey the main street felt.

It felt like stepping back in time to a place where your grandma sent you to the corner store with a nickel to buy some bubble gum. It felt peaceful, like I could take a deep breath for once in the last… well, I couldn't remember the last time I'd felt free enough to breathe without the overwhelming sense of dread flooding my system.

I noticed the lampposts, each one adorned with a small American flag. Because of the lack of any semblance of a breeze, they hung limp from their sticks. I'm sure if there was a small breeze blowing, they'd be flapping majestically. In between each lamp post sat a waist high planter, each one filled with overflowing greenery and summer blooms. The sidewalks were meticulously maintained, showcasing how much the residents cared about this little town.

It was enthralling to take notice of the sheer beauty in the little things. Had I really let my the oppression of my past life rob me of seeing things like these little details before?

I shook the thoughts from my head. After all, Charlie and I were starting over. We weren't hostages of our circumstances any longer.

As I walked, I made a mental note to check the coffee shop for a help wanted board, a current available rentals list, or anything else that could help us quickly find some permanent lodging. We weren't going to be able to afford to stay in the inn for more than a couple of nights. So, I was going to have to work fast.

Stepping into the coffee shop, I felt the immediate side effects of small town living. Every single set of eyes looked up from their drinks, crosswords, or conversations to stare at the non-local who'd just stepped foot in their watering hole. I felt their stares like a brand and glanced down to make sure that I had put pants on before leaving the inn.

Yep, I was wearing pants.

Feeling uncomfortable, I immediately turned to walk back out the door and ran right into a wall. Scratch that, I ran right into the muscled chest of a man - same difference. His rough grasp reached out to grip my elbow and steady me before I tumbled to the ground, baby and all.

I bounced back and kept my eyes down as I attempted to sidestep the person I'd just accosted with my body. Steeling myself for the harsh words I expected to come, I was thrown off when a familiar voice greeted me instead.

"Stella?" a gruff voice came from beside me just as my hand once again reached for the door handle of the exit. The slight southern drawl was familiar, but I'd only been in this town for approximately twelve hours. I didn't know anyone here, except for Connie at the inn and…

I raised my eyes to the wall of a man in front of me and was met with the shy smile of my white knight in cowboy boots.

Max.

max

"WOAH THERE, GIRL." I chuckled playfully as I steadied Stella with a gentle hand on her elbow. She tensed, and I released her almost as quickly as I'd reached to help.

Interesting.

I noted the flinch instantly and again found myself wondering what her story was. Women didn't generally flinch out of reflex. I concluded that she had probably been hurt before, either physically or emotionally. This woman was a mystery. Lost on the side of the road with a crying baby, needing a place to stay, and now frequenting the local coffee shop that hardly anyone but townies ever set foot in.

"Sorry, I was just on my way out," she said as she attempted to sidestep me, refusing to meet my gaze.

Stepping in front of her to block her exit, I fortified my position. I was treating her with the same quiet demeanor that you'd use to approach a skittish foal. I didn't want to spook her, but I needed to make sure she was okay. She looked scared and alone. It sent a protective thrill through my body. I wasn't used to caring for people other than myself, but something about this girl had me rattled.

"Don't be sorry, darlin'." I said as I took my Stetson off my head, running my fingers through my hair, attempting to fluff up the hat head I knew I was undoubtedly sporting.

Ma always enforced the rule of taking off your hat upon entering a building, sitting at the dinner table, or being around a lady. She instilled in Wade and I that manners made a man and that boys disrespected establishments and women.

I let the hand holding my hat fall to my side as I regarded the smiling little girl on Stella's hip. "And how are you today, little one?"

Her grin was infectious. Even around the pacifier she had in her mouth, she smiled so wide that her chubby cheeks squished, her eyes almost closing. She grabbed for the pacifier and shook it at me with an endless string of babble. I couldn't understand a single thing she was trying to tell me, but her animation made me chuckle. I nodded along enthusiastically, pretending that I had any inkling about what she was trying to say.

She didn't have those same emerald eyes as her mother. Hers were chocolate brown. She looked like Stella, but her features were less sharp, more pudgy. Stella had bright blonde hair that fell in gentle waves down over her shoulders, but Charlie's hair was darker, closer to brown, and curled in little spirals that currently were stuck up in every direction.

Stella hoisted her higher on her hip as she stepped out of the way of oncoming foot traffic. We were at the coffee shop's entrance, yet I couldn't be bothered to move. This mystery woman and her adorable, toothy toddler occupied every single one of my thoughts.

"I'll just be heading out." Stella said towards the floor as she attempted to skirt around me, hiking a thumb in the direction of the door. I again put my hand out to catch her elbow, making sure to keep my touch light.

"Don't leave on my account. I know I'm not the best thing to look at, but you should at least get some coffee in ya first before passing judgement." I smirked.

I felt an undeniable pull, a potent chemistry that sparked a sudden urge to flirt; I couldn't explain the inexplicable attraction to her. She had me absolutely twisted up in knots.

I had fought my thoughts of Stella last night at the bar with Wade. I started with beer; however, when those emerald eyes still haunted me, I'd promptly switched to bourbon, attempting to drown out the thoughts of the sadness that radiated in them and the primal urge to hunt down whoever had put it there.

"I wasn't..." she started, but stopped abruptly as I approached the counter, ignoring her.

With a sly smile, I glanced back before shifting my attention to Angie, the local high school student who pitched in on weekends at the counter. I'd assisted her momma and daddy over on their farm on more than one occasion with herding their wayward livestock.

Stella's gaze was nearly feral as she watched me ignore her and order coffee. Good, that was better than the sadness that seemed to follow her. She still had some spark left in her, this girl.

"Mornin' Ange," I greeted the barista. "Can I get my usual, plus an iced caramel latte with oat milk for Stella, and a blueberry muffin for the little one?"

"Sure thing, Max," she said as she punched the items into the register.

Her slight head tilt, as she attempted a look at Stella

brooding behind me, didn't escape my notice. I handed over my card and dropped a ten-dollar bill in the tip jar that read 'college is expensive, tip your barista'.

Turning to face Stella, I saw a scorned woman's stern expression. If she didn't look so cute, I would have been a little worried, but the set of her shoulders and her crossed arms gave her the look of an overgrown petulant toddler.

"I can order my own food and drinks." She huffed before stomping to a nearby table, grabbing a high chair for Charlie, and plopping into an adjacent seat with a thunk.

"I'm sure you're capable, Trouble." I remarked, inwardly chuckling as I slid her drink over to her on a single finger and put the bag with the muffin beside it. A peace offering.

"My intention wasn't to belittle your ability to take care of yourself. I was just doing something nice because you look like someone pissed in your Cheerios this morning."

She cocked her head to the left and narrowed her eyes. "Trouble?" she questioned as she broke off a piece of the muffin, setting it on the napkin she'd dutifully laid out in front of Charlie. The toddler fisted the muffin chunk, crumbling it into minuscule pieces before shoving her entire fist into her mouth.

"Seemed fitting - given the first time we met, you looked like you were *in* trouble, or looking for trouble to get *into*." I responded with a quirk of my brow and a slight lift to one side of my lips.

I saw her face flush with a tinge of pink; this blush just made my desire to know her and the arousal I felt when her emerald eyes locked with mine stronger.

"Whatever you say, Cowboy." She said with a slight uptick to the side of her own plush lips.

This girl was going to be the death of me. Cue instant hard-on.

Giving her a quick once over, I noticed that her bottom lip was plumper than her top, giving the impression that she'd been biting it. She had an angular face with a slender nose. Her gaze was gentle, yet not naïve. I sensed there was more to this woman than she let people see. She looked jaded, but not broken. My gaze was drawn to the slight smattering of freckles across the bridge of her nose that spread up the apples of her cheeks and towards the edges of her eyes, giving her an air of innocence. She was breathtakingly beautiful.

"Mo! MO!" Charlie shouted, breaking me from my lust heated perusal. She slammed her tiny fists down on the table and stretched in the high chair for the muffin sitting in front of Stella. Stella's breathy chuckle sent another rush of blood straight to my cock.

This woman's impact on me felt unlike any other before. I'd always been the type to either take care of my needs myself or pick up a one nighter at a bar a couple hours west in Atlanta. This sensation of unfiltered desire was throwing me for a loop, yet I couldn't seem to stop thinking about what she'd feel like with my hands gripping her waist, her head thrown back in ecstasy as I towered over her tiny frame.

Stella broke off a couple chunks of the muffin and placed them on the napkin in front of Charlie, who immediately continued her decimation of the breakfast pastry and seemed content with the mess she was making.

I watched as Stella shuffled crumbs off the top of the table into her awaiting hand at the edge, dumping them onto a napkin that she kept spread out in front of herself. I knew little about being a parent, as the thought of being a dad had rarely ever crossed my mind and the only true comparison I had was my own Ma - but if I had to take a guess, I'd say Stella was an excellent mother.

I watched as she sipped her coffee, eyes closing, as she relished the cool hit of caffeine she looked like she could use desperately. I averted my eyes before I started thinking again with my southern most head instead of the one between my shoulders again.

I found Stella captivating, yet knew nothing of her background. She'd turned up in town out of nowhere and looked like she could use a friend. I couldn't let myself get attached to an enigma. I was at the point in my life where I needed stability and to settle down, not a one-night stand with this green-eyed blonde. Cresting thirty, and being a perpetual bachelor, only held appeal for so long.

Clearing my throat, I sipped my black coffee. I didn't drink it for the taste; I drank it out of caffeine necessity. The bitter hit of adrenaline did little to quell my persistent exhaustion.

"So."

"Thanks.."

We both chuckled a little as we broke the awkward silence with small talk simultaneously. I gestured for her to proceed, then waited.

"I was just going to say thanks again for saving my ass yesterday. I know it probably wasn't how you wanted to use a 'favor' from Connie."

Brushing off her comment, I shrugged. I had no use for favors from locals. I helped our town's people because I was raised that way. My Ma and Pops taught me to never do things intending to get something in return, to do things out of the goodness of your heart and because it's the right thing.

People liked to rag on small towns for our ability to take

care of each other - but that's what kept small towns alive. We were a family, through and through. When one of us hurt, we all hurt.

"Really, it was no problem." I took another sip of my coffee. "I'm going to assume that you didn't have any trouble getting a room? It's not really busy season around here, so I figured Connie probably enjoyed the bit of company."

"Yep," she said, popping the 'p,' at the end. "Now, if I could just afford to stay for another couple of nights while I find something more permanent, that would be a miracle." She mumbled quietly enough that I barely caught it as she averted her eyes and traced the ridges of the wooden table in front of us.

I couldn't miss the fact that she wouldn't look me in the eyes. She was constantly focusing on her lap, hands, or Charlie instead. I dismissed that minor detail, thinking it was simply a matter of her adapting to her new surroundings and getting to know a new person - but a niggling fear inside of me said that I could add that to the column of traits she'd inherited from her past.

"I'm sure Connie would love to have you girls stay a couple more nights if you need to. I can call and make sure the room cost is covered."

"Oh, no, you don't have to do that. We can figure it out." She replied hastily.

Her eyes darted from the table to the door, then to Charlie, then back to the table. It almost looked like she was planning a quick escape. Reaching over, I softly placed my hand on her arm in reassurance.

"I know you don't know me from Adam, but I wouldn't offer if I didn't want to. I'm not a man to mince words or intentions. You look like you could honestly use a friend." I released her arm and snagged my coffee back up, taking another sip as I waited for her reaction.

I saw her deep intake of breath before the resolve drained from her features. Her nod was shallow and barely perceptible, but I caught it and gave back a soft smile.

I could feel the ice around her thawing as she opened up to the option of letting someone help her. I could tell that life hadn't been kind to Stella and Charlie, and I couldn't help the overwhelming feeling of wanting to change that. If giving her a safe place to stay by paying for another couple nights at the inn helped, I'd call Connie right this minute.

"Thanks, Max." Those emerald eyes met mine, and I felt an instant tingle of electricity in my gut. I'm not one to believe in love at first sight. Honestly, I'd never believed my Ma and Pops when they'd recount their intensely romantic, and often cringeworthy, love story. I figured that love was just as real as the Loch Ness Monster, Big Foot, or unicorns.

I should probably call Doc Jericho about this nagging tingle - it was becoming slightly concerning, and it only seemed to happen around Stella.

In the blink of an eye, Charlie went from shoveling the muffin from her tiny fists into her awaiting mouth to screaming at the top of her lungs and banging her fists on the table. It was as if a switch had flipped and she went from blissfully happy to a complete nuclear meltdown in the blink of an eye.

Stella's gaze grew wide as she stood to pick her up out of the high chair. She cradled the little girl against her body, one hand cupping the back of her head, the other under her butt holding her on her hip. She pressed her face to Charlie's chubby cheek and began shushing her. Her attempts at soothing her were futile.

I didn't need to turn around and look to know that all the eyes in the coffee shop were on her and the crying baby. Looking up at the two of them, I noticed water gathering on Stella's lower lashes, threatening to fall. My gut clenched at the pleading look of desperation clouding her features.

"How can I help?" I asked, pushing my chair back and standing up. She shook her head and continued shushing as she rocked back and forth.

"She's just tired. She slept like a rock last night, but that doesn't make up for the eighteen hours of driving we did and sleeping in seedy motel rooms."

About the time she mentioned sleep, Charlie let out a yawn that almost split her face. She rubbed those tiny fists into her eyes as she continued to wail.

"I'll just take her outside and walk her around.. Thank-"

"Can I try?" I interrupted, standing and raising my hands in offering to give her a minute of reprieve.

She hesitated, looking down at Charlie with concern. I can imagine the struggle she must be warring with to allow someone else to help soothe her child.

"I don't want to overstep..." I added.

I'm not sure how long she'd been on her own, minus the driving, but it looked as if she was used to handling things without help. If I could give her a minute of peace, I'd do it in a heartbeat. She looked like she needed it.

Resigning herself to the help, Stella shushed Charlie a couple more times as she carefully transferred her into my arms, settling her on my right side in the same hold she had been using.

I wasn't intimately familiar with how to hold a baby, but she seemed pretty self sufficient. She could sit upright, so I knew I didn't need to support her neck. I moved her until her cheek rested against my shoulder. I copied Stella's shushing, as that seemed to comfort her. I gently bounced her from side to side as I shushed her quietly.

After a minute, her screaming subsided and her breathing turned to shuddering pants. Her tears had soaked through my thin tee shirt, but I didn't dare move a muscle to stop my ministrations. Keeping up the shushing and bouncing motions, I continued until her breathing evened out.

I bent my head down to see that her eyes were closed, long lashes brushing across her chubby cheeks. Relief washed over me as I looked up at Stella. The tears that had been threatening to fall were tracking down her cheeks in gentle rivers.

I tensed and prepared to hand Charlie back, but she stopped me with a raise of her slender fingers in a 'don't' motion and pulled out my chair so I could sit down. I carefully settled into the chair, positioning Charlie on my lap so her cheek rested on my chest and her body nestled in the crook of my arm. She curled into me and let out a contented sigh.

I'd never been a big kid person. I wasn't around them often enough to feel comfortable saying I wanted ones of my own right now. It had always just been Wade and me - no other siblings. Ma used to tell us we gave her enough grief for a basketball team's worth of kids. She would then regale everyone else with stories that she had gotten it perfect in one fell swoop and never felt the need to go for another round.

I'm sure she would have loved seeing me now - sitting at a coffee shop table with a beautiful woman, a sleeping baby in my arms, and a lot of townies wondering what in the hell just happened. Ma loved a little bit of drama to keep the day interesting.

Stella took the seat across from me and heaved a lung clearing sigh. I was afraid to speak, for fear that I'd wake Charlie up. She watched me with rapt attention. I assumed she could sense my discomfort.

"You can talk. She won't wake up." She said, adverting her eyes down to the table again. I shifted Charlie on my lap further into the crook of my arm, a protectiveness washing over me. Despite her small size, she was remarkably heavy. I could feel Stella's eyes on me and I looked up to a small smile and her fighting back a chuckle.

"What?" I whispered, still slightly terrified I was going to wake the little girl up.

"You look so uncomfortable." She said behind her hand as she continued to fight the laugh. "I'm going to assume that you're not around babies much." She added.

"You'd assume correct."

Charlie shifted in my lap, and I looked up at Stella with panicked eyes. I had gotten her to sleep, but I wasn't sure what to do with her now. Stella let loose the laugh she'd been holding back, and I marginally relaxed. Her laugh was a shot of electricity to my soul. I wanted to hear it over and over again.

"I can take her back." She said while extending her hands to shift Charlie onto her lap. I shook my head from side to side and tucked her into my hold tighter. Stella stiffened, and I realized I had made her uncomfortable. I back peddled, attempting to soothe her anxiety.

"She's comfy. I'm pretty squishy under all this glorious muscle." I teased with an exaggerated eyebrow waggle, trying to lighten the mood.

Stella's cheeks pinked, and she looked back down at her hands.

So, I wasn't the only one affected here. Good to know.

"Sorry, I'm not used to having help. It's taking a lot of restraint to not hole up inside the inn and just stay in our little bubble. It's almost always been just Charlie and I."

I watched as she chewed on the cuticles around her nails - a nervous habit - one I was familiar with as I sometimes did it.

"Well, it looks like we're going to be here a while." I joked, blowing one of Charlie's wayward curls aside as it attempted to shove its way up my nostril. "Wanna tell me what brought you to Firefly Cove?"

FIVE

stella

THE TIGHTNESS IN MY CHEST, which had been easing for the past couple of days of driving, returned. How much of my past was I willing to share with this stranger in the middle of a coffee shop?

Was I going to tell the truth about what happened or create a false narrative to protect myself and my daughter? Max seemed trustworthy enough. But could I just dump all the bullshit we had been dealing with in his lap and expect him not to run or turn me into the authorities?

Taking a fortifying breath, I opted for a semi-watered-down version of the truth. I picked at my cuticles and opened my mouth to speak, but no words came out. I promptly closed my gaping mouth and placed my hands in my lap.

I must have looked ridiculous, a deer in the headlights, struggling to articulate my thoughts; my throat felt tight, my tongue thick and clumsy. The unspoken words hung heavy in the air. I didn't know if I could do this.

"Uhm…" I started.

Sensing my rising anxiety, Max's hand left Charlie's back,

his touch reassuring as it settled on my arm, a silent gesture of support. The gentle touch on my arm, a silent act of comfort, gave me the courage I needed to confide in him.

"Where do I start?" With a sigh, I leaned back in my chair, the wood creaking slightly beneath me, and crossed my arms firmly over my chest.

"Charlie and I have always been a team. It's always been us against the world." I was stalling, and I knew it. I knew it would hurt to go back to that dark place, but I needed to just rip this off, like a bandaid.

"My ex-boyfriend, Charlie's father, isn't a good man." I tensed just mentioning Dean. The memory felt like a faded photograph, its colors muted with the passage of time and lost innocence. He had manipulated me into a version of myself I no longer knew. He became the only constant in my life, forcing me to rely on him alone.

9 YEARS EARLIER - 18 YEARS OLD

Standing outside of Bonneville High School, I tapped my combat booted foot on the concrete. Dean was late, again. The constant checking of the time on my cell phone only served to amplify my feelings of frustration, a wave of irritation that built with each passing second.

It was twenty minutes past the time he promised me he'd be here. With a determined stomp, I stuffed my phone in my pocket and headed toward the closest bench, fully intending to wait there until his ass showed up.

At least he hadn't bothered with an excuse. I knew it was all bullshit. I'd been fed enough bullshit from Dean to smell it a mile away.

He had probably gotten caught up in his buddy Waylon's garage smoking dope again and forgot to set an alarm to come get me. He was unreliable at best.

Dean was already out of school. He'd dropped out midway through his senior year to focus on his 'music career' - I was currently trudging my way through my senior year.

If you ask me, his music career was a crock of shit. He wasn't even that good at playing the drums, yet his buddies all blew smoke up his ass, claiming he was going to be the next Travis Barker.

We'd started dating at the beginning of this school year. My friend Bethany was dating Waylon, who was the lead singer of Dean's band, 'Die Trying', and I'd gone with her to one or two of their practices.

I instantly found myself drawn to Dean; He had that bad boy, rocker-esque, stick it to the man vibe about him. He had shaggy black hair that he let swoop over one of his eyes, a tongue piercing, and a couple of inky black tattoos swirling up his arms. To this rebel girl with abandonment issues, he was a walking wet dream.

Before we knew it, we were inseparable, a bond formed in shared experiences and mutual understanding. Dean was adopted after spending years bouncing around in the foster care system. He knew what it was like being abandoned by those who were supposed to love you the most.

Bethany and I showed up to every single one of 'Die Trying's' practices in Waylon's garage. We thought we were hot shit getting to date guys in a band.

After a couple months of dating, Dean started making little suggestions about the way I dressed and did my hair. He begged me to buy a pair of Doc Marten boots, some fishnets, and exceptionally inappropriate length skirts. I complied, telling myself that it was for my benefit as well as his.

He turned me into his personal 'emo' Barbie doll. At first, it was flattering. He always claimed he was trying to make us the 'it' couple. The skirts and fishnets, he said, made me look sexy. He'd follow that up with a comment here or there about what I ate or drank and how it would affect my body, sandwiching his jabs between compliments.

Eventually, Bethany and I had a falling out. She claimed Dean was emotionally manipulating me. She said she'd seen a huge change in the way I dressed and acted, and it wasn't the Stella she'd become friends with. She said that I'd been moodier and snappy, especially when it came to conversations about Dean.

I told her she was just jealous because Waylon didn't think she was sexy or ask her to wear clothes that made her look more grown up. I didn't need her meddling in my relationship when she couldn't even handle her own.

She had called me delusional, screaming that I'd come running back when Dean broke my heart, and we hadn't talked in weeks. Dean told me it was for the best and she was just jealous of the relationship we had because Waylon had been cheating on her throughout their relationship, anyway.

I believed him, my heart trusting his every word. I always believed him. Even if there was a little part of me that wondered if Bethany was right after all.

7 YEARS EARLIER - 20 YEARS OLD

Dean and I had officially been together for two years. He'd started working a construction job, and I'd been serving down at Granny's Diner on the corner of First Street & Landmark Road. It wasn't glamorous, but it paid the bills.

Shortly after graduating high school, we found ourselves in a small, single-room apartment, the sounds of the city a constant hum in the background. It sure wasn't glamorous, but for two twenty-year-olds out on their own for the first time, it was perfect.

I could look past the occasional roach or leak if it meant I was with the boy I loved.

My parents disapproved of Dean and my relationship, but I knew in my heart we were soul mates. They constantly voiced their disapproval, citing different ways he'd molded me to fit a vision that was so much unlike my true self. It had almost always ended in an argument. I didn't understand how two people who'd spent the majority of my childhood letting me be raised by nannies could suddenly care about who I spent time with.

Every time we talked, the chasm grew wider and wider until I didn't feel as if there was any way we could bridge that gap. After a while, I'd stopped calling home. I didn't want their constant ridicule. I was an adult, I could make my own decisions.

Dean treated me like a princess. After a long day at work, he would come home and sit at the kitchen table with a beer, eager to hear about my day. He was everything I'd ever dreamed about in a partner, and I couldn't wait for our life to truly begin.

Now, if I could just get him to take off his dusty work boots at the door instead of tracking mud and debris all over the place, that would be a plus.

We'd climb into bed each night, make love, and fall asleep to the sounds of the hustle and bustle of the town outside our window. We didn't live in the best area, but it was all we could afford.

We often fell asleep planning how we envisioned our future. Dean promised me a house, his eyes shining with dreams of rock-star wealth, once the band made it big. I held onto that dream, even when things started to feel bleak.

3 YEARS EARLIER - 24 YEARS OLD

I stood in line outside the dingy club in St. Louis, rubbing my hands over my exposed arms to keep warm. It was the middle of October, and the fall chill was setting into a winter briskness. Goosebumps popped up across my skin as a cool breeze blew past. The thigh-high boots, sweater and short leather skirt I wore did little to staunch the cold.

I was in line to get in to see Dean and the rest of 'Die Trying' play their set tonight. I'd asked Dean why he hadn't put me on the approved guest list and he'd patronized me, saying "that's just not how it works babe" with a kiss on my cheek.

I was pretty sure the opening band can leave a list of approved guests, and you'd expect that the drummer's long-

term girlfriend would be an acceptable addition, but who was I to argue?

Each small, cutting remark, like that one, chipped away at my confidence, leaving me feeling stupid. They were starting to wear me down. But, after six years of being together, starting over with someone else seemed like a fresh form of torture, so I sucked it up.

I approached the bouncer at the front of the line and handed him my ID card. He scanned it lazily and waved me inside without a second glance.

Stepping into the club, the thick smell of stale beer, cigarettes, and sweat overwhelmed me. I never would have come to a dive bar like this had Dean not been playing tonight. I'd much rather curl up at home with a warm blanket and a good book.

I looked around, trying to spot him among the sizable crowd of people gathering in front of the stage. When I didn't immediately see him, I walked up to the bar and flagged down a bartender. He gave me a brief nod, letting me know that he'd seen me and would be down my way in just a minute.

While I waited for the bartender to take my order, I did another once over on the crowd. I spotted what looked like it might be Dean over to the left-hand side of the stage, but there was a skinny, scantily clad brunette standing next to him with her hand resting intimately on his arm. Because their backs were to me, I dismissed it as a coincidence and returned my attention to the bar.

I ordered my beer, paid my tab, and turned around to continue looking for Dean. The couple I'd spotted earlier had since made their way closer to the stage and I could see now that I was wrong - it was Dean. A quiet rage flowed through my system as I watched him head towards the rest of the band.

He jumped up onto the stage with finesse and the brunette stood on her tiptoes as he leaned down and gripped her behind the neck, planting an obscene kiss on her red painted lips.

What the actual fuck?

He retreated to his drum kit, wiping the lipstick off his mouth as he sauntered over and straddled his stool. Despite knowing that what he was doing was wrong, his confidence suggested that he believed he wouldn't get caught. I guess that's why he didn't put me on the guest list. He wanted his plaything to see him play tonight.

The rush of fury that invaded my body had me vibrating as I chugged my beer. I couldn't believe him. I had undeniable proof that he was cheating on me; his actions left no room for doubt or any other explanation. How long had this been going on? How had I not seen something sooner? Lastly, why didn't it surprise me?

With a frustrated sigh, I turned toward the bartender, wiping the condensation from my empty bottle as I slammed it down onto the bar top, and ordered two more beers. I was about to get royally fucked up.

I LEFT *after Dean began his set; not staying to see the rest of the show. I caught an Uber back to our apartment and paced. I felt lost; my whole life revolved around Dean, and I didn't know what to do. Six years, a lifetime of shared moments, now felt like a dwindling ember threatening to extinguish. All because he couldn't keep his dick in his pants.*

The meager furnishings of the living room blurred through

my tear-filled vision as I stumbled into our shared bedroom, the emptiness echoing the hollowness in my heart.

I sat down on the edge of the bed and untied my well-worn Doc Martens and slid them off one at a time. When I got the first one off, I reared my arm back and slung it across the room. With a deafening crash, it shattered against the mirror on the far wall, sending shards of glass scattering across the floor.

I slid off the edge of the bed and clutched my knees to my chest. Tears dripped off my cheeks onto my knees and I didn't bother wiping them away. I felt stuck. I had intertwined my life so thoroughly with Dean's that I couldn't see a way out.

The sudden, sharp bang of a slamming door ripped me from sleep, my body stiff and aching from lying curled on the floor. I must have fallen asleep at some point and not bothered to remove the rest of my clothes or climb into bed.

Another slam came from the kitchen and I stood up, righting my skirt and wiping the salty crust from my puffy, tear-stained eyes. I didn't bother looking in a mirror. Dean could see me at my worst for all I cared.

Tiptoeing from the bedroom, I entered the adjacent living room and open-plan kitchen; the silence broken only by the gentle hum of the refrigerator. Dean had his head in the fridge, rifling around for something.

"Looking for something?" I asked without hesitation.

He jumped, and in his haste to remove his head from the fridge, smacked the back of it on the shelf.

"Fuck, Stell. You scared the shit outta me." He complained as he rubbed at the back of his sweat soaked hair. I had secretly hoped he'd have knocked himself out, but I couldn't get that lucky.

To appear stronger, I pulled my shoulders back, the fabric of my shirt rustling slightly as my arms crossed tightly over my chest. I felt the tremor of insecurity bubbling beneath the surface of my forced confidence. My heart was racing and I could hear the beat thumping in my skull.

Dean walked over to me and put both his hands on my hips. His grip was not only firm but verged on painful, causing me to wince. I uncrossed my arms to push against his chest. He reeked of cheap perfume, alcohol, and cigarettes. A lethal combination of bad decisions.

"What's wrong, baby?" he slurred as he pulled me closer, kissing down the slope of my neck. "I'm sorry I'm a little late, took us longer to pack up than we expected."

I pushed against him again and took a fortifying step back. I steeled my spine and willed myself not to cry. If I was going to get through this, I was going to have to pretend that my entire life wasn't falling apart at the seams.

"I saw you, Dean."

"I'm sure you did, babe. We fucking killed it up on that stage tonight."

"No." I said firmly, leaving no room for interpretation or pacification. "I saw you with that girl before the show."

A quick flash of fear crossed Dean's face, but his self-control was swift and soon his expression was devoid of emotion again.

"I'm not sure what you thought you saw, but it wasn't what it looked like," he said as he turned and walked back towards the kitchen in search of a beer, quickly dismissing me.

"I SAW YOU KISS HER!!" I shouted at his retreating form, not giving a fuck if the neighbors heard. I wasn't going to stand here and be lied to again.

A chill coasted down my spine as he stopped dead in his tracks and turned around. For the first time in six years, a bone-chilling fear, sharp and sudden, paralyzed me. A look of untamed fury, eyes blazing, flashed across Dean's face, his jaw clenching. His pupils were pinpoint as he stepped closer into my personal space.

Hoping to create distance, I took a step back. I was shaking.

I'd never once feared Dean before this moment; his presence had always been comforting, a familiar warmth. He'd raised his voice to me a handful of times, but it was always something I did wrong. Stalking toward me, his footsteps like drumbeats, he backed me into a wall. He leaned close, hands framing my head. His breath coasted across my face, it's warmth doing little to combat the chill that was washing over me.

His nearness was suffocating, the oppressive feeling of his authority weighing down. I turned my face away and squeezed my eyes shut.

He skated his nose from my collarbone up my neck to my ear, stopping to grab a handful of my hair hard enough to bring tears to my eyes and tilt my head back.

"Once more, I'm going to tell you this, you stupid fucking bitch. I'm not sure what you saw, but it wasn't what it fucking looked like." he hissed close enough to my ear that I could feel the humidity of his breath.

I kept my eyes shut, pressing my lids together so tightly that my head throbbed, and stood as still as a statue, my muscles tense.

"Are we fucking clear?"

I nodded, but apparently that wasn't answer enough as he gripped ahold of my hair again and I let out a tiny whimper of pain.

"I said, are we fucking clear?"

"Yes." I stammered out.

He released his punishing grip on my hair, and I sank to the floor in emotional agony. I couldn't hold back the sobs that wracked my body upon release.

He stormed into our bedroom, his anger a palpable force, and slammed the door with a resounding crash, effectively sealing me out.

I tucked my knees to my chest and wrapped my arms around them. I felt like I was physically trying to hold myself together. Letting go would allow my complete collapse. A tremor ran through me as the first guttural sob escaped, each subsequent wrack threatening to shatter my composure.

I lost track of time while curled up on the floor until my lower half became numb and I ran out of tears. I padded my way to our bedroom door and silently twisted the knob.

Dean was naked, sprawled out on the bed face down. I padded my way to the bathroom and changed out of my grimy club clothes and into an oversized tee shirt and panties. I didn't bother cleaning off my makeup. My tears, I figured, had sufficiently washed that away.

Tiptoeing to the bed, I eased myself down; the springs sighing softly beneath me, and curled into the smallest ball I could manage. Sweet release washed over me as I drifted into a dream where laughter and love reigned, a blissful respite from the harshness of truth.

For the first time, I was scared of my future.

MAX'S FACE was a mask of indifference, but the barely perceptible twitch in his jaw betrayed his calm demeanor. A silent storm brewing beneath a calm surface. I didn't need his sympathy. Charlie and I were safe - for now.

"Yeah, so.. Things were okay for the next couple years. I forgave him for cheating. He said it would never happen again. He only put his hands on me a couple more times. Most of the time it happened when he came home high or drunk. But, I stayed. Young, dumb, naïve, hopeful, whatever you want to call me, I've probably already said it about myself." I took another sip of my coffee as I waited for him to respond.

When he didn't, I looked up and was met with the blazing look of a man who was on a hair trigger and looking for a fight. He still didn't respond, so I continued.

"Anyway, we found out I was pregnant. Dean stopped using me as his personal punching bag and I just became a verbal sparring partner. I knew I needed to get out. I knew if I didn't, he'd end up killing me. After we found out about Charlie, Dean got really heavy into drugs, cocaine, to be exact. I always turned a blind eye to it, afraid to be on the receiving end of a junkie's wrath. But, about two days ago, things got bad." A nervous chuckle escaped as I sipped my coffee. "I mean, I guess they got *worse* - they were already bad."

This is the part of the story I dreaded the most. The thought of returning to that moment felt like drowning. I could feel that tightening knot of anxiety threatening to close my throat, urging me to keep quiet. I wanted to put the past in the past, but I knew that this wasn't over.

They wouldn't stop until I paid for what I knew, and I was realizing very quickly that I wasn't going to be able to do this on my own.

stella

SITTING *on the edge of the living room sofa, I glanced over at the clock above the stove - twelve-thirty.*

It had already been a while, and I was starting to wonder where Dean was because he should have been home by now. He told me he was heading over to drop off some sound equipment at Waylon's after work, then he'd be on his way home. That was hours ago.

I had already eaten dinner. His food was still sitting on the counter covered in tinfoil, waiting to be eaten.

Tapping my finger on the face of my phone, I willed it to ring. He should have been home, watching Charlie, freeing me up to head to work. I'd picked up a couple of night shifts at the local hotel checking in guests. Though it wasn't glamorous, the weight of the unpaid bills settled heavily on my chest, a dull ache mirroring the emptiness in my wallet.

Unlocking my phone, I clicked on Dean's contact and hit the phone icon to ring out. It rang once, twice, three times before going to voicemail.

"Leave me a message, fucker!" His voicemail screamed.

With a frustrated grunt, I stood up and paced the length of the apartment. Why didn't this surprise me? He'd never proven himself reliable. I just needed him to be a fucking father one or two days a week so I could make sure we had enough money to keep the lights on in this shit hole we called home.

I couldn't stand around idly waiting for him to get home. If he was going to be late, I was going to at least get some things done around the house to ease up the burden on my days off.

I grabbed a basket of dirty clothes and trudged into our makeshift laundry area in the hallway next to the kitchen. Although our apartment wasn't well-equipped, we were fortunate to find a unit with connections and room for a stackable washer and dryer. It prevented us from constantly walking down to the corner laundromat to use the commercial machines once or twice a week.

I opened the lid of the washer and started throwing in the clothing. I grabbed a pair of Dean's jeans and turned the pockets inside out. A small plastic bag dropped softly onto the floor. My blood ran cold, the thud of it hitting the floor echoing in my ears like a gunshot, each beat of my heart a frantic drum against my ribs.

I didn't have a under privileged upbringing, but I wasn't naïve about the drug scene. What had fallen on the floor, I knew, wasn't rock candy in a baggie. I did not know what the substance was, what it did, or how it was used, but I knew for certain it was out of place in my home and it sure as shit wasn't legal.

Reaching down, I pinched the edge of the baggie between my pointer finger and thumb. I regarded the crystals with the care that one might use when disarming a bomb.

About the time I held it up to my face for further inspection, the front door of the apartment slammed open, hitting the wall on its back-swing.

I fumbled the baggie in my haste to hide it and almost as if in slow motion; it hit the ground and broke open, shattering those clear crystals into a mixture of shards and fine dust. Doing my best to sweep it up with my hands into a pile and brush it into the now broken baggie, I cleaned up the majority.

Footsteps thudded behind me. They sounded heavier than I was expecting. Their approach was almost deafening. Fear flooded my veins as I refused to turn around. I closed my eyes and braced myself for what was to come, knowing I wouldn't see my boyfriend's face.

"Well, hello there, pretty thing," came a sickeningly vile voice from behind me. His southern drawl made each word come out with a hiss, reminding me of a snake.

There's something about facing your biggest fears in life that either shrivels you into nothingness or builds you up to be a badass bitch. I steeled my spine and turned towards the intruder, choosing the bad ass bitch road even if I felt like shriveling into nothing.

I'm sure he could smell my fear. Nasty men like him preyed on the weak. He seemed to slink around me, circling his prey.

He spotted the small baggie I'd unsuccessfully tried to hide by the humming washer, and his eyes instantly found mine, a haze of fury washing over them. Before I could think, he had me gripped by the throat. My breath came in strangled pants as I struggled to inhale through the tiny space available in my windpipe. His grip was punishing, and his eyes were staring straight through me.

My limited knowledge of the drug scene, gleaned from

late-night TV dramas, told me he was high; his pupils were dilated, and his speech was slurred, though what substance coursed through his veins was a mystery.

I gripped at his hand around my throat, attempting to pry his fingers from their hold. It was no use. Whatever drugs were flowing through his system gave him an inhuman like strength that I would never overpower.

"You've made a mess of my fucking product, little girl," he spat. "I'd add that to the tally for your man, but that debt's already been paid."

His breath reeked of poor dental hygiene and cigarettes. I studied his face, aiming to remember it if I lived. He was grimy - grimier than I'd ever seen a man before. He looked and smelled like he hadn't showered in weeks. His jet black hair parted down the middle and fell to his shoulders. It looked wet, but I realized quickly that it was just dirt and oil. His eyes were wild - looking in stuttering darts from left to right, attempting to focus on what was in front of him and failing.

Two teardrop tattoos adorned his left cheek; the artist had filled one in, but the other was only a shaky black outline. He had a scar that crested from the top of his right cheekbone to his hairline, bisecting his eyebrow and leaving a jagged slice through the hair.

"Got anything to say, or does the cat got your tongue?" Leaning down, he ran the tip of his nose down from behind my ear to my collarbone, scenting me like a dog.

His intentions unclear, my hands trembled, fearing his next action. His grip on my neck loosened marginally, enough for me to take a deep inhale and cough.

"Please, I did nothing." I whimpered. His grin was feral as he moved his hand from my throat to behind my head and *grabbed a handful of my hair, yanking my head back to look him directly in the eyes. A wave of remembrance struck me as I saw his actions mirrored Dean's. Again, I found myself trembling in fear.*

"You didn't, but your bitch of a man did."

I had no clue what he was talking about. The thought of Dean's actions leading to this brutal confrontation left me with a hollow ache in my chest.

Dean wasn't even here. How did this guy get in? My brain buzzed with questions, a chaotic swarm of confusion as I struggled to make sense of what was happening.

"Good thing he won't be a problem anymore." He spat as he released my hair and gripped my arm, pulling me roughly into the living room.

The moment my feet crossed the threshold of the main living area, a wave of dizziness washed over me as all the blood drained from my head.

Dean was on the floor, face down, in front of the sofa. He was motionless. I couldn't see the rhythmic rise or fall of his chest.

My attacker grabbed my shoulders, pushing me toward Dean's body and preventing me from turning away. Another man stood overtop, as if keeping watch to make sure he stayed put. I was sure that Dean wouldn't be going anywhere.

I'd never seen a dead body before; the sight was shocking and surreal, the stillness unnatural. I'd never even been to a funeral. My parents didn't have many friends or living relatives, which had worked to shield me, preventing exposure to life's harsher realities.

Looking at Dean lying lifeless on the floor in our shared living room, I felt the darkness. I wasn't inherently sad that Dean was gone, but there was a cloud of dread that sat suspended over the scene. Was I going to be next? What would happen to Charlie?

Charlie...

I fought the urge to look down the hall to our bedroom, where our little girl was sleeping. I didn't want to bring any unwanted attention towards her. If I could shield her from the destruction and devastation, even for another couple of hours, until a neighbor found our bodies and called for help, I'd do anything to keep her from this.

A cold sweat slicked my palms as I whispered a desperate plea, every breath a tremor in the face of Charlie's uncertain fate. A mother's job was to keep her children fed, happy, and safe.

The hulking, dirty man who'd been holding me pushed my shoulders towards the ground. My knees buckled underneath, and I caught myself by my hands, my head dangerously close to Dean's body. I fought the urge to vomit the contents of my stomach.

"This is what happens to fucking snakes." He punctuated his words with a kick to Dean's gut. His head lolled to the side, and I got a glimpse into his wide, terror-stricken eyes.

"Your man here decided to eat through my product that was meant to be sold. He owes me a whole lot of money."

The lifeless orbs looked through me and I choked out a sob. The sad part was, I wasn't crying for Dean. The punishment meted out by the thugs was probably deserved, given his past actions and behavior. He was a shitty partner, an absent father, a drug addict, an abuser, and I was relieved that he was dead.

Not knowing what was about to happen, I cried. I was crying for our daughter, who was going to grow up an orphan. I was crying because I could sense death hovering - waiting to take me with him.

"Scuzz, you offin the girl or what? We've gotta get the fuck outta here." The other intruder asked, his eyes just as beady and expressionless as his partner's.

"I don't think so," he replied with a predatory tilt to his head. "There's still a debt to pay, and she looks like a fun little play thing."

A door slamming down the hallway had both men looking over their shoulders. The seconds ticked by as they waited for whoever was outside the door to leave down the hall. Sensing that the coast was clear, he crouched down in front of me and used his thick pointer finger to lift my chin, averting my gaze from Dean.

His smile was wicked as he licked his lips and leaned in close to my ear. "I didn't plan on having a pretty piece of ass like yourself follow me home, but I'll be back."

His promise filled my veins with an icy dread. "You can run, but you can't hide," he whispered as he licked my earlobe. I found myself fighting against the urge to vomit again, not from the dead body, but from the insinuation of what this man could do to me.

As he pushed himself up to his feet and he and his partner disappeared down the quiet hallway, a choking sob escaped my throat, leaving me in stunned silence.

As soon as they shut the door behind them, I crumpled. The heaving sobs choked through my chest, making it hard to breathe. I scooted backwards on my hands and feet to rest my back against the closed door.

The tears flowed in rivers down my cheeks, my eyes becoming swollen and puffy by the minute, obstructing my vision.

A small whimper came from our bedroom and broke me from my pit of despair. In my desperation to keep myself from falling apart, I'd forgotten that Charlie was still in the other room, completely oblivious to our life crumbling around us.

With one last choked sob, I tore myself away from Dean's stillness, the desperate need to survive overriding all else, and started packing.

SEVEN

NOT EVEN THE peaceful warmth of the sleeping child in my arms, her gentle snores a counterbalance to my pounding heart, could diminish the searing rage that consumed me after hearing all that Stella had been through.

A ragged breath caught in my throat; a burning rage ignited within me, the need to hunt this motherfucker down and end him with my bare hands overwhelming.

Although Stella had talked in riddles and half-truths, mincing words because of our current locale, I'd gotten the gist of the danger these two girls were in - and danger was an understatement. I had just inserted myself into something I had no business being involved in, all because a pretty woman had occupied my thoughts.

"Say something." Stella begged, breaking me out of my rage induced stupor.

Unable to articulate my emotions, I began, "I..." I raised the arm not holding Charlie and scrubbed my hand down my face. "I'm not sure what to say."

Her face fell, a look of utter devastation washing over her features as I fought the urge to reach over and take her hand. The way she hung her head and the tremor in her voice told me she felt utterly defeated, a sense of hopelessness radiating from her.

I took a minute to sit with my feelings as Stella sipped on her coffee. I was completely at a loss for words, unsure how to articulate to Stella the whirlwind of emotions I was experiencing following her shocking revelation. After all, I'd only met her yesterday.

Even then, something inside of me screamed that I couldn't just let her deal with all of this alone. What would happen to her and Charlie if these men did find her?

She sipped the last bit of her coffee, sucking the remnants of the liquid up the straw, creating a loud gurgling sound. I watched her plump lips slide to the end of the straw and her tongue dart out to catch a stray drop of the drink.

What was it about this woman with her enigmatic, hard fought smile, and piercing gaze that caused such a visceral reaction in me even after hearing how she'd left her dead boyfriend on the floor of their apartment and bolted for safety?

I felt an overwhelming need to slay all her demons, lock her up in my tower, keep her safe, and fuck her simultaneously. It was unsettling.

I looked down at the little girl in my arms, wondering what it would be like to live in a constant state of oblivion to how cruel the world around you is.

I brushed a stray curl away from her forehead and watched as she shifted, pursing her pouty lips. She was so innocent in all of this.

Ma had always called me her 'little thinker,' but in that

moment, the urge to act overtook my usual careful nature, a rush of adrenaline replacing my contemplative mind.

I looked up to meet Stella's eyes and without hesitation said, "move in with me".

Her reaction was immediate; a sharp intake of breath, a tremor in her hands. The expression of defeat on her face quickly transformed into one of utter shock as she recoiled.

"Excuse the fuck out of me?"

"Move in with me," I repeated. "You and Charlie can come stay on the ranch with my brother Wade and I. We have the room and you need a place to stay. It's outside of town, off the beaten path, and you'll be safe there." I shrugged like the suggestion of moving in with two strangers was a normal conversation for a Tuesday morning in a small town coffee shop.

"Wade and I moved into the big house on the ranch a couple of years ago. It's basically a bachelor pad, but it has five bedrooms. We're only using two currently, a third when Wade's best friend Ray stays over. We can set you up in a room until you can get on your feet. The house has a security system, and my dad lives right next door in the old bunkhouse."

The voice in my head was barely audible, a faint breath of a suggestion—'or you can just stay forever'. The thought came unexpectedly, and I shook it off, completely baffled by where it was coming from. This girl had me thrown completely off my rocker.

I had never been this impulsive, even with Shannon. Our relationship hadn't been the type of instantaneous, passionate whirlwind romance you often read about in novels; instead, it unfolded more gradually and steadily. Nearly eight years of building our life together, I popped the question - and, well; you know the rest.

Stella's mouth opened and closed like a fish as she attempted to gather the words she was looking for. I was sure she was about to curse me six ways to Sunday when she looked down at Charlie. I could see the resignation etched across her face, a visible shift in her demeanor that spoke volumes.

She knew they needed safety and stability more than she needed her pride. I could see the war between what she needed and what she wanted flashing through her mind. I knew that her hesitance was deep-rooted in her fear of being controlled again.

I wasn't trying to take away her independence or staunch her resilience. This girl was fierce. I was trying to offer her the opportunity to lean on other people for help.

"How do I know you're not a serial killer?" she prodded.

With a quiet chuckle, I twisted, feeling the smooth fabric of my pants shift as I reached into my back pocket for my wallet. I flicked it open and handed it to her.

"Maxwell Jason Daniels, born August 15th, 1997 - address is 407 D and D Ranch Way. Social security…" she cut me off by putting her hand up.

I could see the subtle shake of her head as she cataloged my ridiculousness.

"Run a background check, Trouble. It will come back clean - minus the time I got caught running down main street in my skivvies on a dare at twenty-one. Ask anyone in this town anything you want to know about me. I promise you and Charlie will be safe."

"Skivvies? What is this, 1950?" she laughed as she handed me back my folded wallet.

I carefully tucked it back into my pocket, taking great care not to jostle Charlie, and looked back up at her. She was chewing on one of her cuticles, and I reached forward to coax her hand gently from her mouth.

"I have the same nervous habit - my nail girl hates it." I joked, flashing my stubby fingernails and cracked cuticles in her direction.

She let out another breathy laugh. I wanted to keep making her laugh, to see the crinkles around her eyes and hear that melodic sound. She rolled her eyes incredulously at my joke before taking a deep breath and releasing it slowly, as if blowing out all the trepidation she'd been harboring.

"Okay." she sighed.

"Okay… what?" I prodded, stunned by her answer, having expected more of a fight.

"We will move in with you and your brother… *temporarily*, but we will have to do some shopping. I have little in the way of a crib, a playpen, or toys for Charlie." she seemed to get lost in her head for a moment. Her shoulders drew inward and her head hung between her shoulders.

I could see the uncertainty gnawing at her. Was this shift in attitude because of the grief of Charlie's father's passing, the unsettling experience of sharing a house with strangers, her bone-deep exhaustion, or some toxic combination of all three? I could see the weight of it pressing down on her.

"I'm sure we probably have some things in the attic from when Wade and I were kids. Ma was a hoarder of sentimental things. I'm sure she probably even kept locks of our hair and some of our baby teeth." I assured, hoping to comfort her with a soft smile.

"Let us help." I added for good measure.

About the time I saw the resignation seep into Stella's

features, Charlie started to stir and rub her eyes. She let out a face splitting yawn, and I chuckled. She startled for a moment, forgetting where she'd fallen asleep and looking around for her mama.

"Good morning, sunshine. Sleep well?" I said with a grin.

Stella sucked in a sharp breath, a sound like air hissing through a punctured tire, and I looked up at her, concern etched on my face. Had I said or done something wrong? Her eyes filled with tears as she reached over to shift Charlie onto her own lap.

I helped plop the toddler into the comfort of her mama's arms and rubbed the back of my neck, attempting to stretch out the kink from holding the little chunk. I sure wasn't conditioned to holding babies for any length of time.

"Did I say something wrong?" I asked hesitantly, thinking back on what I'd said.

"No, Max. You didn't." Her emerald eyes met mine, and from just one look, I felt my world shift. "You said nothing wrong at all."

AFTER WALKING Stella and Charlie back to the Mayfair to gather their things, I gave her directions to the ranch. Though not far from town, the back roads leading there were barely more than narrow, winding tracks, easily missed by an unfamiliar driver.

As she strapped Charlie into her car seat, I instructed her to stay close behind me. I noted the way she adjusted the straps, tightened them down, and shifted the clip to right over the center of Charlie's chest.

Never having strapped a baby into a car seat before, I found it oddly complicated. It looked like there were twenty or so straps, and I had no clue how they all clipped together. I made a mental note to watch some YouTube videos about car seat safety later, in case of an emergency.

The drive to the ranch, a scenic route through rolling hills and past grazing cattle, took approximately fifteen minutes. Stella stayed close behind my truck the entire way. When we pulled onto the property, I hooked a right to head towards the big house.

The left of the property was mainly stables for our personal horses and a barn to store hay in for the winter. There was also a walking trail that my Ma and Pops had worn down that went through the woods to one of my favorite spots. I made another mental note to show Stella around. I figured that having an overview of her surroundings would show her that she was going to be safe here.

Pulling up to the house, I parked on the right-hand side. We had a makeshift parking area that could fit four or five large sized trucks comfortably, side by side. We rarely filled it, but with the extra vehicle, I wanted to make sure Stella had enough room to get Charlie in and out of her car seat comfortably.

Stella pulled in right beside my truck and killed the engine. Before I even had a chance to hop out and help, she had Charlie unbuckled and propped on her hip. Resigning myself to the fact that Stella didn't need constant coddling, I motioned for her to walk towards the front porch.

The big house wasn't fancy; its weathered clapboard siding and mismatched windows spoke of a long, quiet history. Most folks thought that every ranch had a 'big house' that was reminiscent of what they saw on Yellowstone, but ours couldn't be further from that. It was a modest five-bedroom house with white siding and a wrap-around porch. Ma had insisted that Pops install a porch swing on the side.

She used to say that every good southern farmhouse needed a rickety porch swing, and she often spent many nights curled up on that thing, drinking a cup of tea and regaling stories of her and Pops' good ol' years.

In the two years since she'd been gone, none of us Daniels men could stomach sitting on it. It stood as a vigil to the wonderful woman we had lost. It brought back the gut wrenching pain of losing our family matriarch, but none of us wanted to remove it.

"Let's see this bachelor pad, cowboy." Stella teased with a grin, knocking me out of my trip down memory lane.

The country air must have given her a little sense of peace. She seemed marginally happier out here in the sticks, away from the hustle and bustle of town. I took in how her hair glowed in the warm summer sunlight and the way her eyes sparkled as she took in her surroundings. She seemed lighter, even in the last twenty or so minutes.

As she sauntered towards the front porch, I noticed a slight sashay in her hips. I'm sure it was just the counterbalance of carrying a child on her hip, but reason flew out the window the instant she cocked her head over her shoulder and called back, "You comin'?"

Fuck.

Yes, yes, I would be coming. Right in my fucking Wranglers if I didn't get a grip on the hard on that was thickening in my jeans from watching her tight ass crest the porch steps.

Maybe I had a mommy kink, maybe I got off on playing savior to the damsel in distress, maybe I just had a Stella fetish. Whatever it was, this woman was playing with fire and

I knew trouble wasn't just going to be a nickname; she was trouble personified.

As we stepped up the couple steps to the wraparound porch, I hesitated. I should have warned Wade that I was bringing a woman.. and a baby.. home. Gripping the handle of the red front door, I twisted it, pushed it open with a creak, and silently prayed that he was clothed. Apparently, the universe thought I didn't need a win in that department.

"Fuck, bro! You scared the sh..." Wade stopped as he rounded the corner from the kitchen into the foyer. He was in nothing but a pair of black boxer shorts with tiny red hearts all over them and his cowboy hat.

For the lord's sake.

I could hear Stella snickering behind me as she turned around, presumably shielding Charlie's eyes from the view of a nearly naked cowboy in the foyer of what was to be their new home.

"Uhm. Didn't know we'd have company.." He stammered, "I'll go put some clothes on."

He brushed past me in a hurry, his feet stomping loudly on the stairs to my left as he rushed up them. I turned around in slight embarrassment to gauge Stella's reaction, expecting to see her just as rattled as I was. Instead, she greeted me with a wide grin and a small laugh.

I shook my head and gestured for Stella to walk ahead of me as we entered the kitchen.

The kitchen had been Ma's sanctuary. She'd meticulously selected every detail in this room, all the way down to the cabinet handles. She'd nearly given Pops a heart attack when she'd insisted on sage green cabinets and the expensive white granite countertop.

He'd tried to convince her to go with something more

neutral, but she pulled out her hidden weapon - the puppy dog eyes. Eventually, he'd forked over design rights completely and walked around behind her with the checkbook. After all - happy wife, happy life.

She spent many nights cooking extravagant dinners, even though it was just us three burly men eating. Her love language was always making sure we went to sleep with full stomachs. It wasn't lost on me how privileged I was to be raised in a house full of love and support.

Wade came stomping back down the stairs in a pair of grey sweatpants and a faded rodeo tee shirt. With a flick of his wrist, he swept his long hair away from his face, revealing a dazzling grin that was aimed directly at Stella.

"Sorry 'bout that," he drawled, extending his hand for her to shake. With a slight movement, she shifted Charlie to the side and grasped his hand in a firm handshake.

"Nice to meet you, I'm Wade. The hotter Daniels' twin." He said, accentuating his introduction with a wink.

"Stella." she said simply and gave him a terse smile. I could sense that she wasn't overly comfortable around men, especially ones who weren't shy, like my brother. Her rigid posture and protective stance gave that away.

"This is Charlie." She added as the little girl made excessive wiggle motions to be put down. Seeking my approval, she looked at me, and I nodded in response. With a gentle lowering motion, she placed the wiggling toddler on the floor, giving the little one the chance to explore the surrounding area.

If they were staying long term, we definitely needed to install some childproof latches and covers to keep her safe.

"So, Stella, what brings you to Casa de Daniels?" Wade

asked, walking over to the fridge and grabbing out a bottle of beer.

I snatched the beer out of his hand before he had the chance to pop the top. I motioned for him to sit on the barstool at the island counter. He plopped down with a huff and waited for me to explain why I'd stopped his mid-afternoon drink-a-thon.

"Stella and Charlie are going to be staying with us for a while. I'd appreciate it if we kept the drinking to a minimum," I said, scratching at the stubble that was forming on my chin. "They've gotten themselves in a bit of a bind and need a safe place to land, so I need you to be on your best behavior."

"Ooooo-kay," he said, lengthening the front of the word in confusion. His eyes narrowed on mine, imploring me to elaborate, but I gave nothing away.

It was Stella's story, and hers alone to share with the world in her own time and way. Confiding in Wade was entirely her decision, and she could do so when and if she was comfortable.

"That's all the.." the front door flying open and a shrill shriek coming from the foyer interrupted my thoughts.

"*A BABY*!!!" a female voice screamed, causing all of our heads to turn in its direction.

"Oh, for fuck's sake." I said, running my hands down my face in exasperation.

Now, I not only had to explain to my brother why I brought a woman and child home, but also to his best friend, Ray.

stella

ROUNDING THE KITCHEN CORNER, a woman with a pixie-like appearance emerged, Charlie in her arms. Perfectly content being carried, she sat propped on her hip, gripping her long, black hair, chubby hands gently twisting the strands.

The girl extricated her hair from Charlie's grasp and pinched her cheeks, causing her to let out a boisterous giggle. This girl definitely wasn't shy around babies.

I stifled the urge to reach over and rescue my daughter from the stranger's arms, but she seemed perfectly at ease in her presence.

"You know, Wade, I knew all those one-night stands would eventually catch up with you," she joked as she patted him gently on the arm.

"Ain't mine, sunshine" he countered proudly, a wide grin taking over his face, confidence radiating from him in waves.

I got the notion that Wade was the more promiscuous Daniels' brother and thanked whatever higher power above that he hadn't been the one to rescue me.

The raven-haired pixie, her eyes widening in surprise, looked over at Max. Her gathering of facts was clearly leading somewhere, and I could see the cogs turning in her mind as she formed conclusions based on what she had learned.

Instead of letting her create her own stories, ones that may or may not include my child being fathered by the hot cowboy standing beside me, I walked towards her and put my hands out to take Charlie.

"She's mine." I said as I lifted her from her arms and tucked her into my side while nuzzling her chubby neck. The sound of her giggles caused the biggest, most genuine smile to spread across my face.

Her radiant joy was a warm sunbeam that chased away the shadows, leaving me in a tranquil state of blissful contentment. In an attempt to ease my worries, I kept focusing on the fact that she was young and wouldn't remember all the struggle we'd been dealing with.

"I got that much," the girl said as she gave me a once-over. It wasn't intended to be negative; rather, it was meant to be protective and cautious. Her gaze was sharp and calculating as she surveyed the scene, and I felt the weight of her appraisal like a brand on my skin.

I could instantly tell that she was fiercely protective of these men. Her eyes narrowed and her stance was unwavering. The familiarity in her eyes suggested she'd known them for years, perhaps even decades.

"Nice to meet you..." she prompted.

"Stella, and the baby you rescued from her great escape to find something to chew on is Charlie." I held Charlie's hand up and waved for her. She giggled and attempted to repeat the motion after I'd let her hand go.

"I'm Ray - short for Rayna Cortez."

"Aka, Sunshine." Wade interrupted as he gazed at her with a sly smile. He looked at her with a familiarity that reeked of long-time secrets.

I wondered what their story was. It wasn't often girls and guys could be friends without one falling for the other. I reminded myself that it wasn't my concern, and that respecting others' privacy was the key to protecting my own.

Ray leaned over and smacked the back of her hand into Wade's gut. He let out a pained grunt and clutched his stomach in exaggeration.

"Wade's the only one who calls me that. Everyone else just calls me Ray."

"Noted." I said with a slight nod.

"So, welcome to small town USA, Stella. Who's the pappy of cutie pie Charlie here?"

She reached over and tweaked Charlie's cheek again, causing her to let out another string of giggles. I hesitated for a second too long and Max answered for me, sensing my unease.

"He's not in the picture. Stella needs somewhere to stay short term, so I offered her one of the rooms here."

A look of curious confusion washed over Ray's face as her eyes flickered between Max and me. I could hear the gears turning as she tried once again to work out the dynamic between us. She was intuitive, I could sense that about her.

"Stop trying to see into their souls, Sunshine." Wade piped up and took a step back to avoid being hit in the gut again.

"You don't find this weird?" she asked him, gesturing between Max and I.

Wade shrugged and went to the fridge to grab a bottle of

water. He handed one to Max, one to Ray, and offered one to me with a slight head nod. I took the bottle with an appreciative smile.

"I mean, sure. It's weird - but it's also not my fucking business why Stella needs somewhere to stay. If Max offered a place, he has good reason, and I trust him."

A wave of relief washed over Ray; I could visibly see her relax, a subtle smile playing on her lips. It was as if her and Wade's feelings were in tune. If he was okay with the situation, she could be too.

I again found myself wondering about their dynamic. They seemed to bicker like brother and sister, but the looks I had caught Wade shooting in her direction were definitely not of the platonic variety.

Hmm, interesting.

"My plan isn't to stay here long term. I need a job to earn enough money for a deposit on a downtown apartment, then once I have that saved up, I'll be out of your hair," I said shyly.

Receiving handouts, particularly from strangers, was something I detested. For so long, the only person I could rely on was myself. I wasn't used to having a 'village', so to speak.

"You can stay as long as you need to." Max reiterated.

The front door clicked open, and another set of boots stomped into the kitchen. The weathered cowboy standing in the entry looked around with a confused expression.

"Didn't know y'all were having a party over here." He said as he walked over to Max and slapped him playfully on the shoulder.

"Pops, this is Stella and her daughter Charlie. They're going to be taking one of the guest rooms here for a while."

The older gentleman rounded the kitchen island and held out a hand in introduction. I shook it, noticing how his palms were full of rough callouses - clearly from years of working on the ranch.

"It's nice to meet you, sir."

"No sir needed, darlin'," he grumped. "Hank, if you're feeling formal, but most of these hooligans call me Pops- Ray Charles over there, included." He hooked a thumb in Ray's direction and she cocked a quizzical eyebrow.

"Ray Charles?" she questioned.

"You've gotta be blind to be hanging out with that ugly fucker over there every day." He said, hooking the same thumb over in Wade's direction.

My hand went over my mouth to stifle the laugh. I didn't know this family well enough yet to be laughing at their expense, but you could clearly tell they picked on each other out of love.

I missed having friends that I could joke with. It had been so long since I'd seen any of my family, and my friends all but abandoned me the longer that Dean and I stayed together.

I should have noticed the red flags that Dean was throwing - but ignorance is bliss.

"Hey, this ugly fucker takes offense to that statement." Wade huffed in mock annoyance.

"Anyway, welcome to the family, Stella and Charlie." Hank said, attempting to turn the conversation back to the original topic at hand.

Family. We had instantly gone from being on our own to having a makeshift family. They had so easily welcomed us into their fold. I wasn't sure how to appreciate all they were doing for us, but I'd make sure we pulled our weight while we were here.

"Thank you, Hank." I responded quietly.

"How old is little Charlie here?" He asked, changing the subject. "Been awhile since I've been around little ones, but I'm happy to help in any way I can. I'll have her riding, shooting, and shotgunning beers in no time."

I chuckled, having no doubt that Hank would make an excellent grandpa to some babies in the future. "She's ten months. It turns out she shares a birthday with the twins." I said with a sly smile in Max's direction.

I had left that out at the coffee shop after looking at his license. Although some might dismiss it as mere coincidence, I saw it as a sign of good faith, a subtle nod of approval from the universe.

Max gave me a small smile back as he reached for Charlie. It hit me at that moment that I'd never seen her held by so many other people. She didn't have aunts and uncles and I kept a low profile with a small friend group. Dean was truly a father in name only. I don't think I'd often seen him hold her, change a diaper, or show her much affection for that matter.

A line of dampness threatened to spill over my bottom lashes, and I bent my head to quell them from falling. I turned to the fridge to busy myself- after all, this was now my home as well. I didn't want them seeing me cry over something as silly as people showing my child affection.

I reached in and grabbed a bottle of water, giving myself the time I needed to pull my emotions into line. I turned and set it on the counter beside the other bottle I'd been given.

As Wade took note of the pair of untouched water bottles remaining on the kitchen counter, a gentle nod conveyed his understanding of how uncomfortable this situation was for me.

Slightly embarrassed, I slowly twisted off the bottle cap, a warmth spreading across my cheeks; I paused a moment to quell the blush before bringing the bottle's opening to my lips.

"Well, there, little one, you can be our third amigo," Max said and tickled her belly. A joyous peal of laughter burst from her lips as she playfully wriggled, a giggle shaking her whole body in his embrace.

The grin that plastered on Max's face melted some of the ice around my heart. How had this stranger taken a liking to my daughter faster than her own father had?

I pushed the thoughts away. It didn't matter anymore. His presence would quickly fade from memory. Maybe someday, I'd meet someone willing to take on the baggage of a single mom with an almost one-year-old baby, no place to live, and no family to call her own.

Ray piped up and snatched Charlie out of Max's arms. "I call dibs on babysitting occasionally. I miss having babies around the house. All the kids are old enough now that they don't enjoy having their older sister cramping their style."

"Ray is the oldest of ten," Wade explained. "She's got tons of experience with little kids if you ever need to get out of the house and have some 'you' time."

His wink, a theatrical, exaggerated gesture, was impossible to ignore. I felt the blush creeping back up my neck and spreading across my cheeks.

"I appreciate it. I haven't been out without her since she's been born. It's been just the two of us for so long. Forgive me if I take a little while to feel comfortable letting other people in." Rubbing the back of my neck shyly, I looked down at my feet.

I felt a heavy hand drape onto my shoulder. I looked over

at Hank and gave him a small smile. The smile he gave me in return was genuine and kind. I could see light crinkles at the corners of his lips, presumably from a life filled with laughter. His chocolate brown eyes peered into mine, as if silently letting me know I wasn't alone anymore.

Those damn tears I'd fought so hard to squash bubbled up again and I swiped beneath my lashes.

"You're one of us now, girl," he whispered. "For however long you're here, we've got you."

At that moment, the weight of the world pressed down on me, and I could feel the overwhelming urge to cry. I sensed a shift, feeling everything all at once. Although I felt supported and comforted, I also felt adrift without a paddle.

I didn't know vulnerability; it was a foreign concept, unfamiliar territory. I couldn't step back and trust others. I hoped that the Daniels family and their community would be patient with me through the process of healing.

I still feared that the other shoe would eventually drop. But, more importantly, I felt hope. I hoped we would carve out a life for ourselves. Even if that life didn't end up being forever in Firefly Cove, I hoped that eventually we would truly be okay.

Max gave me a knowing nod as he rounded towards Ray to take Charlie back. He walked my girl back to me and held her out in offering. Somehow, in the brief time we'd been around each other, Max could sense the shift in my mood. He knew I needed the assurance of having Charlie safe in my arms.

I gave a watery chuckle as the tears I'd been holding back streamed down my face in silent rivers. I held my girl close and breathed in her fleeting baby scent. She was so innocent in all of this, and I relished in her unfiltered joy for a moment.

"Let me show you where you're gonna stay. I'll get up in the attic tomorrow to bring down the crib and whatever other baby things Ma stored up there," he said as he put a hand on my lower back to guide me down a long hallway.

Ignoring the pleasantness of his touch, I followed obediently. I turned my head over my shoulder to acknowledge everyone else.

"Thank you guys. I'll see you around."

"See you! I'll run by the house and snag a pack-n-play for y'all to use tonight if you'd like." Ray added.

"I'd love that. Thank you again." I responded.

Max pushed open the last door on the right side of the hallway and held his hand out in offering.

"I hope you'll find your accommodations suitable, ma'am." He gestured into the room.

I chuckled, surveying my surroundings. A queen sized bed sat against the far wall with crisp white linens and what seemed to be a handmade quilt draped over top. There was an end table on the right side with a small lamp. A small TV and an armoire stood across the room.

I walked over to the bed and ran my hand over the quilt. The stitching was jagged, obviously hand sewn, and the color was a mixture of sage greens and yellows. It reminded me of a field of daffodils in the spring. It was obviously a family heirloom, and I wondered who had made it. A pang of sadness hit me straight in the gut, reminding me that I never had the luxury of family heirlooms or anything handmade. The difference between the family that Max had grown up with and the one I'd endured couldn't have been further apart.

Max cleared his throat behind me, bringing me back to the present.

"Um, yeah, so. That door leads to the bathroom. I figured

you might want the room that had an en suite, so you don't have to share with me or Wade." he said sheepishly.

"Thank you. I don't need my own bathroom, but I appreciate it."

"Charlie's room is right across the hall. I'll ask Ray if they have a spare baby monitor we can install in there. I'm not sure if she had her own room at your previous place, so I figured you might want to be able to see her during the night. Anything else you need for her, I can take you into Atlanta and we can hit the Target..." I stopped him with a hand on his broad arm.

He was rambling and although it was cute as hell; I wanted to give him the peace of knowing that I appreciated everything he was doing for us.

"Max, thank you. I don't have words to even convey how much this means to me. You've seriously gone above and beyond, and I don't know how I'll ever repay you."

He smiled sincerely and backed towards the door.

"I'll let you two get settled. We will probably have frozen pizzas for dinner tonight since I didn't plan on extra mouths to feed." He hesitated before asking, "Uhm.. will Charlie eat that?"

It was endearing how clueless he was when it came to raising children.

"She will probably gnaw on some pizza. She's still partially breast fed, but I've been giving her bits and pieces of whatever I eat when it's something she can handle."

A deep crimson blush crept over Max's cheeks, making me inwardly chuckle at his embarrassment. When flustered, he looked almost boyish.

"Okay, well, you two have a couple of hours before

dinner. Make yourselves comfortable and let me know if you need anything."

He scrambled out of the room like his pants were on fire and I laughed lightly. I looked down at Charlie with a wide smile.

"All men go soup-brained when women talk about their boobs." I said with a subtle shake of my head in exasperation.

stella

CHARLIE'S ROUTINE made things easier for everyone and before we knew it, two weeks had already passed since we'd moved into the big house, with Max and Wade as our roommates.

Except for the first couple of nights, which proved difficult, as she refused to sleep in the crib Max had painstakingly dragged down from the attic, things were going well.

We'd gone that first week into Atlanta and snagged some baby essentials that Max and Ray hadn't been able to supply with hand-me-downs. Mostly things like diapers, wipes, pacifiers, a crib mattress, and obviously a few cute outfits. Max had been such a good sport as I pawed through the racks of endless baby clothes. He even offered his opinions when I held a couple up for inspection, never once looking like he wanted to be anywhere else.

I had put away a small amount of money in preparation for leaving Dean. During his working hours, I had babysat for a neighbor in our apartment complex. I left our apartment immediately after he went to work, returning before he got back home. If he would have found out my intention to have money for myself, he would have drained my account dry on the notion that what's mine was his and what's his was also his.

In the weeks of living with Max, I'd managed to snag a job at one of the local boutiques in town. I didn't remember how freeing it was to have something to call my own. It had been so long since I'd been anything more than just a mom. Going to work each day was the welcome reprieve I needed to fill back up my proverbial cup.

I'd only ever held jobs here and there, but working at the shop was easy enough to learn. The boutique focused on affordable but stylish clothing for the mid-twenties to early thirties crowd. I always managed to find a new piece or two that I fell in love in each new shipment.

This week, we'd gotten in a pair of rhinestone encrusted heeled booties and I was desperately hoping were still available in my size come pay day. I didn't have any idea where I'd wear them to, but they had called to me, whispering sentiments of how sexy I'd look strutting around town.

While I was at work, Ray had taken over Charlie duty. I offered to pay for daycare or a sitter, even if it meant I was essentially working for free. It took a lot for me to leave Charlie with a certifiable stranger, but in the end, I'd rather her be looked after by someone I trusted in a home I knew, versus a childcare center where she was out in the open and vulnerable.

Ray would hear nothing of it and literally shooed me out of the house when I had to leave for work each day. Charlie had taken to her like a pig in slop. Ray even called her 'tiny bestie' when they ran errands together, often stopping in to say hi when they were near the boutique.

Ray had the luxury of working from home, which afforded her an exceptionally flexible and adaptable schedule. She ran a virtual interior design firm, something I'd never heard of, but found extremely fascinating.

She met with clients virtually to discuss their needs and expectations for a design project, then sourced all the items online or at local retailers, paid to have them shipped to the customer, and hired a local moving company to move everything in.

After all the main furniture was staged, she walked the client through staging with items they could find at local retailers or thrift stores.

She held the philosophy that a clear vision of the desired mood or feeling within a space eliminated any significant difficulty in the process of interior design. She taught her clients how to thrift, DIY, and use what they had to their advantage.

The entire experience utterly captivated me. I found myself enthralled by the fascinating process of watching her work.

I often came home from work to find her curled up on the floor with Charlie while she "colored". Charlie would jab crayons into a piece of construction paper while Ray was poring over magazines, finding inspiration and using that to sketch ideas into her notebook.

We had all settled into a comfortable routine. In the evenings, after I'd closed the boutique and came back to the big house, I'd make sure there was dinner on the table before the guys got done with ranch work.

I had learned quickly that they were up early and done late. Ranching wasn't for the faint of heart. Max explained that, technically, they owned a 'ranchette,' but that name sounded too feminine, so no one really called it that.

They were a small, thirty-five acre ranch with only a couple of horses, chickens, and a small herd of cattle. They didn't have a large operation, but it still required a lot of manpower and even more physical labor.

Max was up early in the morning mucking out the stalls of the four horses they kept in the stables, making sure the cattle had ample hay and water, and checking crops as needed.

They mainly grew corn during the summer and harvested it for the local markets. Their primary income came from Wade's riding and roping lessons he'd started with the 4-H kids and grew wider from there.

He held classes daily in the paddocks to the right side of the property, teaching anyone old enough to get on a horse how to ride like they'd been born with a saddle between their legs. You could tell that when Wade was on a horse, he was in his element. He rode with the grace and skill of someone who'd been riding as long as they could walk.

Wade was still a bit of a mystery. Max had mentioned that he used to frequent the rodeo circuit as a champion tie-down roper. He'd made it all the way to Vegas for the NFR, apparently the Super Bowl of rodeo events, and had gotten injured, putting his career on hold. In the seasonal interim, he had opened his training up, hoping to keep his skills sharp. Max said that he'd found a love for teaching and never went back to competing.

Max hadn't gone into detail on the extent of Wade's injuries, but it clearly made it so he wasn't comfortable professionally competing, sending him into retirement.

I spent my days off walking Charlie around the property,

getting the lay of the land. Though I hadn't covered all thirty-five acres, my extensive hikes had given me a good feel for the land, its smells, and the sounds of the rustling leaves. The ranch was so peaceful. Something about the quietness of the ranch acted as a balm to my soul. It should have unnerved me, with all that we had endured, but instead, it gave me a sense of comfort.

Charlie loved stopping by the stables, the scent of hay and leather filling our nostrils as she watched the horses stomp and prance in their paddocks. You could hear her squealing a mile away when they reached their long snouts over the top of the stable doors and sniffed their whiskery noses on her tiny hands.

One afternoon, Max had shown her how to present them with treats safely. She had watched with rapt attention as he held his hand flat with a sugar cube in the center, and his horse, Joker, had gobbled it up.

The sound of her laughter, light and carefree, was so contagious that I couldn't help but laugh along.

Max had taken her from me, propped her up in front of him with an arm banded under her legs, and flattened her hand as he had with the sugar cube in the middle of her palm. He patiently guided her, holding his large hand under hers to keep her palm flat, to the horse's mouth and let it nuzzle up the sugar cube.

In that moment, you would have thought that Max had hung the moon and stars in the sky. I had never before witnessed such a look of pure, unfiltered wonder as the one that spread across my child's face.

I pondered what our lives would have been like had we not made it here to Firefly Cove. How many experiences would she have missed out on because of our unsavory circumstances? I thanked my lucky stars every single day that we ended up here with our little "family".

That evening, as I was cleaning the last dish from dinner, elbows deep in the sudsy water of the sink, Ray had burst through the front door and stormed into the kitchen.

"We're going out this weekend!" she exclaimed, as if it had already been decided.

I fished a dish from the sink, rinsed it, and placed it on the drying rack before turning towards her. I propped my hip on the counter, wiping my hands with the dish towel that was slung over my shoulder as I regarded her with my eyebrows raised.

"Oh, yeah?"

"Yeah, we all need a night out. You need to celebrate making it through living with these nasty ass men. I need a babysitter's night out, and the guys could probably use a beer or two after having to pull baby cows out of asses this week." She plopped herself into one of the dining room chairs and I walked over to take the one beside her.

I set the baby monitor down on the table and Ray quickly snatched it up, taking a peek at the angelic sleeping baby in her crib.

"God, she's so fucking cute." She sighed, then set the monitor back down, turning the screen to face me, and propped her hands under her chin, batting her eyelashes inno-cently in my direction.

Ray had quickly grown on me, her spitfire personality never giving me any question about where she stood. She didn't hold back in her words or emotions, and it was refreshing knowing exactly what she was thinking. Over the last couple of weeks, we'd become pretty close.

"So, what do you say?"

"What do I say to what? Going out this weekend?" I asked, fiddling with a string on my shirt that I'd noticed was coming unraveled. I made a mental note to grab a couple of fresh shirts from the boutique when I got my first paycheck.

"Duh. I've already talked to Angie down at the coffee shop. She said she would be more than happy to watch Charlie for parent's night out."

"I don't know, Ray," I hesitated. Leaving Charlie here at the house with Ray was one thing. Leaving her with a stranger who'd only seen her in passing was another.

While Firefly Cove was a small enough town, I just questioned if it was acceptable for a mother to get a babysitter to go out to a bar with her friends.

"I can smell your brain burning with all the thinking you're doing," Ray joked. "It's okay to take some time for yourself every now and again, Stella. Also, Angie has babysat for my dad on occasion when he has to work an overnight shift and I'm not available. I'm sure if she's reliable enough for the chief of police to allow her to watch his kids, she can tackle Charlie."

She reached over and laid her hand on top of mine. I rolled my lips in contemplation. Could I go out for a night out with my friends and not feel the overwhelming weight of mom guilt?

"Okay, how about this?" she said, tapping her chin in thought. "We go out on Friday night. Angie will come over AFTER you've put Charlie down for bed. She's been sleeping really well, so it should be a breeze. We will have you home before you turn into a pumpkin at midnight."

She held her hands up in front of herself in question.

One thing I'd learned quickly about Ray is that she talked animatedly with her hands. If her mouth was moving, so were her hands. It was as if she had an excess of energy that needed to be expelled when she was passionate about something, and it came out as hand gestures.

"Have you talked to Max and Wade about this?" I asked.

"Talked to us about what?" A deep voice came from the hallway.

Max walked into the kitchen wearing a pair of grey sweatpants that slung dangerously low on his hips, a fitted navy blue tee with a white outline of a saddle bronc rider on the left chest, and his hair was still damp from a shower.

My mouth suddenly went dry, and I fought for a coherent thought. What was it about a man in grey sweatpants and straight out of the shower that made every woman a bumbling mess?

Ray answered for me, much to my detriment.

"The fact that we're all going out to Jack's on Friday night after Charlie goes to bed," she answered definitively.

Well, I guess that was that.

"Is that so?" He questioned, quirking an eyebrow in my direction.

"I've already asked Angie if she will come and sit over here while Charlie is asleep," Ray once again answered for me.

I nodded and averted my eyes from that delicious eyebrow quirk and the little smirk that was playing on Max's lips.

In the last few weeks, things have been nothing but cordial around the house between Max and I. I had managed to live with him and Wade with no issues. Though, I will not say that it's been easy, at least not for my libido.

Max is sex personified. I'm also not confirming nor denying that I may have used his likeness as inspiration for my alone time material.

There was something about how he cared for those around him, Charlie and I included, that made him damn near irresistible.

I had made a solemn promise to myself that I would never, under any circumstances, cross that particular line. Charlie and I were finally in a stable environment and were working towards getting on our feet again. I wasn't about to fuck that up for some good sex, and I knew being with Max would be more than just a one time fling.

There had been no news or sightings from anyone associated with Dean, a situation I knew wouldn't last forever, but for the moment, things were good. I had replaced my original phone with a pre-paid temporary fix, keeping my original turned off and in the bedside table drawer.

"Well, Trouble, are you finally ready to break into the Firefly Cove scene and go out on the town for a night at Jack's?" Max asked, bringing me back to reality.

Oh yeah, we were talking about going out.

"Uh… I guess we could go out for a couple hours," I conceded. "It *will* give me an excuse to pick up some of the new items in the boutique I've been eyeing."

Not missing a beat, Max held up a finger as if telling me to 'pause' and walked back down the hallway and to his room. A soft rustling filled the air, punctuated by the hard clang of a belt buckle as he rummaged through something. He walked back into the kitchen and held out a credit card.

"I know you haven't gotten a really steady paycheck from the boutique yet. I don't want you spending your hard earned money on a night out, so here," he pushed the card in my direction. "Grab yourself a new outfit. Don't worry about the cost. I want your night out on the town to be more than just a break from being a mom; I want you to feel truly special and indulged."

Instant swoon. A fiery blush, encompassing at least fifty shades of red, crept across my cheeks as, with the utmost gentleness, I accepted the card from his outstretched fingers.

I'd never had someone offer to buy me an entire outfit just for a night out. I knew Max wasn't exceptionally wealthy. He worked damn hard for all the money he had. Was it wrong of me to squash the thoughts that I should give the card back? Should I play coy and insist that he not pay?

Nope, I'm going to get those fucking sparkly boots and look like a snack out at the bar this weekend.

"You don't have to do that," I said, looking up into Max's eyes.

He grinned down at me and my heart melted even more when he said in his deep timbre, "I know. Just let me take care of you, Stella."

max

THE WEEK CRAWLED BY, the stress of each day compounding, but before I knew it, Friday night arrived with a sigh of relief and the promise of weekend freedom. I was preparing to head out with Wade, Ray, and Stella to the local dive bar, Jack's.

I'd just finished the evening chores, the scent of hay and earth still clinging to my clothes, and was getting ready while Stella settled Charlie down for the night.

After showering, I changed into a clean black tee shirt, my one good pair of 'going out' jeans, and my dark brown Lucchese boots. I'd run some pomade through my damp hair and let it dry in what Wade liked to call 'fuck boy chic', which comprised an intentionally messy effect.

I wasn't sure if I was getting dressed up because it had been awhile since I'd been out to Jack's on a Friday night and I was hoping to get lucky, or if I was holding out hope for a certain blonde-haired, green-eyed, single mom that had worked her way into our crew.

I checked my outfit once over in the mirror and grabbed a

black Stetson off the hat rack by my bedroom door. Ma had always made sure that Wade and I had two distinct sets of boots and hats. We had our work set, a pair of broken-in Tecova boots and a straw Stetson that wouldn't blanch in the sun but would still keep us shaded. Then, we had our 'nice' set that was kept for church, funerals, weddings, and special events.

I definitely wouldn't want to be seen with the most stunning girl in Firefly Cove—her beauty radiating like the summer sun—while wearing my muddy work boots and faded jeans. I had been raised with a little more class than that.

Going down the hallway, I passed Charlie's cracked door. I could hear her sound machine softly playing lullabies and Stella's gentle voice whispering the lyrics in accompaniment. Their quiet time together felt sacred, filled with unspoken words and gentle smiles, so I decided not to intrude.

I walked down towards the kitchen and pulled out one of the barstools to sit down and wait. Wade and Ray had already made their way into town already, citing the need to get a prime real estate table near the pool tables. I'd never seen Jack's full, so I'm assuming they were attempting to play cupid's assistants and force Stella and me to ride together.

As I heard the soft sound of a door quietly shutting down the hallway, my attention was immediately drawn to the sound, and I froze instantly.

Stella wore a black sundress that hit mid-thigh. The top was a corset style that pushed her breasts up to a point that I was sure would be dangerous with some vigorous dancing, and the tiny straps did nothing to help the situation. The fabric flowed in soft waves over her silky skin and I wondered if it felt as soft as it looked.

On her feet was a sparkly set of heeled booties that hit

above her ankle and gave her outfit a bit of extra sass. Her hair was curled in soft waves and her makeup was heavier than I'd ever seen her wear, but accentuated the darker flecks in her eyes.

Although she was naturally beautiful, a captivating smile played on her lips, and in this moment, she took my breath away.

I imagined what her skin would feel like under the rough calluses of my palms. I wondered if that blush I'd seen creeping up her face extended to the top of those perfect tits. Those tiny little straps wouldn't stand a chance if I got my hands on her.

A throat clearing brought me back down to reality and out of the daydream of Stella, spread out beneath me on my bed. I raised my eyes to meet hers and that blush that I'd been fantasizing about made an appearance across the bridge of her nose and tops of her cheeks. My mouth had suddenly gone dry, so I cleared my throat with a rasping sound before I spoke.

"Uhm, you look…" I started, before running a hand down over my mouth and shaking away the haze of lust. "Fuck, Stella, you look stunning."

Shyness overcame her as her blush deepened and her eyes darted down to her boots. It's clear that compliments made her uncomfortable, but I just couldn't help myself. She looked stunning and deserved to know it.

"I picked up a few new things from the boutique. Thank you again for paying. I'll make sure I get that money back to you when I've gotten a really steady check." She said demurely, smoothing out the skirt of her dress nervously.

I scoffed and stood up, swiping my hat off the counter and stalking towards her. With a slow and deliberate movement, I used my index finger to lift her chin, ensuring our eyes locked in a direct gaze.

"Trouble, it was worth every fucking cent if I get to experience how beautiful you look and feel. You deserve to feel sexy and confident. I can see that you feel both in that outfit, and that's all the payment I need." Rubbing my thumb softly across her jawline before taking a step back and putting my hat on, I crooked my elbow in offering and smiled when Stella broke out of the haze my words had caused, chuckled and slid her arm through mine.

The heat from her touch coiled down from my arm all the way to my toes and back up to my dick. I sure as shit wasn't immune to how beautiful Stella was, the last thing I ever wanted to do was make her feel uncomfortable in her own home, and this house was her home just as much as it was mine, but I couldn't stop myself from complimenting her tonight.

Stella put up her pointer finger in a 'wait just a second' motion and walked into the living room to find Angie posted up on the couch. She grabbed a small black clutch off the coffee table and handed Angie a piece of paper with what I can only assume are the instructions should Charlie wake up.

There was one thing I was absolutely certain of, no matter the circumstances, Stella was a kick ass mom.

I listened as she prattled off the instructions listed on the sheet to include phone numbers for everyone in attendance at Jack's, the local hospital, poison control, and because she couldn't help herself, 9-1-1. Angie's nod accompanied Stella's words, a clear sign that she understood the anxiety Stella felt about leaving Charlie, even for such a brief period.

I padded into the living room and put my hand on the

small of Stella's back. She instantly went rigid, but after taking a second to realize who was touching her, relaxed.

"Stell, I promise you, she's going to be perfectly safe. If it will make you feel better, I'll have Angie text me once an hour to let us know Charlie is still sleeping, and we promised to have you back before midnight." I reiterated, hoping to give her an ounce of courage to leave Charlie behind for only a couple hours of 'self-care.'

She deserved a night out more than anyone I knew. After watching how she and Charlie functioned for the last month, I was in awe. She made it look effortless, though I knew it was anything but.

"Thanks again for helping Ang," I said to the teen taking up residence on our couch. She waved me off and grabbed the remote from the end table.

"It's really no big deal. I've got nothing going on and a couple of episodes of Jeopardy to catch up on," she said with a smile. "Now you two, go! Have a good time." she shooed us towards the door. I wasn't sure if she was sixteen or sixty, but I was thankful for her help.

Stella and I made our way towards the door and I once again crooked my elbow in offering. A light chuckle escaped her lips, and with a delicate movement, she once more linked her arm through mine. We walked out to the truck, and I rounded the passenger side, opening the door for her to help her in.

"You don't have to do that," she said with another breathy chuckle. "I can surely open my own door."

I held her hand as she put one foot on the running board and balanced precariously on those booties to step into the truck. My truck wasn't as lifted as Wade's, but its height was still enough to make it impossible for her to step in from the ground. Once seated, I reached across her lap and buckled her seatbelt.

"I'm aware, Trouble, I don't have to. I want to." I said as I leaned back out of the cab, the hitch in her breath audible as I invaded her space. As I walked around to the driver's side, I took a second to adjust my cock in my jeans. Tonight was about to be a long night if just being gentlemanly and buckling her into the truck was enough to give me a semi.

The ride was short and relaxed, neither of us feeling any pressure to make conversation; the comfortable silence was preferable to forcing small talk. It only took about fifteen minutes for us to pull into the bar.

I parked the truck next to Wade's and hopped out, grabbing my hat off the dash on the way, popping it on my head. I rounded the front of the truck just as Stella pushed the passenger door open and put one of those sparkled booties on the running board.

I held my hand out in help and tried to keep my eyes from roaming over the creamy skin of her legs where her dress had ridden up on her thighs.

"Listen here, darlin'," I drawled. "My Ma raised a damn gentleman and if you don't let me open the door for you, I'm sure she'd haunt me from the other side."

She hopped out of the cab of my truck and stood toe to toe with me, our boots barely grazing each other. Though she was small, only coming up to my shoulder, the intensity of her gaze from beneath those thick, black lashes made me feel about two feet tall.

"You listen here, Cowboy," she said, poking a slender finger into my chest. "I'm glad your momma raised a gentleman. The world sure could use a few more of them, especially my world - but I can open my own doors and get my own seatbelt. I don't need a white knight in Wranglers and cowboy boots to save me. I will save my damn self."

Her tone was fierce in her declaration of independence, and that semi I'd been able to squash on the way over here reared its head again. The confidence in her eyes, the way she carried herself—everything about a woman who knew what she wanted was undeniably sexy.

The last month of living in Firefly Cove had sure done wonders for Stella's self-assurance. I smirked down at the little spitfire, tipped my hat back and dipped my head to settle my lips right next to her ear.

"Yes, ma'am," I whispered, letting the tickle of my breath skate across the shell of her ear. I could see her visibly shiver as I took a step back and held a hand out for her to walk ahead towards the door.

"After you, Trouble," I added with a wink. I watched as her cheeks were tinted with a rosy blush and in that moment, that particular shade of pink became my absolute favorite color.

ELEVEN

WALKING into Jack's behind Stella was a lesson in self-restraint. I found myself completely mesmerized by the elegant way her dress swished rhythmically against her hips with every graceful swing, my jaw practically scraping the floor in awe.

She was stunning in her newfound confidence. I'd found her beautiful from the first day I'd laid eyes on her, but the radiance she exuded now as she strutted those rhinestone boots up to the bar and bent over at the waist to order a drink.

Fuck me, I was a goner.

It had been ages since a woman's charm and wit had captivated me, leaving me breathless. Since Shannon's infidelity, I avoided getting close to anyone for more than a night. I enjoyed being able to just come and go as I pleased, not having to answer to anyone or their agendas. It kept me from inevitably getting hurt again.

The accompanying feeling of self-loathing that comes after being cheated on is a beast that's hard to tame. I learned that it's better to keep people at arm's length, so they don't have the power to hurt you.

Somehow, this spitfire woman on the run and her mini-me, with their fiery spirits and infectious laughter, had wormed their way into my life, slowly melting the ice around my heart. Their orbit drew me in, and I didn't want to leave.

I sidled up next to Stella at the bar and nodded at the bartender. Not surprisingly, the bartender's name was not Jack, it was Hayes. I'm sure that somewhere out there, there is a manual on small town dive bars that states the name of the bar is not to be in any way related to the owner, bartender, or long-time patrons.

Jack's had been a staple in Firefly Cove for as long as I could remember. Not that I remembered much about a bar as a child, but I remember Wade and I sneaking in here with fake IDs in our late teens. Now, as an adult, I'm hyper aware that there was no sneaking involved. We'd grown up in this town and everyone knew we were underage. The bartenders never served us alcohol, but I'm sure they kept an eye on us.

Between the ages of eighteen and twenty-two, Wade and I spent many nights creating chaos and facing consequences in and around Jack's, marked by the blur of rowdy nights and close calls.

We had spent our twenty-first birthday bellied up to this bar taking tequila shots and promptly scrubbing the floors the next morning when we inevitably puked those same shots all over the dance floor.

Here at Jack's, surrounded by locals, we learned to line dance on that same worn oak dance floor at the back of the bar.

We'd also attempted, and only sometimes succeeded, to

pick up chicks with our cowboy charm over by the pool tables under the neon lights.

We weren't strangers round these parts, but Stella was. I could feel the heat of all eyes converging on the stunning blonde currently half bent over the bar waiting on a drink, the hem of her dress barely covering her ass.

I tried to appear calm, but the predatory gazes of the men in the dimly lit bar, all focused on Stella, made my senses sharpen, a primal instinct taking over. She was here to have a good time, not to be ogled by some dirty ass cowboys with a penchant for bottom shelf bourbon and a lip stuffed with tobacco.

Before I had a chance to turn around and order a beer, one was thrust into my chest, the wet label seeping through my henley and causing me to let out a slight hiss at the chill.

"Who pissed in your Cheerios, cowboy?" Stella drawled, batting her eyelashes as if unaware that every hot-blooded male in the bar was staring at her taut ass.

I shook the thoughts from my head and out of the corner of my eye, spotted Wade and Ray waving us over to a four-top table in the back corner.

Wade always tried to find a spot near the pool tables. He was a shark at pool and loved showing off in an attempt to get one of the single ladies to let him show her his stick handling skills, pun intended.

I nodded my head in their direction and steered Stella with a gentle hand on the small of her back towards our crew. She shivered slightly at my touch, and I promptly removed my hand as we approached.

"Why do you look like someone kicked your puppy?" Wade asked, using his pointer and middle finger in the shape of a 'V' to gesture up and down at my rigid stature.

"I'm good." I said, sitting down in one of the unoccupied chairs around the table, refusing to acknowledge the surge of desire I was fighting being in close proximity to Stella.

Suddenly, the music in the bar shifted from a slow, twangy, oldies country song to a more up-tempo and popular beat. Ray let out a hoot of excitement and grabbed Stella's hand, twirling her towards the dance floor.

"Come on, girl! Let's show these lame ass cowboys how to have a good time." She said as she flicked the brim of Wade's hat and shimmied her hips while walking away.

Stella let out a giggle and kicked back her beer with the grace of a college party girl, plopping the empty bottle on the table and proceeding to follow Ray.

I glanced over to Wade, whose eyes hadn't strayed from his best friend. If I was anyone else, I'd see an overprotective brother-like figure watching out for a girl on the dance floor, but seeing as how Wade and I had once shared a womb, I *felt* his tension.

"When are y'all gonna sort your shit out and fuck already?" I asked as I took a swig of my beer. The bubbles danced along my tongue and the acidic finish was just what I needed to ease my tension.

"Don't know what you're talkin' about," he responded, averting his eyes from the tiny Latina, shaking her ass with the grace of Shakira out on the dance floor.

Ray was in her element. She was a people person and the life of the party everywhere she went. I knew without a shadow of a doubt that it was Wade's charm and charisma that captivated her. They were twin flames, almost more so than him and I were actually twins.

Wade and Ray's relationship had always been a bit of a mystery to our family. We thought they'd be dating by this point, but they were comfortable in their friendship—until now. The longing in my brother's eyes as he looked at his best friend betrayed the unspoken romantic tension. I wasn't sure when his gazes had become less platonic and more romantic, but it was obvious he was struggling with his feelings for Ray.

I let out a slight chuckle and dropped the topic- for now. I wasn't the type of brother to pry into my sibling's life. I knew that when he was ready to talk, he'd talk. The subject of his relationship with Ray was clearly a painful one for him, causing obvious discomfort and making it apparent that it was a sensitive topic best left untouched.

"When are you and Barbie on the run over there gonna fuck?" he asked nonchalantly, projecting his tension back at me.

I nearly choked on my beer, the resulting foam escaping my lips, which I hastily cleaned with the napkin I found on the table.

"Don't know what you're talkin' about," I echoed back. His smile was wide and accusatory as he tapped the neck of his beer bottle against mine in solidarity.

"Cheers to women who have us so twisted up, we don't know our dicks from our elbows, brother," he murmured.

I took a moment to look out on the dance floor. Moving to the music, Stella seemed so naturally free, dancing with an untroubled spirit, as though nothing could burden her. It warmed my heart to see her happy and smiling.

Knowing what I did about her history, it seemed as if she needed this more than anyone. At the moment, she wasn't a mom, anyone's woman, or a girl on the run. She was just Stella.

I continued to watch as the pair, she and Ray, made their

way back to the bar and requested another round of drinks. Wade's hiss from beside me caught my attention.

"Aw, fuck." He said, scrubbing a hand down his face in frustration.

"What?" I asked, looking between the girls at the bar and my brother in confusion.

"Two words- Jose. Cuervo." he sighed.

"Aw, fuck is right," I murmured.

Ray held her liquor like a champ, especially tequila- but it brought out her feisty side. Get the girl riled up after a couple shots, and she'd be jonesing for a fight with anyone who looked at her sideways.

Countless times, we've had the unpleasant task of removing her, a highly reluctant participant, from this particular bar—the situation always because of her friend and frequent drinking partner, Jose Cuervo.

To slyly monitor the girls at the bar, I left my seat under the ruse of getting another drink. As I slid up to the oak top and placed both palms down to order, I heard Ray shouting at Stella over the booming country music.

"Lick it, drink it, suck it." Ray instructed.

I turned towards the girls just in time to see Stella's tongue dart out to lick the line of salt off the back of her hand. Her throat bobbed as she took back the tequila shot, and her plush lips wrapped around the lime wedge. That semi I'd been fighting the entire night was now rock hard as all the blood from my head went straight to my dick. Stella threw her head back in a laugh and I fought the urge to throw her over my shoulder and take her home like a caveman.

"Let's do body shots!!" Ray shouted as she smacked her hand down on the bar for Hayes to pour them another round.

His eyes met mine in question, and I slowly closed them,

letting out a deep breath of resignation. This was about to be a long fucking night.

After the girls had successfully sucked down three tequila shots, they took back to the dance floor. Their moves had become more fluid with the alcohol now flooding their veins and I could see Stella swinging her hips slowly to the beat. She looked ethereal and carefree under the neon lights of the bar.

I was just about to turn around and watch from our table when I saw a hand curl around her waist and a man step up behind her, lowering his lips to her ear. I couldn't hear her stilted laugh over the thrum of the music, but I could sense the tension radiating off her in waves.

In two long strides, I was on the dance floor and standing beside Stella and Ray. I glared at the man who had his hand currently gripping Stella's hip and gave him the 'man nod' that insinuated he better fuck off before I start swinging.

He immediately let go of Stella and backed off the dance floor, mumbling about needing to find the pisser as he left. To check on her and make certain she was alright, I positioned myself behind her delicate form and swayed to the rhythm of the music.

"Ah, my white knight in Wranglers," she lightly slurred as she turned towards me with a wide grin and a slight chuckle. "Come to save me from the big bad man who wanted to dance?"

"Like you've said before, you don't need savin', but I figured a pretty girl like you deserved a better dance partner than a wanna-be cowboy in brand new Ariat boots." I smirked down at her, and that favorite color of mine crested her cheeks.

Her usual strong front was clear, but I could tell she had

appreciated my intervention. I'd give her the grace of pretending that she didn't need saving just this once, if it meant I got to get my hands on her.

"Show me what you've got, Cowboy." She teased as she twirled around so her back was to my front.

The song was upbeat, a driving beat that took a moment to fully sink into. I could feel the heat radiating from her small body in front of me, but we were still inches apart. I didn't want to risk startling her, so I maintained a safe distance between us.

Her hips swayed in time to the beat and I felt myself becoming more and more comfortable in the rhythm. I chanced brushing my fingertips over the highest portion of her hipbones, and she instinctively moved back into my body. Euphoria surged through me as the warmth of her back pressed against my chest, a perfect fit.

I settled my hands on her hips and coasted through the motions with her, fighting to keep the blood in my head from rushing back south.

I dipped my chin down and placed my lips close to her ear, just like I'd done earlier.

"Looks like you're enjoying yourself, Trouble." I teased as I took a second to pull her even closer. I skated my hand across her belly and I felt the sharp intake of breath as she melted even more into my embrace.

Our bodies swayed to the music as the song ended. The music shifted to a slower tempo, a change marked by softer notes and a wistful tune, and I felt Stella's body move just an inch away. Before she could get too far, I took another leap of faith and tipped my hat back to meet her gaze.

"One more dance?" I asked, my southern twang a little thicker as the headiness of lust clouded my judgement. I really shouldn't be letting myself cross the lines we'd silently drawn over the last few weeks, but I couldn't help but feel inexplicably drawn to this woman.

Her smile was electric as she put one hand on my chest and leaned in close, her lips in danger of brushing against mine, as she whispered, "Just one dance."

stella

THE TEQUILA definitely contributed to the electric thrill that shot through me as Max's fingers intertwined with mine, the pleasant tingle amplified by the alcohol.

A sane individual would surely remind themselves not to get close to a random cowboy met on the roadside. Despite the existence of multiple ways in which this situation could turn out poorly, I currently couldn't find a single fuck to give.

The three shots I'd taken at the bar with Ray had loosened my hips and lips, but this feeling of a static connection with Max wasn't new. The feeling had been building for a while during our time living together, a constant presence that I fought against daily, a battle that had grown increasingly difficult to endure.

I kept telling myself that getting tangled up with another man after the shit I'd been through was a bad idea - but clearly, our attraction to each other was undeniable.

I'd never felt this drawn to someone so quickly. It was as if every nerve ending in my body was on a hair trigger and as soon as Max entered my orbit, those nerve endings fired. I constantly felt a hum of need flowing beneath my skin when I caught his eyes on me. But more than that, he felt safe. He was a soft place to land at the end of a hard day. I never once felt myself questioning his intentions. He was, at his core, a good person.

He gently placed the hand that was not currently curled around mine on the soft spot of my hip. With anyone else, I would have been self conscious of him feeling the squishier parts of me, but with Max I knew I was cherished and safe. His touch was soft and reverent as he allowed himself the opportunity to explore. His hands were wide and rough, but he touched me with a tenderness that I'd never experienced.

He splayed his fingers around my hip and edged them towards my back, slowly and gently tugging me forward until our bodies were a hair's breadth away from each other.

"Where'd you learn to dance?" I asked quietly, attempting to break the tension with some idle chitchat. My voice, tight with a nervous tremor, produced stilted, awkward words; I couldn't meet his eyes, the silence punctuated by the frantic beat of my pulse.

I knew that one look at his face would scramble my brain, leaving me a whimpering mess begging for him to take me home.

His chuckle was gentle as he swayed us from side to side through the crooning melody. "Would you believe me if I told you I learned it riding horses?"

My bewildered expression must have been clear because, when I looked up, his smile transformed into a dazzling megawatt grin, crinkling the corners of his eyes.

He extricated his hand from my hip and gently brushed a lock of hair behind one of my ears and then replaced his grip. Even after he'd moved his hands, I could still feel the pressure, the phantom imprint of his touch, lingering like a radiant heat on my skin.

"When Wade and I were younger, just learning how to ride a horse, my Pops used to have a saying." He paused for emphasis. "'keep your hips loose like a two-dollar hooker.'"

My eyes blew wide at the crude words as I looked up at him. His laugh was soft as he pulled me closer, our bodies now flush. He leaned down and his breath crested the shell of my ear, a whisper only for me playing on his lips.

The shiver that wracked through my body was involuntary and I could feel his sharp intake of breath as my body touched his. The air crackled with a strange energy; it was obvious that our proximity was affecting us both.

"That saying, although not quite appropriate for little ears," he whispered. "Has helped me many times."

He drifted his hand to the middle of my back, pressing my body tighter to his. I felt the press of his erection into my thigh through his jeans. It was abundantly clear that we were venturing into perilous territory, yet I couldn't be bothered to extricate my body from his embrace.

His lips coasted along my ear as he continued.

"Riding… Dancing…" he paused for continued dramatic effect and pulled back to look me directly in the eyes. A sexy smirk adorned one corner of his mouth, and his dilated pupils clearly revealed the lustful thoughts consuming him.

"Fucking."

That one word hit me so hard that I felt every ounce of air rush out of my lungs in a single, shocking whoosh. Who knew something so vulgar could make me weak in the knees?

I could feel the heat as it crested across the top of my cheeks and down my throat. I watched as Max's gaze danced all the way from the tip of my nose down to my chest. He was shameless in his perusal of my body, clearly willing to cross those lines we'd drawn if I gave him the okay.

I hadn't felt that flutter of anticipation in my chest from someone's eyes in what seemed like a lifetime. Max didn't just see me as a mom. The fact that he could so clearly see the woman underneath filled me with a simultaneous feeling of excitement and terror.

Letting out a heavy sigh, I dropped my gaze, his name lingering on my lips as I acknowledged the urgent need to create some space between us.

I tried to step back, but his arm encircled my waist. As I lifted my gaze, my eyes connected with the most profoundly sincere expression I had ever encountered in my life. The feeling of being trapped in his embrace should scare me after what I'd been through, but I knew I was safe with him.

"Stella… when I saw that man put his hands on you earlier…"

"Don't, I was fine." I reprimanded, placing my hand on his chest in comfort. I could feel the steady beat of his heart under my palm. The powerful, rhythmic thumping of his racing heart echoed the frantic beat of my own, creating a synchronized rhythm of anxiety.

"I knew you were fine." He took a fortifying breath as he tipped my chin up so that our eyes would meet.

"I knew you could handle yourself if you got uncomfortable. I knew you were strong enough to fight your own battles. You won't allow yourself to be trapped by another man. I knew that. It wasn't that I wanted to save you. It was that I couldn't stand the idea of another man touching the woman that I hadn't gone thirty seconds without thinking about. There was a neanderthal part of me that wanted to stomp over, plop my hat on your head, throw you over my shoulder, and take you home." His smile was tender as he looked into my eyes.

"Might as well have pissed on the floor in a circle around me, because even though you didn't do any of those things, I'm sure no man will get anywhere close to me tonight," I said with a chuckle.

"That was the fucking point, Stella. I don't want another man close to you. I want to be the man that's close to you."

My breath hitched, a desperate, ragged gasp in the suffocating silence. What had begun as witty banter and slow dancing was now a tense conversation, the air thick with unspoken words, far from the boisterous music and flashing lights of the dive bar's dance floor.

"Max, we can't…" I said, as I again attempted to extricate myself from his embrace.

"Let me take you out," he said simply, loosening his hold just a fraction.

He wasn't keeping me caged, and he wanted to make sure I knew anytime I needed to leave, he would let me go. The truth was, I didn't want to go. I reveled in the comforting, secure feeling of being held in his arms.

"Max, I don't think this is a good idea. You know all I've been through, I've got Charlie to think about, and I don't know how long I'm going to be in Firefly Cove."

I surveyed the dance floor carefully, trying to see if anyone had been close enough to overhear our argument. Lost in their individual worlds, each person was absorbed in their own thoughts and actions, including Ray, who was joyfully dancing away.

"One date," he pleaded. "Let me show you what it's like to have someone fall at your feet and worship the ground you walk on. I want to show you the power of having someone believe in you. Let me show you how much I want you…and Charlie." He said, pulling me back into his embrace.

I felt myself melt at his words, but words were just empty place holders for the actions that I'd been shown would never happen. With a history of letdowns, I worried Max might also end up hurting me.

I wasn't worried that he would hurt me physically, but this man could obliterate my heart and my child's.

I hesitated, not knowing what to say. I wanted to open my heart and let Max in, to embrace him fully and completely. The fragile hope of happiness felt like a candle flickering in a storm.

I deserved to go on living my life, not knowing how things were eventually going to pan out. Charlie deserved to know that not all men were like her shit-bag father. The thought that Max could be the perfect person to give us the fresh beginning that we deserved swam through my mind, but my fear was, unfortunately, overwhelming and paralyzing.

"Can I think about it?" I asked hesitantly, not daring to meet his eyes.

He insisted, once again, that I raise my chin and meet his gaze directly, so that I might fully appreciate and feel the sincerity of his words.

"Take all the time you need. From the moment we bumped into each other again at the coffee shop, I've been fighting an attraction to you. I know that you've been hurt deeply. I wish I could take back all the damage that fucker did to you, physically and emotionally. Showing you that you deserve to be happy will take as long as it takes. You deserve people in your corner, Stella."

I sighed. He was right. I knew deep down that I deserved to move on.

We'd been in Firefly Cove for over two weeks now and we hadn't seen or heard anything out of the men who killed Dean. I was aware that the probability of them ever locating us was incredibly low, bordering on nonexistent, but the fear was still there.

I deserved to move on with my life and eventually stop hiding behind the shadow of my past.

I knew that regardless of if I wanted to or not, there was an undeniable attraction between Max and I. One date couldn't hurt, could it?

"Okay..." I mumbled, looking at him directly this time. The confidence he had in the fact that he could do right by Charlie and I was giving me the second hand confidence to let him. "One date."

A wide smile spread across his face as, taking my hand, he twirled me around before gently dipping me at my waist.

The combination of spinning and tequila wasn't the best idea, but I honestly didn't care enough to be concerned about the consequences. I felt so free and light when I was with Max.

I giggled as he pulled me back into his embrace and I lifted his hat off his head and deposited it on top of mine. Wide with desire, his pupils revealed the intensity of his lust. Apparently cowboy hats and women were an aphrodisiac round these parts.

"Do you know what it means to wear a man's cowboy hat?" he asked gruffly, his voice coming out tinny and strained.

"Uhm, no?" I asked, grabbing the top of the hat to remove it and hand it back. His fingers closed around my wrist, effectively stopping my movements, placing the hat back on my head.

"Wear the hat, ride the cowboy," he smirked down at me. I looked up at him from beneath my lashes, not bothering to hide the thrill that coursed through my veins.

"You get a pass this once, because you didn't know." Dipping his head down and looking me directly in the eyes, he continued, "but, make no mistake Stella, that hat looks damn good on you and when you're ready, I'll give you the ride of your life."

stella

THE BRIGHT MORNING light assaulted my senses, waking me from my alcohol induced slumber, and I rolled over with a groan. The heady feeling of a good night's sleep was tinged with a bone weary exhaustion, the kind you can only feel after sleeping deeply without waking.

Reaching over onto the end table, I smacked around for my phone before checking the baby monitor. Judging by the light streaming offensively in through the blinds, both Charlie and I had opted to sleep in this morning.

We had gotten home at precisely midnight, fulfilling Ray's promise that we would get in just before the clock struck twelve. I popped my head in as soon as we got home and gave Charlie a brief kiss on her forehead before padding across the hall to my own room and flopping on the bed fully clothed.

Things between Max and me at the end of the night had been surprisingly easy. There wasn't any heavy awkwardness that I'd expected after agreeing to go on a date with him- it all felt so natural.

After we danced a few more songs, we finally managed to

persuade Ray to leave with us, and then we carefully helped her into the passenger seat of Wade's truck, which he had pulled up out front and was already waiting for us. She had somehow weaseled her way into a few more tequila shots, but we escaped the night without a fight. Wade had ensured that he would get her home safe, having only had one beer, then switching to soda for the rest of the evening.

Max, being the gentleman that he is, had done the same and drove me back to the ranch as I rambled on and on in his passenger seat about everything and nothing at all. It was a good night, and one I desperately had needed.

Forcing my eyes open in order to check the time, I sat straight up in bed with a jolt.

It was already ten in the morning. How in the hell had Charlie and I slept in that late?

A cold dread seeped into my bones as I snatched the monitor off the end table, each frantic heartbeat a hammer against my ribs.

What if something had happened in the middle of the night and I was so irresponsible about coming home drunk that I didn't even register it?

Heart pounding, I scrambled out of bed, noticing the empty crib on the monitor, and raced to the door. I threw it open and tried to calm my rapid pulse as I ran down the hall to the living area. I wasn't bothering to look in her room. The monitor had told me all I needed to know - she wasn't in there.

Why didn't I hear her cry?

What if she got injured?

How had someone gotten into the house to take her?

Why didn't the house alarm go off?

The questions in my head swirled like a tempest, each one

a sharp jab, and my breath hitched in my throat, tears threatening to spill. The overwhelming urge to scream and cry was weighted down by my drive to find my daughter. When it came to fight or flight, in Charlie's instance, I'd always fight.

I sprinted into the kitchen and came skidding to a stop. The scene before me had me transfixed, not in fear, but in awe.

Sitting at the kitchen table was Max, scrolling through his phone. He had his thick black-rimmed glasses on and a cup of coffee steaming in front of him. Beside him, in her high chair and happy as a pig in slop, sat my beautiful and safe baby girl.

I released the breath I'd been holding and leaned against the archway into the kitchen in relief, willing my pulse to slow.

She was safe.

She was safe.

She was safe.

I repeated the mantra again and again, feeling my racing heart gradually settle into a calmer rhythm, each syllable a soothing balm to the overwhelming anxiety that had taken over my body.

I was so engrossed in my thoughts that I didn't notice Max standing before me until his large hands, calloused and warm, gently grasped my upper arms. I flinched, still coming out of my panic induced haze, and he quickly released me, a pained expression flashing across his face.

"Stella, I'm so sorry.. I didn't think.."

Placing a hand on his arm, I paused, taking a deep breath to steady myself before speaking.

"She's safe." I repeated out loud this time.

As soon as the words left my mouth, Max pulled me into his arms. My body went limp against his chest as the adrenaline drained away; the scent of his cologne filled my nose, grounding me in the moment. He rubbed gentle strokes up and down my back while keeping me tethered to him in a warm and comforting embrace.

"She's safe. I've got you," he whispered into my hair, never stopping his ministrations of gentle coasts of his fingertips up and down my spine.

Once my ragged breathing subsided, I cautiously took a half step back, still remaining in his arms, and looked up at him. He smiled gently down at me, his eyes crinkling at the corners, a warmth spreading through his features.

"Good morning, Trouble."

"I was so scared that something had happened to her." I said, looking down at my bare feet in embarrassment. He resumed his gentle up and down strokes across my back, easing the tension and pulling me back into his embrace.

"I should have left a note. I'm sorry," he mumbled. "She woke up around eight and I was already up for the day. I figured I'd let you sleep in a bit and get her some breakfast. I took her out with me to feed the horses and then made her some eggs and toast…"

He looked almost boyish, a shy smile playing on his lips as he recounted his efforts to do something nice for me. The sound of his voice was gentle and sincere. My fear and the subsequent panic attack I had nearly caused me to ruin everything. When would I be able to live without the constant fear of having to look over my shoulder every second of every day?

Sensing that I was calm enough, he let me go and walked to the coffeemaker. A fresh pot was just finishing brewing, and he poured some into a cup. He added a dash of cream and a couple heaping tablespoons of sugar, stirring it around. As a symbol of peace, he walked over to me, presenting the cup with an outstretched arm.

I gave him a gentle smile and took the coffee, bringing it to my lips. It was perfect - just the right amount of cream and sugar and brewed dark like I liked it.

I have no idea how this man managed to stay hidden from all the women in the world, but I can tell you that he was certainly unlike any other man I'd ever met.

In all the years Dean and I had been together, I'm sure he couldn't tell you even close to how I liked my coffee in the mornings. I'd been here a little over two weeks and Max had managed to make it perfectly.

"Thank you." I conceded, walking over to the table and brushing the curls off Charlie's forehead, leaning down to give her a quick kiss, lingering to take in the feel of her warmth and her quickly fading baby smell.

"I'm sorry about the freak out." I added, sitting in a chair next to Charlie's high chair and looking over at Max, who'd taken up residency on the other side of the table.

He scooped some more eggs onto Charlie's high chair tray and subsequently scooped up the mushy bread she'd been gnawing on to throw in the trash.

"Stella, please don't apologize. If anyone should apologize, it's me. I didn't think about how scary it would be for you to wake up and not know where Charlie was," He said sheepishly as he sat back down at the table. "This is one hundred percent on me."

"For as long as I can remember, I've done everything myself. I'd get up every morning with her, change her, feed her, and make Dean's breakfast before the sun even rose. I can't remember the last time I slept past eight."

Max's jaw tightened, the movement sharp and angry, and

the grinding of his teeth was almost audible, a low, tense rasp. I became aware of the depth of his discomfort, caused by his realization of the significant amount of independent responsibility Charlie and I had shouldered.

"Anyway, she probably needs to be changed," I said, standing up. "I'll be right back."

As I shoved my chair away from the table, Max reacted swiftly, extending an arm to grasp my wrist firmly.

"Yeah, that's the one thing I didn't do," he said, looking over at my daughter. "I figured you didn't stink too bad, and that Mama should be the one changing your diaper."

Boundaries. He was drawing boundaries when it came to Charlie. He wasn't going to overstep and assume I was okay with him changing her. I think, at that moment, I fell a little in love with Maxwell Daniels. I shook my head at him in disbelief as I sipped my deliciously perfect cup of coffee.

"You're something else, Maxwell." I said over the lip of my cup, a gentle smile gracing my lips.

"So are you, Stella," he grinned back flirtily.

Charlie broke our heated gaze as she flung a handful of scrambled eggs right at Max's cheek. I set my cup down and covered my mouth in an attempt to hide my laugh.

The experience of parenting was a strange mix of necessary scolding, balanced by a far greater need to discreetly conceal your laughter to avoid undermining one's authority in the eyes of their children.

Max swiped the egg from his cheek and leaned down to get eye level with my girl.

"Now, is that how you treat the man who walked you out to see the 'bawk bawks', the 'neighs' and the 'moos' this morning?" He asked her, keeping eye contact.

If watching him make animal sounds at my nearly one-year-old wasn't enough to make me break out into laughter, the sound of eggs slapping against his face as Charlie chucked another handful at him was.

I hopped up out of my chair and went to the counter, grabbing some paper towels to hand over. I waited on bated breath for Max to get angry.

Dean would have been fuming at the first splatter of egg on him, but Max was unflappable. He just wiped them off, wiped off Charlie's hands, and scooped up the rest of the breakfast she had in an effort to unload her arsenal.

After cleaning up the remnants of the one sided food fight, he lifted her from her high chair and held her in his muscular arms. In that instant, I swear my ovaries combusted.

"Charlie, no throw," he scolded gently, all while keeping a stern face and eye contact. She shook her head from side to side and giggled.

"No, no, no," she chanted back at him, all while still shaking her head.

"Right, no throw."

"No tow!" she screeched back.

I could see his resolve slipping as he attempted to keep from smiling down at the cuteness in his arms.

"No throw, good girl," he repeated, tickling her ribs lightly. She let out a squeal and wiggled in his arms in an attempt at escape.

"MOOOOOO!" she shouted at him while squishing his cheeks together between her tiny hands.

"Yesh, we ca go see da moo," he said from pursed lips. Charlie giggled and continued to squish his cheeks. "Why don we wet mama go get dwessed an meet us at da moos?"

I laughed lightly as Charlie attempted to decipher what

Max was saying between squished lips. She giggled and looked over at me with a cheeky grin.

"Mama go!"

I looked up at Max, who'd been relieved of squishy egg covered hands pushing his cheeks together and he smiled.

"Yeah, mama. Go! Little one and I will meet you out at the grazing field. Take your time. Shower, shave, wash your hair. We've got this," he said with the confidence of a dad who'd been doing this job since day one.

Without a moment's hesitation, and with a voice certain and strong, he readily took the reins and assumed the parenting role this morning. It almost seemed like he *wanted* to spend time with my daughter.

"Let me just change her first, then you two can go on your farm adventure," I said, taking Stella from Max's arms and quickly running back to her room to change her diaper.

When I got back to the kitchen, Max was back reading something on his phone; those hot nerd glasses were back on his face. When he saw the two of us, his smile beamed and I was struck stupid by the intense happiness that radiated from him.

He reached out his arms and Charlie all but threw herself into them, ready to get started with her day.

I let out a light sigh in concession as I transferred her into his arms and I brushed the curls away from Charlie's forehead to lean in and give her a kiss.

I was met with not only the sweet smell of my little girl, but the manly smell of what I can only assume was Max's aftershave. It was a heady mixture of leather, spice, and vanilla. It took nearly all my willpower not to lean in and sniff a line up his neck like a creep.

"Be good for Max." I reminded my daughter, waving a finger at her.

"Mass!!" she repeated in her attempt at saying Max and patting him gently on the cheek. She laid her head on his shoulder and tears welled up in my eyes.

My girl was falling for this rugged cowboy just as fast as I was. Neither of us had ever known unconditional love, but we were learning quickly what it was like to have people in our corner who genuinely cared.

"Go." Max said sternly, pushing me towards the hallway.

With a light laugh, I retreated to my room for the longest shower imaginable. I was about to shave everything, exfoliate, wash and blow dry my hair, the works. Eventually, Max would reap the benefits of all of this work, I'm sure.

If he continued to shower my daughter and me with the kind of love and attention one reserves for the most precious people in the world, I wouldn't be able to resist his charms for much longer.

FOURTEEN

THINGS HAD FALLEN into an easy routine around the house over the couple of weeks post parents' night out. Stella's initial reluctance to let me assist with Charlie's care lessened each day, replaced by a growing trust. I could almost see the layers of her distrust, like an onion, slowly peeling away, revealing a core of vulnerability. She was broken, and I was a man determined to build her back up.

Charlie was a surprisingly easy baby, though it's not like I had much to compare her to. Around seven o'clock each morning, she'd wake up, which was a couple of hours after I'd already begun my day, having risen early to tend to the animals.

I would get her out of bed, take her out to collect the eggs from the coop, and she'd keep me entertained while I fixed breakfast. Stella would take over with changing her, getting her dressed for the day, and feeding her.

While not world-changing, allowing Stella some extra rest gently nudged her toward accepting support. She deserved a break after having done everything herself for so long.

In the last week, Charlie's newly acquired skill of walking had resulted in an unprecedented amount of chaos throughout the house. She suddenly decided one morning to stop crawling around on the floor and started toddling up and down the hallway as fast as her little legs would take her.

Subsequently, she had also decided that she was done breastfeeding. That was a sore spot for Stella, and I could see the disappointment in her eyes as she imagined missing her quiet evenings with her girl. The realization that this long and challenging chapter was ending brought a mix of relief and melancholy.

I wished I could turn back time, erasing the looming dread of a terrible father and letting her relive those precious moments with her daughter, filled with joy and laughter instead of worry.

I hadn't considered the realities of parenthood, but watching Charlie, a sharp pang of regret struck me—I'd missed key moments in her life. I had to remind myself that I was not her father, and as much as I was enjoying our time together and falling more and more for her and her mother every day, I couldn't just jump right into being a family man.

Charlie and Stella were a solid unit, their combined strength felt like an unbreakable wall against the world. It was going to take more than fixing breakfast and letting Stella sleep in each morning to prove that, to me, this was a long-term commitment.

I found myself daydreaming of a time farther into the future and envisioning a little boy or girl with Stella's emerald eyes staring up at me from my arms. Those quiet moments where I dreamed of creating a life together always filled me with an effervescent sense of calm.

We hadn't known each other long, but the warmth of her

smile and a flash of white teeth against rosy cheeks sent shivers down my spine, melting my heart instantly.

My phone pinging with a text on the counter broke my daydream of a future with Stella. I picked it up and swiped it open, a grin breaking out across my face. The past two weeks had been a whirlwind of planning, a meticulous strategy taking shape in my mind, all for the chance to finally get a date with Stella.

Angie: You got it. I'd love to watch her!

I had texted Angie late last night as a thought came to me about what I wanted to do for our date.

We had made no plans beyond her agreement, but I'd been silently plotting the perfect first date for the perfect woman.

"*Masssss!*" Charlie yelled from her high chair, bashing her fists down in defiance. Since she'd learned to walk, she hated being confined. Apparently, that also included meal time.

Having just finished her breakfast, I knew it was almost time to get her ready for her day at Ray's. Stella had to work at the boutique, so Ray offered to keep her at her house for a while. If I could keep the little girl with me all day around the ranch, I would, but I'm sure heavy machinery and nap times wouldn't mix well.

"Okay, okay!" I said, as I walked over to extricate the toddler from the apparent prison conditions of her high chair.

I knelt and set her down gently on the floor before taking a cloth and wiping her hands and face clean.

"I think it's time we go get mama up. What do you think, little one?" I asked, ruffling her curls.

"Mama!!" she shouted as she took off like a shot down the

hallway towards Stella's room. I hung my head, taking a fortifying breath, and followed behind her.

It was Charlie's world, and we were just living in it.

She waited impatiently outside her mother's room, her small hands outstretched, unable to reach the doorknob. Her tiny fists clenched, and her brow furrowed in toddler frustration. Her look was so reminiscent of Stella, it made me chuckle.

I tapped lightly on Stella's door before twisting the knob to release the spitfire she called her child into her sanctuary. Charlie dashed toward the bed, her small feet padding softly on the carpet, while I watched from the doorway. She tried to scramble into bed with Stella, but her short, chubby legs, like little sausages, couldn't quite make it.

Stella rolled over and picked her up over the side of the bed, depositing her with an exaggerated plop on her lap. Her mussed hair and the pillow creases on her face showed she'd slept well. The soft light of dawn illuminated her face, highlighting the calm in her eyes, a beauty so profound it transcended understanding.

"Mama, up!" Charlie said, taking Stella's hand in hers and attempting to pull her from the covers. A burst of laughter escaped Stella's lips as she over-animatedly tumbled backwards onto her pillows, the sound a stark contrast to the previous quiet of the room.

"Mama sleepy," she sighed dramatically as Charlie continued her attempt to pull her from the bed.

"Mama UP!" she groaned, growing increasingly frustrated at the fact that her twenty-pound frame couldn't move Stella even an inch. With a groan, Stella slowly rose, the effort palpable, as if Charlie's pull was working. Charlie's resounding laughter was infectious as she "pulled" Stella into a sitting position.

"Okay, I'm up," she said, finally looking up to catch my gaze. I couldn't help but smile as I saw her; she looked absolutely stunning, radiating a calm confidence.

"Morning, Cowboy."

"Mornin', Trouble"

Since that day at the bar, our tension had only grown. We were more open in our perusal of each other and aware of the intense attraction between us.

There had been many times of accidental touches that left me rock hard and fisting my cock in the shower. There had even been an accidental ass grab one morning when she almost fell off the counter trying to reach something on the top shelf. That singular moment had left me tending to the horses with a raging hard on for the next hour.

Every interaction felt electric, a dangerous spark threatening to ignite into something more; I was tired of acting like there wasn't something there. Hence, why I was planning the perfect date.

"I'm about to head out to go get some stuff done, but I wanted to make sure you didn't have plans for Saturday." I said as I scratched at the day old scruff on my chin.

Stella had made mention in passing that she liked the unshaven look and I'd been all too keen to agree, causing me to forgo shaving this morning. I had no objection to letting my facial hair grow, but my ex had always demanded that I shave because she hated the "prickles" from my beard when we kissed.

It had become such an ingrained part of my daily routine that it was nice to change things up. Plus, it gave me a couple extra minutes in the morning since I didn't have to stop to shave.

Stella looked at me quizzically as she slid back the covers and set Charlie on the floor to toddle around while she got ready.

I wasn't a stranger to the sight of Stella in her tiny sleep shorts and cami set, but they still caught me off guard every time. Her long legs had gotten tanner in the summer months as she spent her off days lounging around the yard while Charlie played. She had barely there tan lines, a delicate etching from the straps of her favorite tank tops, on her shoulders.

"I'm off on Saturday and I have no plans..." she drawled as she squinted her eyes in trepidation. Her eyes, intense and probing, made me feel like she could read my mind, eliciting a nervous chuckle.

"Good. I've got a sitter for Charlie, and we're going out on that date you promised me." I said as I tapped the top of the door frame.

Turning around, I caught the tilt and shake of her head in exasperation. The wide smile that stretched across her face as I left for the kitchen was impossible to ignore; I could almost feel the warmth of it on my back.

If I could do only one thing for the rest of my life, it was going to be making this woman smile any chance I could. Now, I just needed to put the final touches on our perfect date.

stella

TONIGHT WAS OUR DATE, and Max had insisted I be ready at precisely eight o'clock. I had no clue why, but the nerves that floated around in my belly had gotten stronger with each minute that ticked by.

I'd spent all week stressing about what to wear, what we were going to do, should I eat or not eat, should I kiss him, would we have sex, and so many more imaginary scenarios.

I'm sure by the end of the week, Ray was happy to be rid of my questions and planning. She'd helped me pick out an outfit that comprised skinny jeans, a black lacy camisole, and a light grey cardigan. I chose an outfit that highlighted my favorite body parts, accentuating my post-baby curves and the shape of my ass.

Max had told me to dress casually. He mentioned that we weren't going out anywhere fancy, but to make sure I wore tennis shoes. I'd settled for a pair of broken-in Chuck Taylors to tie together the 'lived in chic' vibe I was giving off.

It had been nearly a decade since I had gone on a date, and to be honest, I didn't believe I had ever experienced a truly traditional or proper date in my life. Dean's idea of a first date was to take me bowling down at the local lanes and attempt to feel me up behind the building next to a dumpster.

I obviously had low standards, but Max had been hyping this date up all week and I could tell that he was excited. He exuded an air of confidence about his plans, any hint of nervousness undetectable. His disinterest toward long-term commitment, a direct result of his past relationship, made me curious about who he was before that pain had reshaped him. He clearly knew how to woo a woman.

Had he been a playboy?

How many women had he been intimate with?

Was he going to expect me to have sex with him?

My mind was spinning as a gentle knock rapped on the door. Another one of Max's insistences. He wanted to do things properly, so he picked me up at the front door, as if he didn't live there. It made my heart flutter that he went to such lengths to make this night special.

Angie had gotten here over an hour ago and was in the process of putting Charlie down for bed, so I was grateful that Max had opted to knock instead of ring the doorbell.

I inhaled deeply, steeling myself, then turned the knob, the door creaking open to reveal the most handsome man I'd ever seen, presenting a dazzling bouquet of wildflowers. The flowers looked handpicked, and if I wasn't already falling for Max, I would have been melting to the floor in a puddle at his thoughtfulness.

"Wow…" He remarked breathlessly as he scrubbed a hand over his mouth in what I can only assume was sheer awe.

Max's gaze made me feel beautiful, a warmth spreading through me like sunshine. It was as if he was seeing me clearly for the first time, and he let every emotion show in his expressions as he openly perused my appearance.

"Stella, you look stunning," he added when he finally picked his jaw up off the floor.

Blushing, a nervous chuckle tumbled from my lips as I smoothed down my tank top. Its "French tuck" (as Ray so cleverly put it) suddenly feeling far too deliberate, the fabric clinging uncomfortably to my skin.

I brushed a stray curl behind my ear; the strands tickling my skin, and refused to raise my eyes from the floor, terrified that the illusion of a man finding me stunning would vanish if I dared to meet his gaze.

I felt the heat of Max's body before his shoes came into view. As always, his fingers gently lifted my chin, his eyes boring into mine.

I loved how he didn't let me shy away from a compliment. He wanted me to see that he saw me—not just as a mother, but as a beautiful woman, someone he desired. It was going to take a while for the overwhelming trauma of being constantly berated and belittled to fade, but it seemed as if Max was steadfast in his intent to breathe new life into my self-confidence.

"I mean it, you look amazing," he said, his eyes sparkling with admiration as he grazed a calloused thumb across my jaw line.

I fought the urge to lean into his caress and close my eyes. The heat of his touch left a trail across my skin and my body vibrated with the electricity of lust. I took the chance to look him directly in the eyes to showcase the sincerity of my words.

"Thank you," I whispered. A thick tension hung heavy in

the air, charged with unspoken desires, as our bodies fought the magnetic pull to come together.

A loud throat clearing echoed from the hallway, shattering the intense moment, the unexpected sound causing us to break apart in a rush.

"Hey, Max." Angie said in greeting, awkwardly holding up a hand to wave.

"Hey, kiddo. Thanks again for agreeing to watch Charlie. I know you probably have better things to do on a Saturday night."

"Nah, watching you two dance around like you're both not attracted to each other is better than anything else I'd be doing tonight," she joked with a laugh.

Modern teenagers were ruthless and I could see the blush creep over Max's cheeks at the same time as mine. Not that we were dancing around our feelings, we were trying not to cross lines that couldn't be uncrossed.

I felt the spark between us, but the reality of my life as a single mom—all the responsibilities and the potential pitfalls of dating—required careful consideration before I jumped in. I ached to be with Max. The thought of diving into bed with him was so tempting, but the thought of my daughter, our shared living situation, and the risks to my own heart halted my desire.

"Cool," Max said awkwardly as he put a hand on my lower back and pushed me towards the door. "We'll just be heading out now. Call if you need anything."

I giggled at his blatant embarrassment and stepped into the humid summer air. It may have been close to sunset, but the air still held that midday heat long into the night.

Max insisted the date location would be a little chilly, a stark contrast to the warm summer air, so I reluctantly agreed to bring a cardigan, even if it clashed with the sex appeal I was trying to exude.

I was nervous and excited all in the same breath as he walked me to the passenger side door of his truck. I fought the urge to argue with him about opening my door, pushing it down since this was our first date and he was just being gentlemanly.

He closed the door and rounded the hood, hopping into the driver's seat with effortless grace. Before starting the truck, he leaned across the bench seat to grab the seat belt above my shoulder. Crossing it over the front of my body, he buckled it with deft fingers.

"Gotta keep you safe, Trouble." he whispered in my ear as he made his retreat to his side of the cab.

Internally, I scolded myself for getting worked up over a man buckling me in as a thrum of want pulsed at the apex of my thighs. I was an independent woman, damnit, and I wouldn't let my traitorous lady bits go all melty over a man doing things I could do myself.

I rolled my eyes at him, and he grinned at my sass. I'm sure he could tell that his insistence on invading my personal space flustered me. He seemed to get a perverse satisfaction from pushing my boundaries, a smirk playing on his lips.

Max rolled down the windows, and we sat in companionable silence on the short drive down to the ranch entrance. We again didn't feel the need to fill the air with mindless small talk. Listening to the peaceful sounds of the ranch was enough for both of us. It seemed to soothe the first date jitters enough for me to prod about our destination.

"So, do I get to know where we're going on this 'perfect' date?" I asked, using air quotations around the word perfect in jest.

"It's only about a five-minute drive from the ranch, but I promise you'll love it." He responded with a wink.

I scoffed and continued to look out the window at the fading sunset and incoming twilight. Before I knew it, we were pulling down an unmarked gravel road flanked by tall oak trees covered in Spanish moss. I quirked an eyebrow in Max's direction and he chuckled.

"Don't worry, I told you I wasn't a serial killer, remember?" he joked.

I let loose a loud laugh at the fact that I hadn't needed to say a word, and he knew exactly what I was thinking. Although the scenery was a little creepy, I didn't feel unsafe. Knowing that Max was with me gave me all the confidence to know that nothing would harm me.

He pulled up to a small clearing and put the truck in park. I looked out the front window with that quirk still in my eyebrow. Nothing around us screamed 'date'. There were no buildings, no other cars, and no lighting.

The surrounding forest was completely still, minus the idling of Max's truck.

"Come on, Trouble," he said after cutting the engine, unbuckling, and opening his door. I didn't wait for him to come around and open mine as I unlatched the belt and hopped out of the passenger seat.

The sigh of frustration that came from Max's lips as he reached for the door handle made me chuckle. I patted him on the chest as I walked into the glow of his still lit headlights and turned around with a grin.

"Gotta be quicker than that, cowboy," I teased.

He chuckled while repeating my words in a mocking manner and opened the back door to his truck to grab something. When he shut the door, I noticed a wicker picnic basket, a thick quilt, and a lantern in his hands.

My heart fluttered with a mix of excitement and nerves as I pictured our date, a hazy image forming in my mind. He'd planned a picnic just for the two of us. I swooned internally at the thought he had put into this night. When Max put his mind to something, he sure went all out.

"Hop on," he said, crouching down so that I could jump onto his back. He carefully set the wicker picnic basket down on the soft grass, motioning for me to climb up onto his muscular frame. I looked at him with slight fear in my eyes and he chuckled.

"You don't think I can carry you?" He teased.

I huffed and put my hands on my hips while shaking my head in exasperation.

"It's not that I don't think you can carry me. It's that you have other things in your hands and I'm afraid you might drop me." I said with a slight air of trepidation.

He stood up and turned towards me, putting his hands on his hips, mocking my stance. He clearly was getting comfortable around me enough to know that he could joke around like this.

"Trouble, I throw around hay bales that weigh twice as much as you do. I'm pretty sure that I can carry you on my back for the fifty yards it's going to take to get to where we're going."

I blushed at the insinuation that he could easily throw me around. A wave of acknowledgement at how it would feel to be manhandled by Max coursed all the way down my spine and settled between my thighs.

I shifted gently on my feet, and Max caught the movement. Even in the dim light, I could see his pupils dilate, dark and wide with an urgent need, his breath catching in his throat.

Clearing my throat and avoiding the incessant desire coursing through my veins, I conceded, "Fine, but if you drop me, it's your funeral."

I turned his shoulders away from me so I could gather the courage to hop on his back. I don't remember the last time someone had given me a piggyback ride, probably grade school. It was juvenile, but the thought of Max carrying me to our date made me feel carefree.

As Max steadied himself in a crouched position, I grabbed hold of his shoulders and hoisted myself onto his back. My raging hormones registered every sensitive part of me pressed against the muscular planes of him, and I adjusted myself for a comfortable ride, minimizing bumps and grinds.

Slowly, and with the grace of a man wearing nothing heavier than a simple backpack, he leaned down and picked up the picnic items. He hefted the basket into the crook of one elbow and used the other to band around my thigh and keep me secured to him.

I laughed loudly at how silly this must look, and I was thankful there was no one around to see when I inevitably fell on this trek.

But, true to his word, Max carried me the fifty yards to our destination and set me gently on my feet. Looking around, I saw little of anything, but the air was cooler and I could hear the faint trickle of what sounded like a stream.

It had gotten remarkably darker as we'd ventured deeper into the woods, so Max lifted the lantern between us.

He reached out a hand in offering, and without hesitation, I placed my palm in his. His rough calluses rubbed against the softness of my fingers, but the warmth and prickle of electricity soothed the grit.

Holding the lantern in front of himself and guiding me forward, we reached a dense portion of the forest. Again, a wave of icy air washed over me, and an involuntary shiver ran down my spine.

Max pushed aside the leaves and branches, their surfaces cool and slick with dew, leading me into a clearing bathed in an almost unreal light.

Dense tree cover concealed a small stream, its banks lined with lush grass and interspersed tiny white wildflowers. My breath caught in my throat. I'd never seen a sight more beautiful. The air was humid but cool and it was quiet except for the soft trickle of water flowing through the small brook.

Without warning, Max cut the lantern, and I gasped, turning towards him in fear. His arms, warm and strong, encircled my waist as he leaned in, his breath ghosting across my ear.

"Shh…" He hissed, stroking his thumb across my hip bone. "Just wait."

As my eyes adjusted to the darkness, tiny flickers of light blinked around us. Tiny yellow stars, each a pinpoint shine, winked in random spots and moments, their appearance sporadic and unpredictable. I felt Max's smile as his lips grazed the shell of my ear.

"Welcome to Firefly Cove," he whispered reverently.

SIXTEEN

THE LOOK of pure wonder on Stella's face was worth all the planning, secrecy, and the dramatics.

Bringing her to one of my favorite places in town was actually an idea from Ray. She'd suggested doing something that let her get to know me on a deeper level. I already knew so much about Stella and her past, but I felt like she was just scratching the surface of mine.

"Wow, Max…" she sighed, taking in the cove's beauty.

I kept my arm around her waist, unwilling to release her, but the date offered more than just a pretty view. With a gentle release, my palm glided down her arm, the smooth texture a prelude to the delicate touch of her hand in mine. As our fingers interlocked, I noticed how smoothly our hands fit together; it felt natural and right.

Tugging on her arm for her to follow, I walked us over to the flat spot on the bank. Although we were only a couple of feet from the babbling brook, the spot was perfect for our picnic blanket.

I reluctantly released Stella's hand and shook out the quilt to spread it flat on the ground. She helped me straighten it and I motioned for her to sit. Carefully placing the woven picnic basket beside us, I settled my large frame into a comfortable position next to her.

"I know you've already eaten dinner, but I figured I'd bring dessert," I said as I opened the picnic basket and pulled out the to-go containers that Ray had helped me pack. Inside were some fresh strawberries, chunks of cheesecake, apple slices, and marshmallows.

I grabbed a thermos from the basket and twisted off the cap, pouring the thick brown liquid into the lid. Stella looked down at the spread with a furrow between her brows.

"Fondue…" I sheepishly remarked, slightly embarrassed and concerned that she didn't like the idea.

Her laughter, bright and clear, shattered the quiet of the cove, and a wide smile stretched across my face. I let out a heavy sigh of relief. I'd been worried that she would find the date cheesy or silly. Apparently, I'd somehow nailed it on the first try, and a triumphant feeling surged through me.

"Max, this is so dang cute," she gushed as she grabbed a strawberry and dipped it in the warm chocolate.

Watching her bring the berry to her plush lips, lick the chocolate off, and bite into its juicy flesh could have easily passed for porn. The way her lips wrapped around the plump flesh caused my cock to thicken in my pants.

I was determined to abstain from sex tonight. Before taking Stella to bed, I wanted to wine and dine her properly. I wanted to show her she meant more to me than just a fling or a single date. She needed the assurance that this was something I planned to commit to long term.

I pulled out a bottle of wine and two plastic stemless wine glasses. My choice of drinkware prioritized practicality over aesthetics. I didn't think glass was a good idea in an outdoor setting.

I held out the bottle of rosé that Ray had insisted was the best with both hands, showcasing the label like a wine aficionado.

"Milady, will the house rosé be to your liking?"

Her giggle and nod were encouragement to pour two glasses. I handed her one and settled in on the blanket, propping myself up on one arm behind me. We sipped our wine in companionable silence while gazing at the surrounding wonders. Fireflies continued their dance through the cove, blinking on and off every couple of seconds.

"How did you find this place?" Stella asked as she looked around, fingering the long grass at the edge of the blanket.

"Ma used to bring Wade and I here when we needed a quiet spot to think or talk." I shared, running my finger around the edge of my wineglass in heavy contemplation.

Talking about Ma after her passing still brought a tight-ness to my chest, even two years later. It was common knowl-edge that I was a mama's boy, a fact I didn't attempt to hide. Ma was my best friend, and she always told me that my pensive nature was something she'd gladly passed down.

Whereas Wade was the rambunctious, outgoing, party boy - I was the silent thinker who would rather enjoy my own company than that of others. Wade often spent his time riding horses with Pops while I spent my afternoons baking with Ma in the kitchen.

After Shannon, I was perfectly content with my solitary existence until Stella's boisterous energy and vibrant person-ality crashed into my peaceful world like a whirlwind. Ma would have loved her. She never was quite fond of Shannon, often telling me that she saw something in her that didn't mesh with my soul. She was always so obscure that I shrugged off her comments.

"The cove is technically on D and D Ranch property. We own the land, even though the boundary lines are somewhat skewed. Since it's technically the namesake of the town, we do nothing but maintain the title. Ma wanted to keep it open to all town residents on the agreement that it remained a place of peace and that we could come here anytime we wanted." I fingered a blade of grass as I felt Stella's hand on my knee in comfort.

Somehow, she could sense my hesitation in talking about my mom. Not that I didn't want to open up to her, it just brought back the grief of losing her so early. I didn't want to burden her with the heaviness that came from losing a parent.

"Will you tell me about her?" she asked softly, leaving her hand on my knee.

I gently lifted the wineglass from her other hand and set it beside mine on the grass. Shifting to create a space between my legs, I pulled her to sit in front of me, her back to my front. She laughed, a tinkling sound, and nestled into the comforting warmth of my embrace, the scent of her hair filling my senses.

"I'd love to," I replied.

I took a moment to figure out where to start. Ma was a lot wrapped up in a little package and I wanted Stella to get an extensive overview of the woman who'd made me into the man I am today.

"You remind me a lot of her. She was an amazing mom." I remarked pensively. "She was full of life, much like Wade - but she enjoyed the quiet moments of contemplation much more, like me."

Stella twined her fingers with mine, urging me to

continue. I brushed my thumb lightly over the back of her hand, feeling the goosebumps rise as she shivered. Smiling, I tugged her closer to my frame under the guise that she must be cold.

"She taught me how to be a good man. She always told me that there were many things in life that would make you successful, but if you weren't good in here," I said, pointing at Stella's heart, "you'd be a failure."

"She sounds like an incredible woman," she whispered, leaning her head back against my shoulder.

"She was," I responded solemnly. "It hasn't been the same since she's been gone. Pops sure hasn't been the same. Truthfully, *none* of us will ever be the same. She had an impact on each one of us individually, as well as being the rock behind our family."

Stella traced her fingers up and down my arm, which was wrapped tightly around her slight frame. I felt the path each one of her digits took long after she'd moved them from the spot. Her touch was like fire branding its way into my skin.

"If you don't mind me asking, how did she pass?" she asked hesitantly.

"A brain aneurysm," I said matter-of-factly. "Here one day, and gone the next. They told us at the hospital that there was nothing we could have done to prevent it. They just… happen."

Stella shifted in my arms to turn and look at me. She was so goddamn beautiful, even with the solemn look that currently blanketed her expression.

I brushed one of her curls behind her shoulder, tenderly trailing my fingers over her slender neck on the retreat. She leaned into my touch and I settled my hand on her hip.

"I'm so sorry, Max," she whispered.

"Thank you," I replied in earnest. I could tell that her apologies weren't the empty platitudes we'd come to expect around Ma's death. People don't know what to say when someone passes suddenly. Their default reaction is an apology and an empty offer to help if we needed it.

"When Wade and I were little, she'd bring us here to the cove every first of May. The fireflies appear when the weather warms up. It became a tradition for us to camp out here and wait for the fireflies to make their appearance, signaling the start of spring."

I looked around at the serenity of the cove and continued, feeling a gentle breeze sway through the trees. I felt as if that breeze was Ma giving me her silent approval. "She always told us that fireflies were magic- that they carried your wishes off into the night to be granted by the moon."

"She would tell us to sit right here on the bank, catch a firefly in our hands, make a wish, and let it go." I cupped Stella's hands in mine and watched as a firefly landed in the middle of her palm. I carefully closed my hands over hers, her soft skin a contrast to my own, and looked up to meet her gaze.

"I've made my wish. Now it's your turn. Make a wish, Stella."

stella

I PEEKED at the tiny orange and black bug crawling around between my palms. Its bioluminescent lower half flickered green in random intervals.

Closing my eyes, I thought of what to wish for. I could wish that Charlie and I wouldn't have to look over our shoulders for the rest of our lives. I could wish for an abundance of happiness. After a long period of contemplation, my countless desires eventually narrowed down to one particular wish: a single, burning hope.

Opening my eyes and my hands, I released the firefly. I watched it buzz away into the night, mixing with the stars in the sky, with a gentle smile spread across my face.

The idea that a tiny little bug that could fly all the way to the moon and grant wishes was silly, but it was the perfect type of silly for tonight. I needed the lightness of this moment in a life full of moments designed to test me at every turn.

"Do I get to know what you wished for?" Max asked, breaking me from my gaze on the bright twinkling stars above.

My smile turned timid as I looked down and picked at a hole in my jeans. I tugged on the barely fraying strings until they began unraveling into a bigger rip. The symbolism of pulling at those strings to what lay beneath wasn't lost on me. Max had been peeling back the threads of my carefully crafted armor designed to protect my heart. He had created a hole that only he could fill.

"If I tell you, does it not come true?" I challenged.

"I'm not sure if wishing on fireflies is the same as wishing on birthday candles, but I can tell you I'll go crazy if I don't know what you wished for."

I thought about suggesting a different wish because I was a little embarrassed by how simple and silly mine was. Instead, I opted for the truth.

"I wished for you to kiss me," I whispered and brought my eyes up to meet his gaze.

His eyes blazed with desire; his grip on my neck, tender yet firm, sent shivers down my spine. There was zero hesitancy in his movements. I was sure he could feel my pulse racing, but I hoped that his was beating just as fast.

Max leaned down and swiftly pressed his lips against mine. His mouth was soft in its caress, as if he was holding back. I shifted to my knees, scooting forward until our bodies were flush, our lips still locked.

Placing one knee on either side of his outstretched legs, I straddled his lap, seating myself gently down on his thighs. I hadn't ever been this brazen, but something about how Max cherished me made me feral with need.

Max groaned into my mouth and tilted my head back to open me up to him more, licking at the seam of my lips for entrance. I moaned softly, and he used the opening to coast his tongue gently against my own. As I ran my hands up his chest and around to the nape of his neck, I scratched my nails through his short prickly strands of hair and shivered at the electric need coursing through my body.

Max kissed with the fire of a man who was desperate to consume me. I kissed back with the wanton need of someone desperate for affection. I felt his rigid length thickening between my legs, and I shifted my hips in exploration. He broke the kiss with a heated groan and trailed tender nips down the smooth column of my throat.

"Fuck, Stella." he remarked, trailing his way back up to take my mouth in another sensual kiss.

"Yes, Max. That's exactly what I want," I teased, nipping at his bottom lip.

He dropped his head back to look at the sky and let out a groan of frustration. I giggled lightly at his attempt at restraint and kissed the corner of his mouth, then his cheek, then right below his ear. He shivered, which caused me to smile against his skin.

I'd never felt so powerful as I did in this moment, having Max completely at the mercy of my touch. I felt a surge of confidence, a newfound sexiness coursing through me, thanks to him; I was ready to seize what I wanted.

He gripped my hips to keep me from grinding myself against what I could only ascertain was his impressively large cock. Pulling me close, he dropped his forehead to mine in an intimate gesture that had me feeling vulnerable.

His eyes locked onto mine, a weight in their depths, before a heavy sigh escaped and his eyes fluttered closed. I hesitated as the self-deprecating thoughts came rushing back in. Did he not want me?

Thoughts swarmed my senses as I started to become engulfed in an overwhelming panic.

Had I been making up the stolen glances in my head?

Had I imagined all the times that I'd caught him smiling at me over his morning coffee?

Was I dreaming, and this was all a one sided infatuation?

Sensing my spiraling thoughts before I even had a chance to vocalize them, Max coasted his hand up the side of my throat and forced my gaze to his.

"No." he said simply, as if that would calm the raging voices in my head shouting all the words I'd worked so hard to erase from my psyche.

Useless. Whore. Trash. Unloveable. Damaged.

I scrambled from his lap and he had the good sense to let me go. I brushed my fingers through my mussed hair and straightened my camisole that had come untucked. Tugging my cardigan tighter around my frame, I attempted to make myself smaller as I searched for the strength to speak.

"Please take me home now."

I couldn't meet his gaze, anticipating the condescending pity in his eyes. I couldn't stand to see his lips, still swollen from our kiss, even though I could still feel the ghost of his touch.

I turned in the direction we had come, not waiting for his response, my gaze remaining fixed on the ground as I stumbled back to his truck in the dark.

I heard him gathering the remnants of our picnic and tossing them into the basket quickly. The snap of the quilt echoed through the quiet cove as he hastily snagged it from the ground and it whipped through the air. Just as I reached the passenger door of the truck, his hand darted out to grab hold of my wrist, stopping me in my tracks.

"Stella… let me explain."

"There's nothing to explain. I understand, Max. I come

with a lot of baggage. Thank you for trying to set up a fun date, but I don't need your pity."

"Pity?" He asked incredulously as his eyebrows furrowed together.

Before I had the sense to know what was happening, Max had me pressed up against the cool metal of his passenger door and had his arms bracketed beside my head. The move should have scared me, but even in my self-deprecating state, I knew that Max wouldn't do anything to hurt me.

I heaved in a gulping breath as my pupils blew wide. Even if this was one-sided, I found him attractive, and his rough handling was an aphrodisiac. He tilted my chin up, his fingers brushing against my skin, forcing our eyes to meet. He then leaned down, his breath warm against my lips as he spoke.

"I don't fucking *pity* you, Trouble."

He slid his nose across my jaw and down my neck, causing goosebumps of pleasure to erupt in his wake.

"Make no mistake, Stella Jacobsen, the reason I stopped was absolutely not because I fucking pity you," his lips coasted the shell of my ear and I involuntarily shivered with desire. "I stopped because the first time I fuck you will not be in the middle of the woods on a blanket my mother hand stitched."

His grin was feral as he gripped my hip bone and drove his knee between my legs. I gasped and felt a tingle of need shoot down to the apex of my thighs, right where he'd placed his knee. I felt his erection pressing into my thigh as I let out a breathy moan.

"Stella, I want you. I want *all* of you. To be completely honest, I want Charlie in my life just as much. I want your morning bed head, your mid day laughter, and your night time yawns."

He placed his callused hands on the side of my neck, brushing his thumb across my jaw. I fought the urge to close my eyes. "I want to make you happy, but I need to be able to touch you without you flinching every time. I need you to let me in to be the man you deserve. I need all of you without reservations."

He paused, making sure I was paying attention to his heated words. "When you can give me all of you, I'm going to ruin you for any other man. I'm going to make you come so hard there's never any chance of anyone else's touch igniting desire in your veins. I will love you and Charlie so fiercely that I will be forever embedded in your souls."

A whimper fell from my lips as I felt a line of tears gather on my lower lashes. His declaration had hit on all the sore spots of my soul. All I had ever wanted was to feel cherished, loved, and safe. Max was doing all he could to show me that he meant every word that crested his lips.

I felt his rough thumb swipe with an unnatural tenderness across the tops of my cheeks, brushing away the streaks of tears I hadn't realized had fallen.

"Please don't cry, baby," he whispered, placing his forehead against mine again in an incredibly intimate gesture.

The overwhelming emotion of the moment caused more tears to fall, and I let out a small chuckle. I had a man standing in front of me declaring his desire to be with me and my child, and I was crying.

"I'm sorry, I shouldn't be crying," I apologized, wiping the tears away with the back of my hand. He once again used the pad of his thumb to swipe beneath my lashes, gathering the remnants of my mascara to keep it from running.

"Don't apologize for feeling," he remarked with sincerity.

"You have every right to be scared and hesitant, given all that you've been through."

I leaned my head back against the window of the truck and closed my eyes, taking a big breath and releasing it slowly to calm my racing heart. Trauma had a way of ruining even the most special of moments. All it takes is one fleeting glance, one wrong word, one second of hesitation to undo all the progress you've made. Max continued stroking his thumb across my hip bone in a silent show of solidarity.

"When you hesitated, my mind started spiraling. All I could hear was Dean's voice calling me worthless, useless, unloveable…" I trailed off, chancing a glance up at him.

I could see the slight tick in his jaw as he fought the urge to rage against a man he had no possibility of fighting in my honor. There would be no retribution for all the hurt and anguish Dean had caused me over the years. I had to learn to live with that fact and if Max was going to be in my life, he would too.

"I wish I could kill that fucker for what he put you through," he seethed.

"Well, it's a good thing someone already took care of that for you, because I don't really think you'd look good in orange ,and you're too pretty to be someone's bitch." I said with a tender smile as I patted his cheek. That got him to crack a small smile, and he leaned down and pressed his lips against mine in the softest of kisses.

"I'm sorry if I ruined the rest of our date," I said solemnly. Max chuckled and brushed a stray tear from my chin.

"The date's not quite over yet. I haven't walked you to your door," he teased while reaching behind me to pop the handle of the passenger door. He held my hand as he assisted me up onto the running board and into my seat. Before he could shut the door, I leaned over, grabbing ahold of the front of his shirt and tugged his lips roughly against mine.

"Thank you, Max," I mumbled against his lips. "Thank you for showing me what it means to be cherished."

"If you'll let me, I'll spend the rest of the days I have left showing you how much you and Charlie mean to me." he said with a quick peck to my lips before buckling my seatbelt and walking around to the driver's side.

When he climbed into the truck and started it, he didn't hesitate to rest his hand on my thigh in a possessive gesture. He acted as if he wanted to keep me constantly aware of his desire, a subtle but persistent reminder.

He was giving me the reassurance I craved.

stella

TRUE TO HIS WORD, Max drove me back to the house and walked me to my bedroom door like a southern gentleman. Even though his intentions were altruistic, we proceeded to make out against the hallway wall like a pair of horny teenagers.

The only thing that broke us from our lust induced haze was a tiny whimper from Charlie's room across the hall. The sound, like a shock of icy water, jolted us back to reality; that we weren't two horny teenagers, but two adults with responsibilities.

His fingers brushed a stray strand of hair behind my ear, his large hands cradling the side of my neck as he leaned down and kissed me with the gentlest touch of his lips, his murmured goodnight barely audible above the beating of my heart.

What I felt for Max was more than attraction; it was a primal pull, a deep yearning I couldn't ignore. Even after all the years I spent with Dean, well, our good ones, I'd never once felt this deep-seated desire that left me breathless. Max made me come alive with every touch, and I was glad that the feelings weren't one-sided.

The next morning, I woke to the sound of soft crooning country music coming from the kitchen. I rolled over with a huge smile on my face and stretched out the stiffness of a good night's sleep. After checking the baby monitor to see that Charlie was already up and cared for, I made my way towards the delicious smell of bacon and coffee.

At eight in the morning, the kitchen was already a whirlwind of activity, filled with the clatter of dishes and cheerful chatter. Seated around the table were Wade, Ray, Max, Charlie, and Pops. Confused by the sudden family breakfast, and the aroma of a full three-course meal wafting from the kitchen, I paused in the doorway.

Beside Charlie, Max spooned scrambled eggs, apparently her new favorite meal, onto her tray. She attempted to use the baby spoon to scoop them into her mouth, but gave up and shoveled the eggs in with her hands.

The sight of the family seated around the table, a warm glow illuminating their faces, filled me with a wistful longing; their happy chatter creating a comforting atmosphere.

Family breakfasts were never a part of my childhood, even on the rare occurrence that both of my parents were actually home on a weekend.

Did Charlie and I have a permanent place here in this little group? Or were we just bystanders that seemed to mesh well into their carefully built institution at the current moment? I squashed down the self-deprecating thoughts that seemed to pop up every time I started letting my guard down and continued my descent upon the brewed coffee.

"Mornin'," Pops called over the top of his own coffee cup.

"Good Morning."

"Saw y'all comin' in late last night." He said, darting his eyes knowingly between Max and I. I lowered my gaze to the floor as a light blush creeped across my cheeks. I risked a quick look up at Max, catching a glimpse of his sly smirk and a playful wink, his eyes twinkling.

As if the universe was throwing me a proverbial bone of avoidance, my phone chimed from the counter. I flipped it over to see who might be texting me. This kitchen held most of the people on my daily call log, so I couldn't imagine who'd be texting me this early.

A gasp escaped my lips as my breathing hitched, a cold sweat breaking out across my brow, and my heart pounding in my chest.

Unknown Number: u can run but u cnt hide

I immediately felt light-headed and gripped the countertop behind me for support.

That was impossible.

It had been a month already, with radio silence. How had they found us? Had they found us?

The questions swirled through my head like a hurricane. I felt the rapid beat of my heart in my ears as I fought to breathe.

I sensed a warm presence step in front of me. He slowly took the coffee cup I'd been absent-mindedly clutching from my hand and set it on the counter.

I felt like I was floating in an ocean and everyone was speaking to me from above the surface, their voices muffled. Max's words of comfort were lost in a blur, his voice a whispered hum against the roaring in my ears.

"Ma!" Charlie's tiny voice called out through the haze,

breaking me from my stupor. I shook my head, trying to clear away the fog of panic, the dizzying rush of fear still clinging to me like a shroud.

"Stella. What's wrong?" Max asked while gently putting his hand around my phone in an attempt to pry it from my clutched hand. I loosened my hold on the device and Max took it, studying the message that had sent me off the deep end. I could see his rage bubbling to the surface as he stomped over to the table and slammed the phone down in front of Ray.

In her defense, she didn't flinch. She read the message over with a furrow between her brows and looked at me in confusion.

"What is this?" She asked, her eyes scanning the cryptic message one more time.

Ray was perceptive, but I'd left everyone but Max in the dark about the danger Charlie and I were in. I didn't want them being dragged into the darkness that I knew would eventually catch up with me.

Sighing, I sat down in one of the wooden chairs around the table. With a sigh, I knew it was finally time to share what had happened.

"I guess it's time to tell y'all what brought us to Firefly Cove…" I started. Max sat beside me, taking my small hand in his, a warm reassurance that he was here for support, but this was *my* story to tell.

After twenty minutes, a million questions - primarily from Ray, and one scrambled egg induced meltdown, I'd finally coughed up a watered-down version of our story. I left out the gritty details of seeing Dean's lifeless body, but gave a comprehensive overview of how much danger we'd brought to their little town.

"I know this is a lot, and I don't expect any of you to just up and throw yourself into the drama that I've brought to your doorstep. These people are unhinged and dangerous. I can't expect you guys to put yourselves in their sights."

The room was silent except for the nervous drumming of my fingers against the table as everyone absorbed the weight of my words. I had expected them to insist that we move, but without hesitation, Pops stood up, placed his hand on my shoulder, and declared with the weathered gruffness only found in a cowboy, "Family takes care of their own. We've got you."

I couldn't stop the tears from falling as I dropped my head in relief. The process of learning to accept help from others had been challenging, but I was slowly getting better at it. I realized that I needed to embrace the community we had built and stop fighting them every step of the way. These people had proven time and time again that they weren't going to run at the slightest hint of trouble.

Ray excused herself with the promise that she was going to call her dad and have him come over with any resources he could supply. Having the Sheriff in your back pocket at a time like this wasn't a bad idea. The thought of retelling the whole story again filled me with dread, but Max's comforting hand squeeze reassured me that I wouldn't face it alone.

Less than thirty minutes later, Sheriff Cortez sat across from Max and me in the dimly lit living room, the air thick with tension as I repeated the story for what felt like the hundredth time. I'd insisted Wade and Ray take Charlie outside; I needed to share the unvarnished truth and I didn't want Charlie hearing all the gory details.

I figured they also didn't need the gruesome specifics, but I wanted to ensure the Sheriff received every piece of information we possessed, no matter how unpleasant it was to recount.

"I can assure you, Stella, we will do everything in our power to catch these guys. I appreciate you being forthcoming in the information you've provided." He had promised.

Instead of Ray coming to the ranch, I'd frequently drop Charlie off at their home, meeting Ray's father in relaxed, unofficial encounters–usually in the midst of cheerful morning chaos. He was always warm and inviting, a loyal family man. He loved to recount how Charlie's playful nature and unwavering optimism kept him young, that she was a constant reminder of the world's goodness.

Having raised ten kids of his own, you could tell he was comfortable taking on that fatherly role. I hadn't heard much about Ray's mom being in the picture, but I wasn't about to pry into her home life. I hadn't ever seen her when I came to visit, so maybe one day she'd feel comfortable opening up to me about her.

Ray's father showed no surprise when Ray placed Charlie on his lap during my first visit, even while she went back to grab things from the car. He'd tried everything to make her laugh: cooing sweet nothings, pulling funny faces, and bouncing her playfully on his knee, making horsey sounds.

Seeing him in his uniform and role as the hardened officer had thrown me off at first. One moment he was jovial and carefree, the next a stern protector; yet, both sides were driven by a fierce protectiveness.

I felt uneasy as I recalled the events to the best of my ability. When I got to the part in the story describing my near assault, I could feel Max's hand tighten around mine. He'd refused to let go at any point between reading the text and now. That grounding touch was comforting, a familiar weight that steadied me and gave me the strength to continue.

Sheriff Cortez, who'd insisted I call him Emmanuel, had assured me he would have his team working overtime on this case and they wouldn't rest until we were safe. He'd made sure I knew I had nothing to fear legally, and that I was a witness, not an accomplice. I had been so scared of retribution; I hadn't even stopped to think about legality.

Hearing his words did little to squash the dread that filled my body. I knew he would do everything in his power to help, but the ease with which criminals skirted the justice system left me on high alert. Somehow, even though I'd driven across state lines and over eighteen hours from the only home I'd ever known, they'd found us.

As we walked him out to his cruiser, Max's hand resting on the small of my back, I once again thanked him for his help.

"If you receive any more messages from unknown senders, please pass them on to our office," he insisted.

I nodded, fearing that if I spoke, I'd break down. A suffocating pressure bore down on me, the weight of the situation a palpable thing pressing against my chest. I was sure that if Max removed his hand from my back that I'd crumple to the ground in defeat.

I thought we had gotten away. How stupid could I be? You don't outrun a murderer set on vengeance.

After the patrol car's tires crunched on the gravel, disappearing down the driveway, Max put his arm around me, turning me back to the house. I'm not sure how he could sense the quiet desperation radiating from me, the way I was barely holding it together, but I wasn't going to question it. I let him guide me back into the living room and sit me down on the sofa.

Retreating to the kitchen, I heard him rustling around in cabinets for a few minutes before reemerging with a steaming cup in hand.

"Tea." He said simply, as if using too many words would snap the tightly wound tether on his restraint.

"Thanks." I replied and brought the steaming cup to my lips. It hinted of cinnamon and clove as I took a slow sip. The warmth trickled down my throat and into my belly, instantly relieving some of my anxiety.

"When I was a kid, I'd have panic attacks," Max stated while picking at a loose thread on the sofa. "Ma would always sit me down with a cup of chai tea. She said that the warmth was good for calming the soul."

"I wish I could have met her." I said, placing my hand on Max's knee in comfort.

"She would have loved you." His gaze met mine and a slight smile tipped up at the corner of his mouth. "She was fierce, loyal, and stubborn as hell. You remind me a lot of her. She would have gone to the ends of the earth to make sure Wade and I were safe, happy and loved."

He used his signature move, a gentle lift of my chin, his eyes shining with sincerity, leaving no doubt about his words as he spoke.

"You're an amazing mom, Stella. You did what you needed to do to keep yourself and Charlie safe. We're not going to let anything happen to you two, I promise." His sincerity met its mark, and I smiled weakly.

The group ambled back into the house, settling with soft thuds onto the plush living room furniture. One by one, they all nodded in agreement, a silent chorus of approval for Max's earlier statement.

"We mean it, kid. You're one of us now." Pops said with a tender tilt of his lips. "Now, who's gonna train this woman how to shoot?"

Laughter bubbled out of everyone in the room, myself included at Pops's brisk change of subject.

"Now, that's a great idea Pops." Max said, scrubbing at the stubble on his chin in contemplation. I could see the wheels turning as he worked out logistics in his head.

I mean, it couldn't hurt to learn.

stella

THE ACRID SMELL of gun smoke, a metallic tang mixed with something burnt, filled my senses as I made my way from the porch of the big house, crunching on gravel, to the shadowy coolness behind the barn.

Max had insisted on starting our shooting lessons immediately, taking Pops' advice to heart. I was hesitant, but reluctantly agreed. I longed for the day when the knot of dread in my stomach would loosen, replaced by the confidence to protect myself. Realistically, I knew that one lesson on how to shoot a gun didn't make me an expert, but I hoped it would give me a little bit of strength to know that I *could* protect myself.

It just so happened that a water main break near the boutique had shut everything down, giving me an unexpected day off. Though disappointed about closing, the thought of having uninterrupted time with Max brightened my mood.

Ray had already planned on having Charlie for the day, so she offered to keep her so that Max and I could work on some shooting lessons.

The sight that greeted me as I rounded the building was nearly pornographic.

Max was standing with his feet shoulder width apart and his arms raised as he aimed at a target approximately fifty feet away.

He looked ever the vision of lethality, and I leaned against the barn in an attempt to keep out of sight and avoid rubbing my thighs together to quell the ache settling between them.

Max's faded Wrangler jeans clung to his muscular thighs as they flexed with each shift of his hips. He wore a tight-fitting black tee tucked into his pants, accentuating his broad back. To top off the sexy hitman visual, he had on a ball cap turned backwards and a pair of aviator sunglasses. Over his hat was a pair of black earmuffs to dull the sound.

I watched with rapt attention at the way his body moved. He was a source of strength and stability, a constant in my otherwise chaotic world. He oozed effortless masculinity with the way he gripped the pistol in his hands. I wondered what it would feel like to have that grip focused on me. I knew that Max would never use his strength to hurt me, but I wanted those strong hands wrapped around my—

"I can feel you staring," he called from his spot, cutting off my thoughts as he took a deep breath, held, then pulled the trigger, effectively shattering one of the beer bottles lined up on the target wall, and my daydreams of him naked.

He handled the firearm with practiced ease, the smooth metal cool against his skin as he detached the magazine, placing the weapon and ammunition on the nearby table in separate spots.

I felt heat rising up my collarbones and across my face as he turned to look back in my direction.

Fuck, how long had I been staring?

He lifted his sunglasses from his face and tucked them in the neckline of his tee, then removed the earmuffs, setting them on the table beside the weapon pieces. A wide grin stretched across his face, nearly splitting it as he saw my flustered reaction.

"You comin' down with something? You're lookin' a little flushed there, Trouble." he teased.

Clearing my throat, I steeled my spine and stomped toward him. His low chuckle, a warm, comforting sound, followed me as I walked past him and stood where he'd been moments before. I wouldn't be the one to shatter the fragile, unspoken peace we had established, the quiet understanding between roommates that kept things strictly platonic… for now.

"Nope, all good. Teach me how to shoot this thing," I responded briskly, not daring to meet his eyes, for fear that he'd see how much he had truly affected me.

My fingers brushed the cold metal of the gun before a hand clamped down on my wrist, halting my action. I shot a warning glare at Max. My eyes narrowed, and he immediately released his grip. He nervously lifted his ball cap and ran his fingers through his hair before dropping it back on his head.

Logically, I knew my reaction to him grabbing my wrist was unfounded. Max had never once made any move towards me that was anything less than gentlemanly. But, trauma overrides logic; rational thought processes become secondary.

"Before we get to the shooting, I want to go over some basic firearm safety. I also want to go over the inner workings of the firearm and proper handling." He said authoritatively, acting as if I was a student in a class he was teaching on firearm safety.

Although the naughty teacher act was hot, the nuances of

learning to shoot a gun, such as proper stance, breath control, and target acquisition, hadn't occurred to me. I figured it was just pick up, cock, aim, and fire.

Sensing my hesitation, Max stepped beside me and pointed down at the weapon.

"Tell me what you see," He commanded.

"A gun?" I asked incredulously, with a quirk of my brow.

Exasperation caused him to let out a heavy, theatrical sigh; then, hands planted firmly on his hips, he let his head droop. I could tell this was going to be a long day if I'd already annoyed him. Why did the thought of ruffling his feathers fill me with so much excitement?

"Yes, Stella. It's a gun. But, it's more than that," he said as he picked up the main component of the gun. I didn't know the exact terminology, but enough TV had taught me it wasn't loaded, and I presumed it was safe for me to handle.

"A gun is more than just a hunk of metal. It is a dangerous object used to injure, or in extreme cases, kill." He held the weapon out in his large hand for me to take. The cool, smooth metal of the gun barrel rested in my palm, its weight surprisingly substantial.

"You need to always keep in the forefront of your mind that this gun is dangerous. That might seem like common sense, but having a slight fear of weapons is healthy. The more complacent you become in your handling, the more risk you run of injuring yourself or someone else without meaning to."

His voice was low and lethal as he walked closer, the scent of gun smoke and leather clinging to him. He stood behind me, the warmth of his hands enveloping mine as we held the weapon together. My heart rate spiked at the feeling of his large palms encompassing mine.

Using his pointer finger, he regaled all the key components of the gun and what they did, his breath coasting along my ear as he gruffly spoke. His deep knowledge of marksmanship was comforting, and I felt at ease knowing he was going to be the one teaching me. Having seemingly mastered the weapon's inner workings to Max's standards, we moved on to stance and handling.

"One thing you always want to remember is to never point the firearm anywhere you're not okay with shooting," he preached, holding the weapon down at his side. "If you're raising your weapon, be prepared to pull the trigger."

I nodded and watched him load bullets into the magazine with deft fingers and push the magazine back into the handle of the gun. With his weapon securely at his hip, finger away from the trigger, he moved me aside so he could take my spot.

He gave me his extra pair of slightly too-large earmuffs with a subtle nod to put them on, the cool leather a subtle contrast to the heat that was coursing across my skin, then put his own back on.

He positioned his feet shoulder width apart, instructing me on the proper stance with his free hand as he went along. His voice was muffled by my ear protection, but I still managed to understand his instructions.

With a slow, deliberate movement, he raised his arms, the gun steady in his hands as he aimed it towards the target, the silence broken only by the rhythmic beating of my heart. He walked me through the proper grip, all while keeping the barrel of the pistol trained down-range and his finger off the trigger.

With a nod backwards of his head in a silent instruction to back up, he steadied his footing and gazed out towards the target, cocking the gun and raising it in front of him. He inhaled deeply, filling his lungs. The stillness that washed over him was eerie as he trained his sights on another bottle.

He was ever the vision of calm and stability. Slowly releasing his breath, I saw him move his pointer finger to rest on the trigger and pull. The gun kicked upwards with the force of the bullet releasing and in the blink of an eye, another bottle shattered.

He unloaded the magazine once again, setting it down on the table beside us, and motioned for me to step up for a turn. With shaky hands, I reached down and grabbed the frame, putting the magazine back in its rightful place.

I mimicked Max's motions in keeping my finger off the trigger and the weapon aimed at the ground. I nervously traded spots with him as he moved to stand behind me. He slipped the earmuffs from my ears so I could hear his instructions.

Pressing his warm chest against my back, he slid his hands down my arms to help me lift them into the proper stance. A loud, frantic thumping filled my ears, the sound of my own heart pounding in my chest. I wasn't sure if my heart was beating out of my chest because I was holding a weapon designed to kill, or because Max's body was pressed tight against mine.

He used his booted foot to kick my feet apart, and I shifted them into a shoulder-width distance, attempting to ignore the jolt of pleasure from being manhandled. He twisted my hips a tick to the right and before righting my ear protection, leaned down to murmur in my ear.

"You've got all the power, Stella,"

I caught his double entendre and steeled my spine. His words hung in the air—a fragile promise of his safety and his heart, now resting entirely on me. He believed in me enough to know that I wouldn't hurt him. I wasn't as confident, but I trusted him.

He carefully lifted the ear muffs, positioning them on my head before taking a measured step back. Nerves fluttered in my belly as I grasped what I held in my hand. This wasn't merely a gun; Max was right, it was power. I was learning how to protect myself and Charlie, reclaiming what had been stolen from me for so long.

I took a fortifying breath and braced myself as I pulled the trigger. The shot rang out, and I felt my arms kick back with the recoil. An adrenaline rush surged through my veins as I watched the bullet drift toward the target, almost as if in slow motion. I completely missed the paper target Max had tacked to the wooden backstop, the bullet ricocheting off the side. The shot didn't hit anything, but it was still a shot.

I lowered the gun, emptied the magazine from its holster like Max had shown me, and placed both halves of the gun on the table. My hands shook with adrenaline, but my body buzzed with excitement. I'd done it.

Looking up, I saw a look of bewilderment cross Max's face. He looked at me, his expression one of pure astonishment, as if seeing me for the very first time. Before I could think, he had me in his grip as his mouth crashed down over mine. The heady rush of adrenaline continued coursing through me as I gripped the front of his shirt to keep him close, deepening the kiss.

His lips were warm and soft as they took control of mine. His hands were demanding in their perusal of my body, gripping my hips like he was drowning and I was his lifeboat. Our emotions snapped like a rubber band, but the kiss I returned was fervent, a desperate tangle of tongues and urgent need.

"Fuck, Trouble," he murmured against my lips. "I couldn't

wait one more fucking second to have my hands on you. You looked so fucking sexy up there protecting yourself."

A light laugh bubbled from my chest as I looked him directly in the eyes. "Right back at cha', Cowboy. It's the Wranglers for me." I patted his taught ass for emphasis.

His laugh was infectious, and I leaned my head onto his chest to feel the gentle vibration. Hearing Max laugh was like a calming balm to my soul.

"How do you feel?" He asked, the brush of his fingers against my skin sending shivers down my spine as he tucked a loose strand of hair behind my ear. His other hand lingered on my back, softly trailing across the fabric of my shirt.

"Honestly? Fucking terrified," I huffed. Although I'd managed to shoot at the target without killing myself or Max, the fear of holding someone's life in my hands, the weight of the gun barrel pressing against my palm, was still terrifying.

"Good," he whispered, as his eyes caught mine again. "I'm terrified too."

"Max," I whispered reverently. His eyes blazed with a fiery desire, the unspoken longing practically crackling in the air as he heard his name on my lips.

"Seeing you up there, holding that gun, taking back the power of your own safety? Fuck, Stella. I've never seen anything hotter."

A fleeting touch, like a phantom's caress, grazed my skin as his fingertip trailed across my arm; a nervous laugh escaped my lips, and I quickly looked away. Max's endless stream of compliments, each delivered with an effortless smile, left me reeling. I couldn't get used to the unexpected warmth in his voice each time he offered a compliment; it felt oddly disarming.

But, that steely resolve he was so good at hiding behind? I

wanted to snap it. I needed to know he felt the same intense desire as I did. "So, what are you going to do about it?" I asked from beneath my lashes, goading him.

"Hold up, just a second." Max instructed as he gathered all the pieces to the weapon and stored them in their locked carrying case. My confusion must have been evident, because as soon as the case shut with a soft snick, he was on me again.

"Safety first," he murmured against my lips as I laughed at his ability to be a walking green flag. Romance authors would have a field day with Max Daniels.

His hands were everywhere as he deftly guided us towards the barn. I'm not sure how his brain was functioning well enough to make it happen, but he did.

Slamming through the door, Max walked me backwards to what appeared to be a small office filled with dangling straps and saddles, his lips never leaving my skin. It smelled like leather and it reminded me of Max's cologne he'd worn on our night out. A twinge of pleasure ran down my spine and settled in my core. I'd never be able to smell leather without getting aroused again.

"Tack room." He managed to grit out, in explanation, between kissing down my neck and urging me backwards.

I nodded in understanding as he backed me against a short workbench on the far wall. His hands were explorative as he skimmed them under the hem of my tee. I had thrown on a pair of jeans and a tee shirt, figuring that since we were just shooting in the backyard, anything too fancy would be overkill.

I wished now that I would have at least put on a better set of underwear and bra, as my nursing bra and granny panties weren't the sexiest things to exist. The thought of new underwear and bras, perhaps some silky ones, popped into my head; I'd pick them up next time I was in town.

Everywhere Max touched, left embers in its wake. Was this normal? I'd never felt this nearly animalistic desire to be with someone before. My skin tingled with a starved longing, and Max's touch sent shivers of awareness through me, awakening a deep, primal need.

He lifted me up and deposited me with ease onto the workbench as he slowed our kissing. He caressed my bare hip bone and coasted his warm fingers towards my ribs.

I leaned my head back in wanton need as a breathy moan escaped my lips. Max took the opportunity of my throat bared to him to kiss up the expanse and nip at the spot right below my ear. Another moan coasted from my mouth as I gripped the back of his head to hold him against me.

"Fuck, Stella. I want you so fucking bad it hurts," he groaned.

"What are you waiting for?" I teased, leaning back to give myself enough room to tear my shirt over my head. His pupils blew wide with lust as I reached behind me and unclasped my bra. Slowly edging the straps from my shoulders, I held the soft cups in place with an arm across my chest.

"You gonna put your money where your mouth is, or are you gonna make me do it myself?" I joked, coasting a hand down the plane of my stomach and teasing at the waistband of my jeans.

Somehow, even though I was still learning to love my postpartum body, I felt sexy and confident. Max's gaze followed my hand as his breathing turned to soft pants. I could feel his rigid length growing hard behind the zipper of his jeans as he shifted between my legs. Max looked at me with a reverence that superseded any doubts I had about my body.

"Well, Cowboy?" I asked again, as I'd somehow managed to short-wire his brain in the process of undressing. As if all neurons fired at once, he snapped forward, gripping my hips and yanking me to him, my ass sliding across the workbench. I let out a light yelp in surprise as he pressed our chests together, my arm trapped between us.

"You keep talking, and I'll give you something else to do with that pretty fucking mouth of yours," he whispered in my ear. I felt my core flush hot with desire at his words and fought the urge to grind myself against him.

"Now, look who's tongue-tied," he said with a wicked grin and a subtle bite of his bottom lip.

max

ALL THE TENSION we'd been pushing down over the last two months was coming to a head. Like a simmering volcano, I could feel the tremble of desire flowing through our bodies, ready to erupt. We'd had enough of dancing around the inevitable. Stella and I were combustible.

Taking a step back, I allowed myself a long look at the beautiful woman sitting in front of me. She propped herself up on her hands angled behind her back, allowing me to look my fill. She had removed her bra and her breasts hung heavy, begging to be touched, her dark nipples pebbled with desire. I could see her breaths quicken as I traced my eyes over her lush curves.

Fuck, was she beautiful.

I wasn't sure what Stella had looked like before having Charlie, but motherhood had given her a lush, soft look that I found myself completely obsessed with; her skin seemed to glow, her curves were the perfect place for my hands, and her breasts looked like the perfect large handful.

Society preached that women should look a certain way post baby. If their bodies didn't 'bounce back', they needed to eat better and hit the gym more often. Looking down at this woman, who'd carried a whole ass human being inside her for nine months, filled me with such immense desire. She exuded raw femininity, and I wanted to bow down and worship at her feet.

I hadn't realized how long I'd been staring until Stella cleared her throat in trepidation. She banded her arm across her chest again, attempting to cover herself. I stepped in between her spread legs and eased her arm away. I threaded my fingers through the soft strands of hair at the nape of her neck, tugging her head back until her eyes met mine.

I sensed the hitch in her breath and her eyelids flutter shut. A wild grin curled up one corner of my mouth as I witnessed her succumb to a flood of longing.

"Don't hide from me." I commanded as I ran my fingers deftly over a stretch mark on her hip. "Never fucking hide from me, Trouble."

She shivered at the gentleness of my touch, accented by the rough tug of my hand in her hair, which spurred me on in my exploration. I traced a single finger across the lushness of her belly and up to the side of one of her ample tits, watching as her nipples peaked in desire. I circled one of her nipples slowly and lowered my head to blow a stream of warm breath across the bud.

Watching the way goose bumps rose on her skin and a gentle shiver coast through her, I smiled. I leaned my head down to graze my lips across her nipple, just enough to tease. I was going to make her work for this.

A small groan of frustration rolled through her throat as she shifted her hips forward, pressing her breasts up, urging me to take her into my mouth. I halted her movements with a hand on her hips.

"Such a greedy fucking girl," I murmured against her skin. "Don't rush me, Trouble."

"Please, Max. I'm on fire," she begged, leaning her head back to bare her throat to me as I slowly trailed my way up with wet kisses, placing soft nips along the way.

"Say it again," I commanded deeply. "I love to hear you beg."

She gripped the short strands of hair at the nape of my neck, pulling my head back to look me in the eyes. With a wild, untamed look in her eyes, she licked her lips; the movement exuding a fierce, almost painful longing. I could see the fire coursing through her eyes as she bit down on her plush bottom lip.

"Please." she begged again, refusing to break eye contact with her statement.

My control snapped at her eagerness and I tilted her hips forward to shift her pants over them. She lifted her ass as I slid them down and kicked them to the side into our growing pile of clothes.

Spreading her legs, I ran a knuckle up the inside of her thigh, relishing in the heat emanating from her core. I teased the edge of her panties with a finger as I lowered myself to my knees.

"Trouble, you may be the one begging, but I'll be the one on my knees." I said reverently as I slid the soft cotton of her panties off her hips and down her legs. I shoved the discarded underwear into my pocket, a keepsake for later.

Kissing my way slowly up her legs, I draped her knees over my shoulders. I gripped ahold of her thighs and scooted her to the very edge of the workbench, feeling her sharp intake of breath and her stomach caving as I coasted my lips across her pussy. I used two fingers to spread her open as I flattened my tongue and ran it from bottom to top, pausing to tease the bundle of nerves at the apex.

Her hips bucked against my lips as I overwhelmed her senses by sucking and licking her most sensitive spot. I alternated with quick flicks of my tongue and long laps along her seam as I brought her to the edge of orgasm. I scissored my fingers inside of her, stretching her pussy in preparation for my cock. Her grip on the back of my head was punishing, as I felt her walls contracting around my digits.

She tasted like honey on my tongue, and I groaned in ecstasy.

"You taste so fucking good, I can feel your tight little cunt squeezing me. Are you getting close, baby?" I whispered directly over her clit, letting the soft caress of my breath tickle her most sensitive spot.

"Fuck, Max." she moaned reverently as I continued my ministrations.

I wanted her coming on my tongue so I could be flooded with the sweetness I'd been dreaming about for weeks. I felt her thighs begin to clench around my ears as she careened closer and closer to climax. Her breaths became quick and ragged as I shifted my focus to her clit.

"Yes.. YES. Just like that!" She moaned loudly, holding my head against her core. I banded my arms around her thighs as I wrapped my lips around her clit and sucked hard.

She bowed off the counter with a loud moan. I felt her pussy pulsating against my tongue as I drew out the remnants of her orgasm. When her pants subsided and her breathing slowed, I lowered her legs from my shoulders and stood.

Stepping between her legs, I pulled her head back by her hair again, forcing her gaze to mine.

Her chest rose and fell with the aftershocks of pleasure, her eyes glued to mine. I took my fingers, soaked in her release, and drew them into my mouth. I greedily licked them clean as I committed the vision of her climaxing on my tongue to memory. She licked her lips, hungry for more, as I slowly pulled my fingers from my mouth.

I took her lips in mine in a searing kiss, allowing her to taste herself. Catching her moan in my mouth, I tangled my tongue with hers. Breaking the kiss, I gripped the back of my shirt and in one fluid motion, removed it and tossed it aside with the bulk of her clothing.

stella

MY PUPILS BLEW WIDE as I took in Max's appearance. To make sure I always felt at ease, he was ever so careful to remain fully clothed in the house. I hadn't been able to even catch a glimpse of his fantastic body.

I bit my lip to hide the smirk that was playing at my mouth. He looked delicious. His muscles were sculpted by years of hard work, the type of strong that only came from manual labor. He had a rugged patch of thin brown hair that dusted the top of his chest and led down to the waistband of his jeans.

Looking down, I noticed the impressive bulge that was pushing behind his zipper.

Spotting a tattoo on his chest, I reached across the space between us and drifted a slender finger over the script below his left pec. He had what looked like a woman's handwriting and the words 'love always, Ma' stamped across his heart. I eased forward and leaned down to kiss the tattoo with a softness that had his breath catching. Easing off the workbench, I sank to my knees.

Coasting my fingers down the planes of his stomach to the thin trail of hair that led to his waistband, I looked up at him from below my thick lashes. His breathing came in rapid pants. For all the bravado this man exuded, I sure had an undeniable effect on him. The thrill of knowing we were matched in our ferocity for each other sent a shiver down my spine.

"Now, it's my turn," I teased as I flicked open the button and pulled down the zipper. I pushed down his jeans and he stepped out of them, kicking them to the side. Watching him palm a large hand over his briefs, where his rigid cock was straining to be released, I licked my lips in anticipation. He groaned in pleasure as I eased the waistband down over his ass and his cock sprang free.

I bit my bottom lip as I took in the sight before me. He was rock hard, pre-cum leaking from the tip. My eyes caught on the metal barbell that was pierced through the underside of his shaft. I flicked my gaze to his hesitantly, and a chuckle rumbled in his chest, a low, comforting sound.

"It was a dare." Max explained, stroking a hand down the length, rubbing his index finger over the metal. "It was either pierce a nipple, or pierce my dick. I lost a bet in my early twenties while drinking with Wade. I didn't think I'd look good with a nipple piercing."

I gingerly stoked a finger over the piercing and lifted my eyes to his, watching the shudder of pleasure course through his body.

"Does it hurt?"

"Not anymore. The healing was a bitch, but it's been years now. It's extra sensitive when you—" He was cut off by a hiss escaping his lips as my mouth crested the tip of his cock and my tongue stroked across the barbell. I smiled around his length as I licked around the head.

"Fuuuuucckkk," he croaked, slapping a hand on the counter behind me to hold himself steady. I used one hand to stroke his length as my wet mouth coasted up and down. I hallowed my cheeks on the ascent, sucking greedily at his most sensitive areas. I could tell he wasn't going to last long by the way he tensed with every stroke of my tongue.

I gently rolled his balls in my hand and licked a line from the base to the engorged tip before taking his entire length to the back of my throat. Max wasn't porn star hung, but his cock was long and thick, hitting the softness of my throat with ease. I gagged lightly on his length and breathed through my nose to do it again.

His hiss of pleasure was just the confidence booster I needed as I felt his balls drawing up in anticipation of release. He gripped my hair and tugged, removing my mouth with an exaggerated pop.

"I'm not going to ask where you learned to suck a cock, but fuck if I'm not thankful to any man who came before me, because mine's going to be the only cock you ever suck after tonight," he claimed. The intense desire to be marked and claimed by this man had my pussy throbbing.

"I need to be inside you." He begged, reaching for his jeans to snag what I can assume was a condom. Before he grabbed hold of them, my hand came around his cock again, stroking from root to tip. An exaggerated hiss left his lips due to how sensitive and close he was.

That got his attention.

"I've got an IUD," I announced, and my heart stuttered at the thought of him being inside me bare. The last time I had let a guy inside me without protection, I'd gotten pregnant with Charlie. But with Max, I knew that I could trust him. "I'm clean. I got a check up right after having Charlie and I haven't been with anyone since."

Turning to face me, he regarded me with a questioning look. I'm not sure if he was shocked, or didn't believe me, so I rambled on in a nervous stream of consciousness.

"After having Charlie, he said things weren't the same. He said I wasn't as tight, and it didn't feel good anymore. He wanted me to get a check-up, claiming that I had to have been with someone else." I said with a shrug, as if it was completely normal for your partner to belittle you post baby.

I could feel the anger radiating off him in waves as he gripped the strands of hair at the nape of my neck to tug my head back and look him head on. Fuck, if I didn't love the way he manhandled me into submission.

"If that man wasn't already dead, I'd fucking kill him for making you doubt yourself. This body," he grazed his hands down my back, cupping my ass in a tight grip. He rounded his hands around my front and firmly gripped my breasts, tweaking the nipples between his thumb and pointer finger. "This fucking stunning body carried one of the most amazing things inside of it for nine months. This body has done things beyond my wildest comprehension. It deserves to be worshiped." Pausing to clear his throat of the emotion that was threatening to spill over, he looked me directly in the eyes as he said, "Let me worship you."

He placed his forehead against mine and I nodded softly beneath his gaze. Lifting one of my legs to wrap around his hip, he lined up the tip of his cock with my entrance.

Slowly edging forward, my warm heat engulfed the head, and I moaned in pleasure. Not tight, my ass. After just a year of celibacy, Max needed to take breaks to allow my body to compensate for his length. Inch by inch, he slowly fed himself inside of me.

"Breathe, baby," he coached. "Breathe."

Reaching between our bodies, he teased my clit as he slowly edged forward. I took in a gulping breath as I felt my body relax enough that he was able to fit his hips against mine and bottom out. We collectively released a moan and took a moment to allow my body to adjust to the glorious stretch.

I relished in the feeling of connection. Max didn't rush or push. He sensed what I needed without me having to utter a word. His uncanny ability to anticipate my every move, to know my thoughts before I voiced them, filled me with fear. I was opening my heart up to the possibility of being broken again.

The pure ecstasy of finally having him inside me was overwhelming as our breathy pants mingled in the air around us. He coasted his hands over every inch of skin available and teased my nipples with his mouth, taking his time in exploration. He savored every piece of my body, taking great care to kiss and suck the parts I always tried to hide.

We explored each other's bodies as he gently edged himself back and forth inside me. The overwhelming intimacy of the moment was enough to have another orgasm slowly building at the base of my spine. I used my heel to dig into his ass, urging him forward, silently asking for more.

I felt his breathing pick up as he skated a hand between my breasts to rest on my throat. He collared my slender neck in his hands and caught my eyes in a search for consent. I aggressively nodded and moaned, loving the feeling of his dominance, which spurred him on as he squeezed the slightest amount on the sides. I felt my throat constrict with a swallow beneath his palm as my mouth gaped open with desire.

I hadn't ever explored anything outside of vanilla missionary sex. This intimacy and exploration with Max was something I couldn't have ever imagined doing. Yet, the thrill of being completely at his mercy left me panting and begging for more.

"Oh, my girl likes a little hand necklace when I'm fucking that tight pussy, does she?"

A loud moan coasted up my throat at his crude words.

I felt the surge of heat rushing down my spine and settling in my core, teetering on the edge of release. Sensing the impending orgasm, Max released his grip on my neck to wrap my hair around his fist.

"Look at me. I wanna watch your face as you strangle my cock when I fill you up," he commanded as he began rutting harder and harder into me. The squeaking of the work bench beneath us intensified as his thrusts became erratic.

Feeling my body clench tight around his length, I let go with a loud moan and chanted his name. The orgasm overtook my senses and all I could feel was tiny pin pricks fluttering over my skin. The intensity of release caused my vision to swim as his balls slapped against my ass with his deep thrusts.

"Fuck, yes, Stella." He panted as hot jets of cum emptied into my core. Slowing his pace, he slowly slipped out of me, picking me up and depositing me back on the edge of the workbench. He spread my thighs and watched as his release dripped from my pussy.

"Max, what are you doing?..." My words were lost to a hiss as he scooped up our collective cum and pushed two fingers into me to force it back inside. Logically, I knew that with an IUD, it made no difference, but the thought of being filled by him had my heartbeat fluttering. He pressed a kiss to my overly sensitive clit and then another to my lips as he tenderly brushed the hair from my forehead.

"Now that we've gotten dirty, let's get you cleaned up." He said with a smirk and handed me back my clothes, minus my panties that he'd claimed ownership of. With gentle hands, he helped me into my jeans, the denim cool against my flushed skin, then tugged my top over my head before straightening his own clothes.

Helping me down off the workbench and banding an arm around my waist as he pulled me into his chest. His brown eyes met mine as he trailed a finger softly across my jaw.

Lowering his lips to mine, he murmured against them, "You've got all the power, Stella. Please don't break me."

My nod was gentle and instantaneous, as he pressed a soft kiss to my mouth, the meaning of his words hitting like a stray bullet to the chest.

"Right back at ya, Cowboy."

TWENTY-TWO

IN WHATEVER PARALLEL universe shower sex exists, it definitely isn't the same one Max and I are living in.

We rushed back to the big house to get cleaned up before I had to go pick Charlie up at Ray's. We stripped each other naked with the same quickness and urgency we'd felt in the barn, and stumbled blindly with our lips locked into the shower, but that's where the magic ended.

One of us was consistently standing in the cold while the other was lathering up their body or attempting to execute something resembling sexy.

Max's attempt to eat me out was interrupted by a stream of water hitting him in the face, causing me to burst into laughter and lose my focus.

I suggested he take me from behind, but a six foot two man trying to sink into a five foot seven woman against a shower wall involved way more acrobatic finesse than we ever dreamed of possessing.

We settled for a steamy make-out session with some heavy petting while we got cleaned up. I washed every square inch of his body, taking immense glee in the way his breath caught as I skimmed my hands across his cock and his glorious piercing.

I'd obviously never been with a man who had a cock piercing before, but the way it had coasted over the sensitive inner walls of my pussy had me seeing stars.

After thoroughly edging each other for the fifteen minute shower, we managed a down and dirty round two quickie before I headed out to the Cortez house to get Charlie.

Being with Max was exhilarating. The passion between us was an all-consuming fire, leaving us breathless and wanting more. I don't think either of us was ever going to be fully sated.

Heat flushed my cheeks as I replayed our afternoon. Cranking the AC to full blast while pulling down the driveway of Ray's dad's house, the cool air was a welcome relief against the memories causing fire to erupt along my skin.

After sufficiently cooling my face, and satisfied that I wasn't sporting a post-sex glow, I walked up the front porch steps and into the house's foyer. As many times as I'd been here, I had earned enough chastisement from Emmanuel that I knew he wanted me to treat his house like a second home and not knock every time I came over.

Walking into the living room of the modest one-story home, I found my daughter giggling on the floor as Ray tickled her feet.

Over the course of the last couple months, they'd become exceptionally close. Ray treated her with the same care and love that I would expect from a sister or an aunt. She made Charlie feel like family, and that warmed my heart.

Wade was seated on the floor, his back against the couch,

a huge smile playing upon his lips as he watched Ray and Charlie play.

We had carved out a little slice of home here in Firefly Cove, and I was feeling more and more settled by the thought of staying.

Finally noticing me, Charlie squealed with delight, her chubby legs pumping furiously as she toddled towards me, Ray and Wade a distant memory as a giggle escaped her lips.

"Mama!" she shouted and raised her arms for me to pick her up.

I'd carry my girl as long as I could. There would come a time when I would pick her up for the last time and the thought of her growing up filled me with dread. I looked at my life, at my current family and my capacity for more, and I wasn't sure if I wanted any more children, unless it was with the right person.

Unexpectedly, a sense of giddiness came over me. I found myself drawn to thoughts of Max holding a tiny baby in his arms. He had already proven that he was an excellent partner. He made an excellent addition to the duo that Charlie and I had forged over the last year. I shook away the thoughts. It was too early in our budding relationship to think about things like kids and a permanent future together.

"You okay, girl? You're looking a little flushed." Ray narrowed her eyes in scrutiny and ticked her head to the side. It didn't take longer than a second for a knowing smirk to find its way to her face. She squealed almost as loud as Charlie had and stood in front of me, hopping.

"SPILL!" she screamed with a giddiness I'd only seen from her upon finding the perfect thrifted dresser in an online auction for less than a hundred dollars.

"And with that, I'm out." Wade said, pushing to stand and giving us a mock salute. He walked over to Charlie, popped a wet kiss on her cheek, gave me a side hug, and headed for the door.

"See ya later, Waddle!" Ray called loudly as Wade opened the front door.

"I told you, Sunshine, stop calling me that." He grumped as he unceremoniously left.

"Okay, now that he's gone, SPILL."

I covered Charlie's ears in makeshift earmuffs as I found the words to explain what had transpired between Max and me in the last couple of hours.

"Long story short… I think Max and I are… *together*?" I said with a slight hesitancy.

"Think? Did you not talk about it?" she asked in confusion.

"Umm… It's a little hard to talk when you either have his tongue or cock in your mouth." I joked.

Her laughter, a joyous sound that seemed to fill the entire room, startled me, and her hand, firm on my arm, steered me toward the kitchen.

"I'm going to need to know details, but first, we have more pressing matters." She grabbed a small notebook off the counter and brought it over to the table where she'd deposited me.

I plopped Charlie on my lap and waited on bated breath as Ray flipped to the page she was looking for. After everything I had been through the last ten years, surprises were pretty high on the list of things I despised most.

Ray flipped to one of the inner pages, and my anxiety ebbed. Written at the top of the page was 'Charlie's Fairy First

Birthday'. The sudden heat of unshed tears burned behind my eyes, blurring my vision. With everything going on, I had somehow forgotten that Charlie and the twins' birthdays were coming up.

"I hope I didn't overstep…" Ray mumbled, obviously sensing a change in my demeanor.

I rarely saw Rayna Cortez demure, but the thought of her taking the time to plan a birthday party for my daughter brought such a lightness to my heart.

"Ray…" I fought to find the words to express my gratitude. I wanted to tell her thank you for loving my daughter. She deserved to hear how much it meant to me that she had done all of this, especially for all the time she spent watching her while I worked, taking an enormous burden off my shoulders.

"It's fine. It was just a thought.." I stopped her with a hand on her arm as she motioned to close the notebook. I flipped it back open and pulled it towards me, getting a look at all the planning she had done.

"This is… everything."

"Are you sure? I just figured, with everything going on, that planning a one-year-old's birthday party would be the last thing on your mind."

She shyly flipped through the pages, showing me all the ideas she'd written down. She had even sketched out a cake idea. A two-tiered monstrosity covered in flowers, mushrooms, and woodland creatures.

I watched with rapt attention as I saw how much love and enjoyment she had put into planning and designing. Her artistic talent went far beyond that of interior design. She was a talented designer and planner as a whole. I wondered if she had ever given any thought to expanding her business into the party planning sector.

"Ray, this is amazing," I said, thumbing through the pages. "I was just planning on getting a cupcake and singing happy birthday over breakfast."

I leaned down to rest my cheek on top of Charlie's head as she pointed at things in the notebook and babbled words only she could understand.

"Faiwee!! Chawee faiwee!" she shouted as she wiggled to the floor. She ran around the kitchen flapping her arms and twirling in circles until she plopped on the floor in a dizzy daze.

"But what about the guys?" I asked. I didn't want to take the spotlight away from Wade and Max's birthday. They deserved to be celebrated just as much as Charlie did.

"Pshh," Ray said with a flick of her wrist. "They have had twenty-nine years of birthdays. You only turn one once." She smiled down at Charlie, still attempting her best fairy impression, with a tenderness of someone filled with love.

Ignoring the familiar ache in my chest—a dull throb that always surfaced when witnessing their familial love—I chuckled at her nonchalant attitude towards celebrating her best friend and his brother's birthdays.

"Fine, but please, let's make sure to do something special for the guys as well. I'd really like to make them feel included."

"I'm sure they'll be perfectly happy to spoil little miss fairy princess over there." She tapped her chin with her pointer finger. "I wonder if I can get them all matching tutus and wings."

Before I had a chance to object, she was pulling out her

phone and searching the internet for adult sized fairy costumes.

I'm not sure how Wade had put up with Ray's antics over the years, but she sure did keep things interesting.

WHEN WE GOT BACK to the house, Charlie had already fallen asleep in her car seat. Ray had warned me that she'd been fighting her naps and cutting down from three shorter naps to one long one mid-afternoon. Just another way that my little girl was growing up before my eyes.

As soon as I pulled into the driveway, Max emerged from behind the house, likely from the barn. He was outfit in his signature Wrangler jeans, boots, a plain tee shirt, and that sexy as hell Stetson he always wore when working out on the ranch.

I fought to control my raging hormones, yet Max's sex appeal was undeniable. He emanated an air of authority everywhere he went and I was happy letting him take charge in and out of the bedroom.

He met me at my door just as I'd swung it open, the furrow between his brows appearing at the fact that I hadn't let him open my door. I got out of the car and softly closed the door behind me, hoping to keep Charlie asleep and avoid a meltdown.

Max bracketed my hips with his hands, and I slid mine up the broad expanse of his chest. I massaged the scowl between his eyes with a single finger and an innocent smile. He huffed in annoyance before gently pressing his lips to mine.

We didn't need words to express our feelings. We could

read one another as if we had been learning each other's nuances for years.

Max snuck a glance over my shoulder into the back seat of the car, and a soft smile appeared on his lips. It never ceased to amaze me how he had folded himself seamlessly into our family unit.

"So, we never got to talk earlier," he said as he took my hands in his, rubbing his thumb over my knuckles. "I just wanted to check in with where your head's at."

He seemed almost nervous as he looked down at our entwined hands. I took a page from his own play book and used my pointer finger to lift his chin and look into his eyes.

"Are you having the 'what are we' talk right now, Maxwell?" I chuckled.

With a nervous rub of the back of his neck, he started, "I mean..."

I stood on my tiptoes and coasted my lips across his in a whisper of a kiss.

"Ask me." I commanded.

"Fuck, Stell. You make me nervous," he chuckled.

"How about this?" I said as I stood on my tip toes, draping my arms around his neck, our lips still a breath away from touching. "I'm yours. As long as you'll have me."

He didn't hesitate as his lips crashed down on mine in a punishing kiss and he pressed me back into the door of my car. He consumed me with an intensity that gave me more than butterflies. It set me ablaze.

Knowing things were about to get more intense, I pulled back from our kiss, only to lightly brush my lips against his one last time.

"My bed...or yours?" he asked with a wicked grin, and I slapped his chest playfully.

"You get the sleeping baby, Cowboy. I'll prep a bath." Sauntering towards the front door with an extra swing in my hips, I heard his exasperated groan as he popped open the rear door to grab Charlie, who was starting to wake up.

"Your momma is gonna be the death of me, little one," he mumbled just loud enough that I heard.

I chuckled as I retreated into the house to start our new nightly routine. This felt good. I could get used to it.

MAX and I being together felt easy. We meshed in a way that felt like we'd been friends for years and co-parenting for all of Charlie's life. The ease of falling into a 'family-like' routine was unsettling but so welcome. For so long, I'd done everything myself, and it felt good to lean on someone else for a change.

Max took almost every morning shift, waking up before me and getting Charlie ready for the day. With my permission, he changed, dressed, and fed her before I got up. I often found them out collecting eggs from the chicken coop or visiting the horses in the barn.

Charlie was very quickly becoming a horse enthusiast, even at just one year old. She loved giving them treats, and no longer needed Max's help when doing so. She confidently held her tiny hand out flat in offering, letting their whiskered lips nuzzle up the apple slices or carrots Max dutifully kept in his pockets. Seeing her joy in something so simple as feeding farm animals breathed new life into my heart. I felt at peace with my decision to make Firefly Cove our new home.

Max and I's relationship had blossomed into something I was terrified to define. He had wormed his way into the facets of my heart, yet I still felt that niggling thread that everything was going to go to shit. I don't know that I would survive if something happened to him. He had taken my broken pieces and fit them together again.

We were currently cuddled up on the living room sofa, recounting our day as we did each night. It was nice to have someone to decompress with. Max's fingers traced idle circles on my knee as I filled him in on the comings and goings of the boutique business. I had asked Tracy, the owner of the shop, if I could help with more of the inner workings of the day-to-day operations. She had happily agreed.

I had blossomed into a little fashionista, often spending a portion of my paycheck on new outfits. It proved worth it to see Max's eyes light with desire when I sported a new outfit for our now weekly date nights. Tracy had offered to let me take a stab at inventory and ordering for the upcoming fall collection. I was nervous, but excited, that I was going to be curating the entire store's collection.

I pored over magazines and fashion blogs, checking for the latest trends. Since our clientele catered to the late twenties through the early thirties crowd, I wanted to find pieces that could transfer from office wear to nightlife. I'm sure Max was tired of listening to me prattle on and on about the latest fashion trends, what influencer was wearing what, or who was coming out with new lines.

Like the good partner he is, he took everything in stride. He nodded and remarked at the appropriate times, adding commentary when the situation called for input.

"I'm sorry, I'm probably boring you," I sighed, putting my phone face down in my lap. I'd been showing him the latest runway looks suitable for the shop's clothing line when I realized I had talked for nearly a full hour.

"Trouble, you're not boring me. I enjoy listening to you talk about the boutique. I can tell that you're passionate about it and it's nice to see you happy," he said, taking my hand in his and rubbing his thumb across my knuckles.

"I know the last couple of weeks have been busy, but it's all going to be worth it when we're celebrating tomorrow," he promised.

I'd been burning the candle at both ends for the last couple of weeks between taking on more responsibilities at work and planning Charlie's and the twins' birthday party with Ray. Honestly, the more stressful of the two was planning a one-year-old's birthday party, knowing that she wouldn't remember it.

Ray and I had spent hours nailing down the details, from whimsical forest decor for the backyard at the big house, to cake flavors and snacks. When Ray had shown me the plans she had started for Charlie, I jumped in to help anywhere I could.

It was proving to be a much bigger soiree than initially planned, and the guest list was damn near all of Firefly Cove. I guess that's what happens when you wind up dating one of the town's golden boys.

I hadn't ever thrown a party of this scale, but Ray seemed in her element. She took everything in stride and I barely had to lift a finger in planning. I had made mention of the idea of spreading her design business into the party planning sector. Her eyes lit with a fire and a gleam only found in those with the entrepreneurial spirit. She began immediately jotting down notes on how to make it happen, thanking me profusely for the idea.

I still struggled daily with letting others help. Being that it was such an ingrained part of my psyche, I constantly questioned everyone's motives or intentions.

I knew deep down that no one in the Daniels or Cortez families would do anything they didn't want to, but I still felt like a tad bit of a burden. After all, I'd shown up in the town with a baby in tow, on the run from a drug-dealing murderer, and with nowhere to go. Nothing screams 'burden' like the damsel in distress.

My phone buzzed from my knee, and I turned it over to check the messages. Seeing the unknown number, I flipped the phone back over, concealing it from Max's view. There was no reason to get him worked up over the one or two messages I had received over the last week. They had all been vague and cryptic, with no discernible information that led me to believe that Charlie and I were in any further danger. I reminded myself that tomorrow, I needed to mention the messages to Sheriff Cortez.

I knew that if I mentioned the messages to Max, he'd have the house locked down tighter than Fort Knox. He'd insist on following me to and from work each day, and he wouldn't ever let Charlie out of his sight. I didn't want to go from living a life of freedom to being stuck in a cage created from fear again. I wouldn't let them win. Charlie and I were safe here in Firefly Cove.

They wouldn't find us here.

Max had insisted on installing a camera doorbell at the big house after the first message had come through. He said it gave him a slight peace of mind, knowing that if Charlie and I were here by ourselves and he was out on the ranch, he could see everything from his phone. That man was so protective of us, it made me fall deeper for him each day.

We had been skirting around saying the big three words. Both of us showed it in our actions, and I knew in my heart that we were both feeling them. I think Max was afraid of scaring me off, and I was afraid of getting my heart broken. My self-doubt was overwhelming, though Max gave me no reason to think his feelings weren't genuine.

What I felt for him was foreign and scary, but it also brought me so much joy and security. I wish I had fallen in love with him first, instead of getting tangled up with Dean. I wished more than anything that he was Charlie's biological father. Regardless of paternity, he constantly showed my daughter what it would like to have a consistent and stable male role model in her life.

Max and I had discussed what we saw our future looking like as we curled up in bed one evening.

Max wanted the standard nuclear family. He saw himself having at least one or two kids of his own. I hadn't ever given much thought to having another baby, but now that I was with a man who treated me with such respect and tenderness, I found it hard not to call the local OBGYN and have my IUD removed immediately.

Max's hand caressing my thigh brought me out of my lust induced day dream. I'd never had a daddy kink, but the thought of Max holding a newborn had me nearly panting.

"You okay?" he asked with a quirk of his brow. My cheeks flushed, and his sexy smirk revealed he knew where my head was at.

"Mhmm.," I mumbled, rubbing my thighs together to ease some of the tension that had gathered there.

"You sure?" He asked as he coasted his fingers with torturous slowness along my inner thighs. My breathing quickened, and I avoided looking at him to give him the satisfaction of knowing just how turned on I was.

We had such an early morning, and both needed to get to bed. Thoughts of all the party details that still needed to be nailed down in the morning swam through my head. Max's fingers continued their ascent as he crested the hem of my cotton sleep shorts.

"I can hear you thinking all the way over here, Trouble. Need me to help quiet that pretty little mind of yours?" he taunted as he teased the edge of my panties with his pinky finger. I was nearly panting with want at such a simple touch, but Max consistently had that effect on me.

I leaned over to the side to check the baby monitor I had placed beside me, making sure that Charlie was fast asleep. Wade and Ray had gone out for the evening to gather the last of the party supplies. He was staying at the Cortez house to put together balloon arches and flower garlands.

What I wouldn't give to see Wade attempt to style a flower garland, but I knew he was in the best hands, with Ray at the helm. With the baby asleep, and the house to ourselves, the world was our oyster.

I felt Max's fingers breach the lace edge of my panties and I damn near tossed the monitor onto the other couch cushion in frustration as I tipped my head back to rest on the back of the sofa.

He chuckled softly at my increasing desire and I spread my legs wider in blatant invitation.

"Such a greedy fucking girl," he tsked as he removed his hand. I groaned in annoyance and that infuriating chuckled rumbled from his throat.

"It seems to me like you need a little relaxing," he purred while fingering the waistband of his gym shorts and boxers.

He palmed his thickening cock through his pants before sliding them off. His rigid length bobbed against his stomach as he removed them, one leg at a time, with a slowness that would make a turtle cry.

He sure wasn't in any hurry as he slowly stroked himself from root to tip. His arousal was clear in the bead of pre-cum that was leaking from the tip. I moistened my lips in anticipation of leaning down to gather a taste.

"Cat got your tongue?" He asked with the confidence of a man who knew what he wanted.

I cleared my throat before answering. "Nope, just thinking about how fast I can have your cock down my throat."

The lust from hearing those words was evident in the way his cock twitched in his hand.

"As much as I love watching you gag on my cock, Trouble, I want to help *you* relax." He stroked the silky crown, using his pre-cum as lube as he coasted his hand up and down. I whimpered with desire and scooted to the edge of the couch to get on my knees.

"No." he commanded. I stopped and lifted my eyes to his. His dilated pupils made it impossible for me to distinguish where they ended and his irises began. His eyes seemed almost black with desire.

I quirked a brow in question.

"I wanna watch," he said with a wicked grin.

Oh, fuck.

TWENTY-FOUR

WHILE SEEING Stella on her knees was one of my favorite sights. I wanted to see her open up and own the confidence she'd been working on building. I knew that this was going to be a huge step for her, but taking charge and matters into her own hands was one of her strong suits.

Her breaths came in ragged pants as she dutifully waited for instructions. Her eyes were lit with a fire of want, and I was sure that if I shoved my hand down those flimsy cotton shorts, she'd be soaked.

I took my time watching her squirm as I stroked my cock. It was hard as steel and borderline uncomfortable, but I wanted myself on the edge as I watched her bring herself pleasure.

Following her eyes as they tracked my movements, she regarding how I stroked the silver barbell pierced through the underside on the ascent. I could see her brain taking mental notes, and that just wouldn't do. I wanted that brain turned off.

"Clothes. Off." I commanded.

She looked back at the baby monitor on the arm of the sofa and I reached past her, snatching it and turning it face down on the ottoman. I had the sound on, so if Charlie was to wake up, we would hear it. But, in this moment, I wanted her attention focused on herself, not all the things that needed to be taken care of.

I glanced back at her, quirking an eyebrow, silently questioning why she wasn't naked. She huffed a sigh of annoyance as she stood up and sauntered over to stand between my legs. She fingered the hem of her broken in sweatshirt as she raised it above her head.

God, almighty.

She was bare under, and her breasts bounced free with the motion, situated perfectly at my eye level. She turned, bending forward to give me the most delicious view of her peachy ass, and repeated the motion with her shorts, sliding them down her toned legs and tossing them across the room to land on the recliner.

Seeing her, in all her naked glory, was like looking at a vision of Aphrodite. She was ethereal and delicate, but also strong and steady. Stella was everything I imagined the perfect woman to be. She was also *mine.*

I resisted the urge to skate my hands up her creamy thighs as she brushed her own across her nipples. The buds peaked with the sensation and my cock twitched again in my hand. I ached to say 'fuck it' and throw her down on the sofa to have my way with her. This was going to be a lesson in self-restraint for me as well.

I was used to being the one to handle everything, but so was Stella. She had come so far in her journey of self reflection, blooming into the confidence I saw growing daily inside her.

She still struggled with letting go and relinquishing the reins, but I was determined to see her spark continue to ignite as I stood beside her fanning the flames.

I raised my eyes to hers as I leaned back and grabbed hold of my rigid cock.

"Other side of the couch, Trouble." I said, nodding my head for her to sit at least two couch cushions away. My self-restraint was threadbare, so I didn't trust myself not to take control with her so close.

She sat on the opposite end of the couch, facing me with her legs tucked under her body and her ass resting on her heels. The subtle position of submission had me closing my eyes and finding anything in my mind to keep me from blowing my load too early.

After envisioning the town librarian, a crotchety older lady with jowls like a bulldog, in a pink bikini, I opened my eyes to meet hers again, content that I wasn't going to come in five seconds flat.

"Lean back and spread those pretty thighs for me. I want to see my favorite pussy." The words came out breathless, and I watched her dutifully follow directions.

I could see the pulse in her neck flutter with my filthy words. I'd very quickly learned that my girl loved dirty talk. Lucky for her, it was turning out to be one of my favorite pastimes.

"Now, take two fingers and spread yourself apart. Are you dripping for me, pretty girl?"

A breathy moan coasted her lips as she spread her pussy open, and I saw the glistening evidence of her desire. She was soaked. I wanted nothing more than to lean over and lick a line from bottom to top, savoring the feel of her clit between my lips and tasting the sweetness between her thighs.

"Looks like my girl is soaked. Is that all for me, Trouble?" I questioned, softly stroking my cock. Her eyes watched my movements as her tongue darted out to wet her lips. She nodded.

"I need your words, baby," I coaxed.

"Yes. Yes, it's all for you," she whined as she used her free hand to play with her nipple.

"Good girl," I praised. "Now, let me see your hand."

She leaned forward, putting her palm in mine. I folded all of her fingers down until the only one that remained was her middle finger, standing straight in the air. Such a vulgar gesture and I was about to make it even more so. I pulled her arm forward and wrapped my lips around her finger, swirling my tongue along the tip.

Her sharp intake of breath and lowering lids gave me all the encouragement I needed. I removed her finger and placed a quick kiss to the pad before releasing her hand.

"Now, use that finger to fuck yourself." I commanded.

In a quick show of defiance, she inserted the same finger into her own mouth and sucked, gathering her taste and mine to rub on the small bundle of nerves at her apex.

Coasting her hand down the plane of her stomach, she swirled her middle finger over her clit. Her head leaned back in ecstasy, her eyes closing. But that just wouldn't do.

"Eyes up here," I scolded.

Her eyes snapped back to mine as her mouth dropped open with a low moan. She continued circling the bud as I stroked my cock in time with her movements.

"I want to watch as you take what you deserve, Stella." I said through gritted teeth. The head of my cock throbbed with the need to cum, and I felt my balls rising in anticipation of release.

Stella's breathy moans came more rapidly as she swirled two fingers around her clit and used the other hand to pinch her nipples.

"I can see you getting close. I bet if I was inside of you right now, your sweet cunt would be gripping my cock like a vice," I purred.

"Yes, yes. I'm so close, Max," she panted.

"Who's bringing you pleasure right now?"

"You are."

"No, Stella. *You* are. *You* are the one in charge. Take control, baby, and let me be the one to witness your beautiful undoing." I gritted out.

"Max.. I'm gonna…" she panted, speeding up the pressure on her clit.

"I'm right here baby, take what you need."

Her eyes rolled back with pleasure as her head tipped back to the arm of the couch. I watched as her body tensed in anticipation and her release dripped from between her thighs. Speeding up my strokes, hot spurts of cum landed on my belly. I continued stroking to coax out the remnants of my release, but it felt like I was an endless well of desire.

Stars clouded my vision as my body came down from the euphoric high of pleasure. I opened my eyes and Stella's flushed face was the first thing I saw. I didn't even bother to clean us up before I launched across the sofa and took her mouth in mine.

A muffled alarm sounded from the coffee table, and Stella reached over to silence it. She stroked a finger down my cheek, and brought her lips back to mine.

"Happy Birthday, Cowboy," she whispered reverently against my mouth.

I smiled softly at the thought that she had set an alarm for midnight on my birthday. I couldn't think of a better way to ring it in than with the woman that I loved tucked into my arms.

stella

AFTER ONE MORE ROUND OF passionate sex, we finally made our way to bed. We were completely consumed by our desire for one another; a craving that left us breathless and desperate.

This was evident in the fact that Max's head was currently buried between my thighs at five o'clock in the morning on the day of *his* birthday.

"Mmm." I moaned as he continued stroking his tongue through me, focusing on the most sensitive spots he knew drove me wild.

"It's *your* birthday. Shouldn't I be the one giving you a present?" I chuckled, running my fingers through his hair, fingering the long strands on top.

"This pussy is the best present I ever could have gotten. It's my favorite meal, and I'm starving." He said as he placed a tender kiss to the inside of my thigh.

I laughed and closed my eyes, enjoying the tender strokes of his tongue, bringing me closer and closer to the edge of an orgasm.

A gentle cry came from the baby monitor propped on the bedside table, immediately halting our passionate wake up call. I looked over at the camera, noticing that Charlie was standing along the rail of her crib, banging her pacifier along the rungs.

"MASSSSSSS!" she shouted as loud as her little lungs would allow. Max groaned from between my thighs and pressed one more tender kiss to my sensitive clit as he extricated himself.

"Happy Birthday, Cowboy." I chuckled as he walked across the room in all of his naked glory to throw on a pair of boxers, grey sweatpants, and a black tee shirt. I bit my lip to quell the rising desire, but the sight of this man in loose fitting sweatpants that did little to conceal his raging hard on made me feral.

I swung my legs over the side of the bed and reached for one of Max's tee shirts to throw on and a pair of shorts. Before he could insist on grabbing Charlie, I was at the door.

"I've got her." I said, knowing that Max meant well in his intentions of handling the morning routine, but I wanted a moment just between my girl and I. He nodded softly in understanding, a small, knowing smile playing on his lips.

I padded to her room and cracked the door. Hearing the soft creak as I pushed it open, Charlie's gaze darted to mine. The wide grin that spread across her face was enough to melt even the most frigid of hearts. My girl was such a sweet soul.

I padded my way to the edge of the crib as she stood and balanced against the rails.

"Good morning, sunshine. Happy Birthday." I said with a wide grin of my own. I hadn't been able to say those words before and they felt foreign on my tongue. We had somehow made it a full year.

A year's worth of laughs, snuggles, learning, and tears. We had braved all of it as a pair.

I felt Max's presence before I could even turn around. I didn't need to see him to know that he was there. He stood just in the hallway, allowing me a private moment with my girl.

I plucked Charlie from her crib and padded over to the rocking chair in the corner. Somehow, she felt heavier, more solid, more grown. Even after just a night, I felt like she had grown so much. I had laid my girl down for bed last night and woke up to a big one-year-old.

I felt a tear track down my face as I settled into the seat with Charlie on my lap. I rocked the seat back and forth as I tucked her into my embrace. She nuzzled her cheek into the space where my shoulder met my neck and I pressed a soft kiss to her forehead. Charlie was undoubtedly the best thing that had ever happened to me.

After a couple minutes of snuggling, Charlie got restless, and I placed her down on the floor with another quick kiss to her chubby cheek. She toddled to the door that I had left cracked and pried it open with her tiny fingers. Quick as a shot, she bolted down the hallway towards the kitchen, in search of her second favorite person.

I waited for the pang of jealousy to hit that she'd sought Max instead of wanting to sit and snuggle with me, but it never did. Max and I were a team. I was afraid to think too long term, but over the last couple of months, we'd become a formidable force with Charlie.

Max had taken on the role of a father figure in Charlie's life as quickly as he'd offered for us to stay here. He was steadfast in his support of us, and it made my heart swell. I wondered if this was what it felt like to be truly loved.

I made my way to the kitchen, following the sounds of excited toddler squeals. Max had Charlie banded in his arms and was kissing all over her face and chanting 'happy birthday' over and over again. I shook my head at the bond those two shared and made my way towards coffee.

The squealing quieted as Max snuggled Charlie into his chest. He pressed his forehead to hers tenderly and whispered, "Happy Birthday, Little One."

She pressed her tiny hands on either side of his face and whispered back, as well as a one-year-old could, "Hap Bir Day Da."

My breath caught in my throat, and it must have been audible as Max scrambled to correct her.

"Max." He coached, pressing his finger into his chest in determination.

"Mass Da." she insisted, placing one of her hands on her hip in a sassy move of defiance. Max hung his head and sighed. He brought his eyes to mine in a 'help me' gesture. I chuckled as I handed him the cup of coffee and took Charlie from his arms.

"Charlie." I pointed at her chest. She nodded dramatically in understanding.

"Max." I said, pointing towards Max, who had stationed himself leaning against the kitchen counter.

"Mass Da," she insisted with a huff, as if I was the one who wasn't understanding.

I sighed and brushed the curls from her forehead, kissing her temple before setting her down in her high chair and handing her a granola bar I'd broken in half. She began fisting the breakfast into her mouth using her chubby hands. We'd work on table manners next birthday.

I walked back to the coffeemaker to pour myself a cup, as I'd relinquished mine to Max.

"I'm sorry, Stella. I promise I didn't coach her to say that," He apologized, placing his coffee cup down and pulling me to stand in front of him, his hands on my hips. I could sense his anxiety in the way he fiddled with the hem of my shirt.

"Max, it's okay," I said, bringing one of my hands up to brush along his cheek.

Sure, hearing Charlie call Max her baby babble version of dad was a shock, but was it feasibly something I was going to fight? We'd lived with him for over two months, becoming fully integrated into the Daniels family. Max was the only father figure she'd ever known and, to be honest, I kind of liked the idea that this would be a permanent arrangement.

"Are you sure? I can reinforce her addressing me as 'Max' if it makes you uncomfortable," he said almost sheepishly.

I placed my hand on his chest and lifted onto my tiptoes to kiss him beside his mouth.

"I'm sure. Happy Birthday Mass Da," I said with a grin. He growled as he snatched me around the waist and tickled my ribs. I laughed until my sides hurt and he gave me a quick kiss and pat on the ass as he started breakfast.

In this moment, I was sure I'd fallen madly in love with Maxwell Daniels.

PARTY SET up was in full swing by the time Stella and I made our way outside. We had taken our time with breakfast, doted on Charlie, and worked through farm chores as a family.

I couldn't remember the last time I'd celebrated my birthday with anyone other than the normal crew. I was pretty positive that the main reason everyone invited was attending wasn't for myself and Wade. They were here to celebrate Charlie, and, subsequently, Stella.

Firefly Cove had welcomed Stella and her daughter with open arms. I knew she was still a little uncomfortable with all the nuances of small town living, but she took each day in stride.

No longer fearing she would be gawked at like a zoo animal, she went to the coffee shop on her errand runs. Doc Jericho knew her and Charlie on a first name basis as she worked to make sure little one's vaccines were up to date and her physical on file.

She even felt comfortable heading into the feed store to

pick up things for me for the ranch. Stella never ceased to amaze me with how easily she took adversity and turned it into something positive. She and Charlie had opened my eyes to all that life offered, and I couldn't wait to experience it with my girls by my side.

Having Charlie call me her baby babble version of dad was an unexpected turn of events. I won't lie and say it didn't give me the warm and fuzzies knowing that she thought of me as a father figure. I had always dreamed of having a family of my own eventually, and if I could choose one, I'd choose Charlie and Stella as mine, ten times over.

As we finished up farm chores and Stella made her fiftieth 'daddy' joke of the morning, I flagged down Ray, who was bustling around the backyard. She was in party CEO mode as she directed Wade on where to hang fairy lights amongst the trees. She nodded back in acknowledgement that she'd seen us and left Wade on the ladder to his demise by fairy lights as she jogged over.

Earlier in the week, I'd mentioned to Ray that I wanted to do something special for Stella on Charlie's birthday. Celebrating a child's first birthday is a special occasion. But, a child's first birthday was also a celebration for the mother, especially if it's your first child.

"There's my little birthday girl!" Ray cooed, snatching Charlie out of Stella's arms.

Charlie squished Ray's cheeks in her signature sign of affection and nuzzled their noses together. I had known that Ray watching Charlie during the day was going to work out well, but what I hadn't expected was the bond they shared. Ray was the aunt that Charlie had never had.

"Can you watch her for a minute or two?" I asked, as if Ray wasn't already privy to my plans.

"Of course! She can help me boss Wade around, can't you, girlfriend?" she cooed. Charlie nodded as if she understood.

"Thanks, Ray." I said, taking Stella's hand in mine and leading her out to my truck. I didn't give her a moment to hesitate before whisking her away, knowing she would come up with every excuse in the book to avoid leaving the party planning in everyone else's capable hands.

"Where are we going?" She asked as I opened the door and helped her into the passenger seat.

"Do you trust me?"

"With my whole heart," she replied instantly, zero hesitation in her response.

I felt a swell of pride course through my chest. I don't know what I did to deserve this woman, but I couldn't imagine any sort of future without her now.

"Good," I stated as I shut her door and rounded the hood to get into the driver's seat.

The drive to the cove took only a couple of minutes, and Stella squinted in confusion as soon as she knew what direction we were heading in. Dutifully, she sat quietly in the passenger seat, not attempting to ruin my surprise.

When we got to the clearing, I parked the truck and leaped out before she could open her own door. Stella had an infuriating habit of insisting that she open her own door and I was bound and determined to beat her to it each time.

I held my hand out in offering and she placed her palm in mine, allowing me to help her down from the truck. I took the opportunity with our proximity to place a searing kiss on her lips. She opened for me and wrapped her arms around my neck, pulling me closer to deepen the kiss. Kissing her never got old. Each time felt like the first time. I pulled back before things got out of hand and touched my lips to her forehead.

"Come on, I've got a little surprise for you," I said, reaching out so we could walk to the cove. Skeptically, she conceded, and we pushed through the dense brush to get to the clearing where we had been on our first date.

I sat down along the water's edge and pulled her to sit between my outstretched legs. She leaned back against my chest with a contented sigh, and I took the opportunity to wrap my arms tightly around her chest.

"Why are we here, Max?" she questioned. "We have so much to do back at the ranch to set up. I'm sure Charlie is giving Ray and Wade a run for their money. I've got food to make, decorations to put out, Charlie needs a nap…" I cut her off by turning her head and placing a chaste kiss to her mouth.

Pulling back, I smirked at her blissed out expression. It never ceased to drive me wild at how receptive she was to my touch.

"Will you shut up?" I chided. She cocked her head to the side in annoyance and I chuckled.

"I wanted to bring you here so I could give you this." I reached into my pocket and pulled out a small velvet box. Her eyes blew wide as I could hear the wheels spinning. I'm sure she thought it was an engagement ring, and although I knew that was part of our future, and I'd already planned on when and where to make that happen, now wasn't that time.

"Open it." I instructed, handing her the box.

She took it with tentative fingers and flipped open the lid. Inside, nestled in the silk lining, was a simple necklace featuring two green stones and a single orange one, swirled in a rose gold pendant. I felt a drop of wetness fall onto my knee and I met Stella's eyes just as another tear tracked down her cheek.

"The green stones are peridot, the birthstone for August. One for Charlie, and one for myself. The orange stone is Topaz, the birthstone for November, your birth month. I had it made special just for you," I explained, fingering the thin chain as I lifted the box from her grasp and extricated the necklace from its resting place.

"May I?" I asked softly, brushing her hair off the back of her neck. Her silent nod was all the encouragement I needed as I undid the clasp and circled the chain around her throat. I re-clasped it and adjusted the pendant so it sat in the middle of her chest.

I had selected a shorter chain to deter Charlie from pulling it and rose gold because it reminded me of my favorite blush that always crested her skin.

"Max.." she whispered reverently, fingering the pendant with the softest touch.

"I know today is Charlie's birthday, but I feel like people always overlook the moms. You spent the last year living in a literal hell, working to design a better life for your daughter. You sacrificed your body, your sleep, your emotions, and so much more to bring her into this world. I can never explain how much having Charlie and you in my life brings me joy, but I wanted you to have a reminder of the family we are creating together."

Tears tracked down her cheeks as she took in my words. I wasn't sure if I had overstepped with the gift as her silence was becoming unnerving.

"Do you like it?" I asked with an air of hesitation.

"Max.. I love it. I've never owned something so beautiful. The fact that you took the time to have something created that embodied both us and Charlie means the world to me." She wiped the tears from her cheeks and leaned back, kissing me with an appreciative tenderness.

"I think I'm falling in love with you, Maxwell Daniels." she whispered against my lips.

I felt my heart soar at her words, and I spun her around so she straddled my thighs. I wanted her entire focus on me when she heard this.

"I love you too, Stella Jacobsen. You and Charlie both. You've turned my world completely upside down in the short time you've been here, but I couldn't imagine my life any other way. I want you to know that I'm all in. For as long as you'll have me."

"What if I want you forever?" she asked, a slight hesitation in her words.

"Then forever is what you'll get," I responded with a smirk.

I was so fucking gone for this woman.

stella

AS WE MADE our way back to the ranch, I couldn't stop touching the pendant that now hung around my neck. Max had been so thoughtful to get me a gift for Charlie's first birthday.

I had never thought much about celebrating moms on their child's first birthday. Max's heartfelt words, detailing all my accomplishments, filled me with a quiet pride, and I couldn't help but smile.

Charlie and I had truly accomplished a lot over the last year. Though I might have been the one to bring her into this world, her daily presence mended the cracks in my weary soul.

We hadn't been gone more than thirty minutes, but it seemed as if in that short time, Ray had enlisted the help of every town's person of Firefly Cove; twinkling lights, whimsical decorations, and the joyful chatter of people had transformed the ranch into a fairy wonderland.

My heart swelled with gratitude, a profound sense of appreciation for the family we had found here.

On the porch, Ray, with Charlie in her arms, was bossing people around to finish decorating. She was clearly in her element as she pointed Wade towards a tree from which she wanted the unicorn piñata hung. I'm not sure a one-year-old was going to be whacking and cracking a piñata, but I wasn't about to burst her bubble.

Max parked the truck off on the grassy side of the barn, amongst everyone else's vehicles. We made our way to the porch hand in hand to relieve Ray of at least one of her duties.

"Welcome back. Did you like your surprise?" she asked with a knowing smirk.

That little traitor.

I once again ran my fingertips over the dainty pendant resting against my skin. I couldn't help the smile that crested my face as I nodded in agreement.

"Yeah, Max did well," I murmured, my hand falling on the warm, corded muscle of his arm that was a comforting weight banded around my chest from where he stood behind me. We couldn't go more than a couple of minutes without touching each other, it seemed.

Charlie made grabby hands and attempted to wrestle out of Ray's grasp to head in my direction. Ray settled her on the ground and she padded her way to the edge of the stairs. Waiting on bated breath, I watched as she easily scaled the four wooden platforms and released a sigh of relief when both of her tiny feet were back on the ground. She toddled over to me and wrapped her arms around my leg, nuzzling her cheek into my thigh.

"Are you sleepy, little one?" Max cooed as he ran his fingers through Charlie's curls. She nearly purred at his touch as her eyes drifted closed and I internally chuckled.

Me too, girl. Me too.

"Let's get you down for a quick nap before all the festivities start around here," I said, scooping her up into my arms and nuzzling my face in the crook of her neck. She let out a sleepy giggle and cuddled into my chest with a wide yawn.

"I'll be right back," I promised Max, as he leaned down and placed a tender kiss on Charlie's forehead.

"Sleep tight, birthday girl," he whispered.

The quietness in the house was a stark contrast to the chaos that was erupting outside. We padded our way down the hallway and into Charlie's nursery. I sat down in the rocking chair to get a few minutes of snuggles in.

Charlie curled into me as I gently rocked her back and forth. I hummed a lullaby softly as I watched her eyelids become heavy with sleep.

A few minutes later, her tiny chest rose and fell rhythmically, the gentle snores a sweet melody to my ears, a peaceful sigh of relief washing over me. I stood and tiptoed over to the edge of her crib, lowering her down onto the mattress, attempting to not wake her. She rolled over, clutching the horse stuffy Max had given her as an early birthday gift in her chubby grasp.

A warmth spread through me, a silent contentment washing over my body as I watched her serene slumber.

"Sleep tight, birthday girl." I whispered, mimicking Max's earlier nickname.

Easing my way out of the nursery, I closed the door with a soft snick. Before I even turned around, a mass of solid muscle pressed me against the wall. Max gripped my hips and pressed a passionate kiss to my mouth.

A soft moan escaped my lips, and he took that as an invitation to tangle his tongue with mine. One of his hands coasted the planes of my stomach, up between my breasts, and rested on my neck. He didn't apply pressure, but the simple fact that he could filled me with an eager thrill.

He pulled back to gaze at me from beneath hooded lids.

"You're so fucking beautiful," he growled as he dove back in for another searing kiss.

A throat clearing down the hallway broke our passionate embrace. Max lowered his forehead to mine before cocking his head to the side to see who had the balls to interrupt the tiny snippet of time we had to be together. His dad stood at the end of the hallway with a shit-eating grin, his arms crossed across his chest.

"When you're finished mauling each other, Ray sent me here to gather her worker bees."

I could hear his attempt at holding back laughter as Max attempted to conceal his rapidly growing hard on.

"We will be out in a second," I retorted, giving us a few minutes to gather our wits before being fed to the wolves of party decorating.

"I love you," he declared in a whisper, his eyes sparkling with affection. I could feel his heart pounding in his chest.

"I love you too, Cowboy. Now let's get this over with so we can go back to where we left off after this party."

AFTER ANOTHER HOUR of food prep, last-minute touches, one emotional melt down from Wade, and dozens of popped balloons, the party was about to start. I looked around at how Ray had transformed the simple ranch into such a whimsical fairytale.

She had draped fairy lights along each of the trees lining

the backyard, giving a subtle ethereal glow to the space. The interspersed paper mache mushrooms and flowers along the tree line enhanced the illusion of a forest.

Someone had outfitted two long tables with white tablecloths, draping them in layers of chiffon fabric in varying muted neutral colors and adorning them with garlands of ivy.

Charlie's highchair sat at the head of one table, a banner with the word 'one' dangling from the front and balloons floating on the back. Fairy lights wrapped around her chair legs would illuminate her in the afternoon glow.

Ray stepped up beside me, and I reached out a hand to take hers. She reciprocated the gesture and leaned her head on my shoulder in an affectionate touch.

"Ray… How can I ever thank you?" I asked in a whisper, still in awe of all the work she had put in to making the party so beautiful.

"Stay. That's how you can thank me," she responded softly, tightening her grip on mine three times in quick succession.

It was such an affectionate moment that it threw me off kilter. I was thankful to have her in my life, and even after fulfilling her wishes to stay, I'd still forever be indebted to her.

I nodded, unsure if she was even watching to see my affirmation, but the appearance of two burly men in matching fluffy tutus and fairy wings, stepping from the house, diverted my gaze.

"Oh.. My.. God." I chuckled, unable to restrain my laughter.

Max and Wade stood on the back porch steps, clad in matching fairy princess attire, holding a tiny version of their outfit between them. Pink tutus encircled their waists, and each man wore a jeweled crown and glittery fairy wings.

"We need our third amigo to finish the vision!" Wade remarked, twirling like a ballerina, causing glitter to sparkle everywhere around him. I put a hand over my mouth and laughed hard enough that I felt tears prick my eyes. These men stopped at nothing for their girl.

I checked my phone clock and noticed how long Charlie had been sleeping. I had forgotten to grab the baby monitor off the nightstand in our bedroom. Assuming she was awake, I walked up the back porch stairs, stopping to give Max a quick kiss and pat on his tutu clad ass as I made my way into the house.

Making way down the hallway, I cracked open Charlie's door. Surprisingly, all was quiet. I had half expected Charlie to be banging on the rungs of her crib, wanting to get out and join in on the fun.

Approaching the crib, the horrifying emptiness of it, the absence of my child's sleeping form, sent shards of ice through my heart. A soul shattering scream escaped from my throat as I fell to my knees and wailed.

Instead of my beautiful baby, there lie a note in a scrawled handwriting that read,

"Come out, come out, wherever you are."

TWENTY-EIGHT

STANDING OUTSIDE BY THE GRILL, I glanced around at all the people here to celebrate Charlie. I'm sure some of them would claim they were here to wish Wade and me 'happy birthday' as well, but I knew deep down that they showed up to support Charlie and Stella.

A tangible electric current pulsed in the air, a strange tickle on my skin that made the hairs on my arms stand on end. The sensation felt as if I was edging close to a live wire of an electric fence.

I wasn't sure whether the feeling was the proximity to the heat of the grill, or a niggling sensation of something amiss.

Wade sauntered off the back deck and headed in my direction, his tutu swishing in the breeze. It almost seemed as if he had an extra swing in his step and I chuckled under my breath.

Ray and Stella had gotten us matching tutus and fairy wings to Charlie's. I'm sure they meant it as a joke, but I wanted to show Stella that I wasn't above doing anything to see my girls smile.

We had, without reservation, rocked the tutus and wings

as if they were a regular part of our wardrobe. Although, watching Wade strut my way, it seemed as if he might enjoy it more than I had expected.

"Looking good, birthday boy," he said, nodding curtly, a smirk playing on his lips as he clapped me on the shoulder.

"You're loving this, aren't you?" I asked with a sarcastic roll of my eyes.

"Fu- I mean, heck yes, I am," Wade responded with a grin. "The ladies love a man who is confident and secure enough in his masculinity to wear a tutu to make his future niece happy."

I shook my head in exasperation. Especially at this moment, the differences between us couldn't have been more clear. I felt like I was itching in this outfit, but I knew it would make Charlie happy to match with Wade and me, so I stuck it out.

Just as I began to speak, a scream so horrific it made my blood run cold ripped through the air from the house. Before I even had time to think, I was bolting up the back steps and slamming through the door in search of Stella and Charlie.

A million thoughts were running through my mind. I couldn't silence the constant barrage of 'what ifs' that plagued my thoughts.

"*STELLA?!*" I yelled out into the vast emptiness of the house.

I could hear muted whimpers and wails from Charlie's nursery and I stopped, rooted to the floor. I tried to steel myself for what I was about to find. The scenarios of what I might find were endless, but I snapped myself out of my fear induced haze as I inched towards the room.

I stopped right outside the door, my hand fiddling with the

handle, and took a deep breath. The door creaked open, the silence inside the room oppressive.

Curled on the floor, sitting slumped against Charlie's crib, was Stella. She looked so small and fragile. I took another step into the room and crouched in front of her, not bothering to look into the crib just yet, afraid of what I might find. Panic clawed at my throat; Stella's frantic whispers and trembling hands revealed a deep panic.

I reached out and tenderly caressed Stella's knee. She flinched, and I startled. It had been so long since my touch had caused such a visceral reaction in her; it caused my heart to clench.

"Stella?" To avoid startling her again, I whispered.

She raised her eyes to mine, and the emptiness caused my heart to break. Grief had dulled the once vibrant emerald green. Red rimmed her irises as she took a shuddering breath and a steady stream of tears dripped down her cheeks.

"Charlie…" she whispered, barely audible above the sound of my pounding heart.

I took a fortifying breath before asking the question I wasn't sure I wanted to know the answer to.

"What happened to Charlie?"

Her hand trembled as she unclasped the note that was crumbled in her grasp. I could see the spots where her tears had dripped onto the paper, smudging the fresh ink. As I unfurled it, the words ignited a quiet fury within me.

"She's gone…" Stella whispered, her voice void of emotion. She was breaking, and I couldn't blame her a single bit.

Vaguely aware of the crowd that had gathered outside the door. I raised my gaze to meet Wade's and managed to utter from between clenched teeth, "Find Sheriff Cortez."

When Wade didn't move, my simmering rage turned to a rolling boil as I took in a deep breath and shouted.

"*NOW!*"

Sensing the urgency of the situation, the house became a flurry of commotion. I managed to usher Stella into the living room, and we sat curled together on the couch, clutching one another like a lifeline. Charlie, our girl, was gone.

Sheriff Cortez had thankfully already been at the house and was able to dispatch a call for units to come out to the ranch. Once his fellow officers arrived, it turned into a constant barrage of questions, recollection of events, and details that could point them toward a lead.

Police swept Charlie's nursery for fingerprints to check against their records. Someone asked Stella to recount the night she left her ex for dead in their shared apartment. She had shared the story no less than ten times in the last hour since we'd left the nursery.

Emmanuel had sat beside Stella, a presence of comfort and stability should she need it. Any other time, I would be banging my chest in protectiveness, insisting that I was her rock, but right now, I was just as broken as she was.

Pops took up the seat beside me, his hand a constant pressure on my shoulder, reminding us we were not alone.

Ray had rushed out to work on the party clean up with Wade, neither of them good at expressing their emotions in the heat of the moment. The ethereal vision they had constructed to celebrate our girl had since turned into a den of chaos as officers skittered about.

"Stella, Max, did you hear Sergeant Walker?" Emmanuel said softly, breaking us from our trance.

I cleared my throat before answering, "I'm sorry, no. I wasn't paying attention."

Sergeant Walker pursed her lips in a gentle sign of annoyance. "That's okay, I know this is all extremely overwhelming, but the more information we can gather, the more chance we have of finding Charlie."

I felt Stella stiffen beside me and I reached over to clasp her hand in mine. I could feel the rage radiating off her body in waves as she spoke.

"You *will* find my daughter." She gritted out through clenched teeth.

"Ma'am... With all due respect, the chances of that ha-"

"I don't give a fuck about the statistics or chances. You'll find my daughter before something worse happens to her." Stella's eyes met the officers and I could see the fire brewing in them.

"I swear on my life that if *you* don't find her, I will, and I can guarantee you that you'd rather be the one putting this motherfucker in handcuffs because if I get my hands on him, he will be leaving in a body bag."

She pushed off the sofa and stormed down the hallway, leaving Sergeant Walker with her mouth opening and closing like a fish.

"Sergeant Walker," I said, garnering her attention. "Do you have kids?"

Her head shook from side to side, telling me what I already knew.

"Then, with all due respect," I responded, mocking her earlier sentiment. "Fuck off."

I stood and followed Stella's retreating footsteps and muted sobs down the hall. They had finished sweeping Charlie's nursery, and I found Stella sitting in the rocking chair she and Charlie had frequented daily.

In a slow, swaying movement, she continued to rock. In

her hands, she clutched the outfit Ray had gotten made for Charlie's party. I sat beside the rocker and placed my hands over hers.

"They'll find her," I reassured, unsure if I was doing so for my benefit or hers.

"What if they don't?" she whispered, stuttering breaths making her words come out stilted and stiff. Her wracking sobs had slowed to a constant slow trickle of tears, but the aftermath had left her exhausted.

"Then we do," I promised. "We're going to get our girl back, I promise."

Leaning in, I pressed my forehead against hers, gently brushing a strand of damp hair from her face and behind her ear. I felt warm drops hit my knees as her tears continued to flow. The intense pain and grief that overtook us was something I couldn't describe.

It was a visceral and drowning emotion that left me feeling hollow. The only thing that could fill the gaping hole where something was missing was closure.

We would get Charlie back. I wouldn't let these girls escape the fiery clutches of hell, only to be dragged back down into its suffocating depths.

stella

TWENTY-FOUR HOURS FEELS like an eternity when part of your soul is missing. Minutes seemed to drag on, somehow morphing into hours. The sun rose and fell, but I couldn't acknowledge its existence. A heavy blanket of gray settled over my senses, leaving only a dull ache where vibrant life used to be.

The moment I became a mother, I felt like the universe had broken off a piece of my essence, and it now lived and breathed outside of my body. There lived a primal part of me that yearned to protect that tiny piece of myself at all costs. Every ache, pain, and emotion that my child felt resonated through me in tandem.

The oppressive guilt of not having defended Charlie from the wickedness of the world consumed me. I felt suffocated in the weight of my grief. Every second stretched into an eternity, and the fear of not finding her soon gnawed at my insides.

Statistics state that if a child isn't located in the first twenty-four hours of abduction, it's unlikely that they will be found alive. As we neared the end of that window of time, my hope refused to wane. I refused to give up on my girl. I would find her, even if it killed me.

Sheriff Cortez and his team had left a while ago. Hours, or perhaps minutes, had drifted by in the unnervingly silent house, leaving me with no sense of how long I'd been there. At least with the officers here, I felt we were constantly working towards the end game of finding her.

"Stella," I heard Max whisper from beside me. I hadn't even registered him coming into the room.

I adverted my eyes from the empty crib I'd been staring at for God knows how long and met his gaze. I could see the turmoil reflected in his eyes that mirrored my own.

It wasn't until I felt his thumb swipe softly under my eyes that I even realized I was crying. How did I even have tears left?

"You need to eat something," he murmured.

I could tell that the idea of eating thrilled him just as much as it thrilled me. Was Charlie eating? Had the sickos who'd taken her made sure she was fed, changed, and taken care of?

Thoughts of my beautiful girl in a soiled diaper, screaming for food and comfort, threatened to overtake my mind.

Sensing my inner struggle without me even having to utter a word, Max tugged on my hand, coaxing me over into his lap. I went willingly, my weary bones heavy with defeat, no fight left in me.

I curled into his embrace as the tears fell harder. Shuddering cries came from my lips and Max brushed the loose strands of hair from my face and rested his cheek on top of my head.

"We're not giving up," he insisted. "Everyone down at the station is working overtime to find her. They have put a rush on any finger prints they lifted earlier and all evidence is being combed through with every set of eyes available."

As much as I wanted his words to comfort me, I couldn't mask my fear. Would we find her? If we did manage to find her, what state would she be in?

"Let's go lay down,"

"I'm not going anywhere."

"Stell.."

"I said, I'm not going *anywhere*," my voice cracked with the desperation of needing to feel close to Charlie. I couldn't leave her nursery. If I did, I felt like I was giving up. I would sit vigil here until they brought us news of where she was.

"Okay, okay," Max conceded, shifting so he could sit with his back against the wall, myself between his outstretched legs. "We'll stay right here."

"You don't need to stay. Go sleep," I huffed in annoyance.

He didn't need to sit here with me out of pity. We'd gone through hell and back before and I was intimately familiar with the ways in and out. I was used to handling the pressures of life on my own. I didn't need my boyfriend to coddle me.

"Don't do this, Stella," he pleaded.

"Do what?" I bit out.

"Don't push me away."

"She's not your daughter, she's mine. I don't need your pity."

I knew that I should have felt a tinge of regret saying the words as soon as they left my mouth, but Max just couldn't understand. He wasn't her father. He hadn't raised her from the moment someone set her on his chest and said 'congratulations'. He hadn't soothed her to sleep through regressions, teething, cluster feeding, and sickness. Point being, I didn't need him here.

"Don't you fucking dare." He seethed, pushing out from behind me to stand. Pacing the floor, I could feel the frustration and anger radiating off him in waves. He stopped in front of me and crouched down so that he was level with my gaze. I refused to look him in the eyes.

"Don't you fucking *dare* assume I'm not going out of my fucking mind right now."

He placed his hand on the side of my throat, angling my face so that our gazes met. I didn't flinch as I looked up at him. I could see the tears threatening to fall on his lower lash line. His eyes seemed almost hollow and in that moment, I could clearly see he was hurting just as bad as I was. I'd underestimated how much Charlie and I meant to him, but seeing his face contorted in grief cleared things up.

"I may not have given life to that little girl, and I may not be her biological father, but I swear on everything I have that I love her more than life itself. Stella, it's *killing* me not to be out there looking for her. I want to find the mother fuckers who took her and make them pay for the pain they've caused this family over the last twenty-four hours. It's taking every ounce of my willpower to let the Sheriff and his men do their jobs. I'd love nothing more than to grab my gun, search the town from top to bottom, and put a bullet between the eyes of the men who did this."

A single tear crested over the edge and tracked down his cheek. I reached my fingers up to silently brush it away.

"I love you and Charlie with everything I am and everything I have. You two are my light and my world. I know you're hurting and I can't even begin to imagine how painful this is for you, but please Stella, don't push me away. Let me carry this burden with you. Please, Trouble, let me in."

The pain in his voice broke me and wracking sobs shook

my body as I threw myself into Max's arms. We held each other like our lives depended on it. It felt as if, in that moment, our embrace was the glue holding our broken pieces in place, and if either of us let go, we would fall apart.

Breaking through the sound of our collective sobs, Max's phone let out a shrill ring. He hesitated to loosen his hold, but released me enough to reach into his back pocket and pull out his cell. I saw his eyes shoot wide with concern as he pressed answer and then switched it to speaker so we both could hear the conversation. He gripped my hand in his, both of us shaking so hard that I didn't know where I ended, and he began.

Before we could speak, a voice answered.

"We've found her."

A guttural cry wrenched from my soul as I bent forward and cradled my head in my hands. The sense of relief that flooded my veins was overwhelming. They'd found her. They'd found Charlie. Before I let myself drown in hope, I had to make sure she was okay. I needed to hear Sheriff Cortez say in clear terms that my girl wasn't hurt.

"Is she okay?" I asked, clearing my throat through the thickness of emotion.

"Our forensic analysts were able to lift fingerprints off of Charlie's crib and it came up as a match in the national database. The guy has a rap sheet a mile long. His name is Silas Price, and he's a known drug dealer in Minnesota. I don't know why we didn't think to search your car before, but we found a tracker in one of the wheel wells. He's been tracking your every move, Stella."

Max cut in before Sheriff Cortez could speak again. "Emmanuel, with all due respect, cut to the chase. Can you tell us if our girl is okay?"

Hearing Max call Charlie *ours* was a shot of lightning to my soul. I never realized how much I craved the feeling of being wanted until that moment. I squeezed his hand in solidarity as we waited on bated breath to hear what Emmanuel had to say.

"We were able to locate our guy just outside of Firefly Cove at an abandoned warehouse off Interstate 285 near Atlanta. Patrol cars are over there now, scoping out the place. I wanted to update you with what information we have, but as far as they can tell, Charlie's okay. They reported that there were multiple individuals coming and going from the property, one of which was a woman carrying a little girl matching Charlie's description. I'll keep you up to date as I have more information, but Max," he paused, gaining our attention, "don't do anything stupid."

"Yes, sir." Max gritted through a tightly clenched jaw. I could see the wheels turning in his mind as he formulated a plan, his brow furrowed in concentration, to find the warehouse and save our girl.

"I'll call when I have more information," Sheriff Cortez promised.

"Thanks." Max clipped and hung up the phone, tossing it across the room. He paced from wall to wall, running his fingers through his hair.

"What are you thinking?" I asked hesitantly, knowing I probably wasn't going to like the answer.

"I'm thinking that I can't just sit by and wait while someone else takes their sweet fucking time to get our girl out safely."

"I feel the same way, but Max, we can't barge in there and break down doors. What if they're armed? Someone could get hurt or worse, killed. I want to go in there and get our girl just as bad as you do, but we have to keep a level head."

I wrapped my arms around his waist and laid my forehead on his chest. Feeling his heart rate slow and his arms come around me, I closed my eyes in contentment. Our girl was okay. Now, we just needed to find a way to get her home.

I held Max tight, knowing that this could very well be the last time I got to be in his arms. He was right. We couldn't sit by and wait while someone else took their time rescuing Charlie.

Even though I'd just told him we couldn't make any rash decisions, my mind swirled with plans. I knew that Sheriff Cortez and his team were doing everything they could to get to Charlie, but I also knew how unpredictable this scum bag was. After all, who lets a woman who saw what I did go, just to play a game of cat and mouse across half of the country?

I wasn't going to let Max charge in there, guns blazing, and get himself killed. But, I wasn't going to sit around with my thumb up my ass waiting for Emmanuel and his team to come up with a plan.

We had already passed the threshold that the experts expected to find a child alive. Every moment we waited was borrowed time. I needed to do something, but I couldn't drag Max and his family into it.

"Let's go update everyone and come up with a plan." I said, knowing that a plan was already coming together in my head. I knew in my heart that as soon as the house was quiet and asleep, I'd be breaking his heart to put mine back together.

stella

WE SPENT the next two hours around the weathered kitchen table poring over ways to get to Charlie. The tension was so thick, you could have cut it with a knife as everyone held their breath, hoping for news. Sheriff Cortez hadn't given us any further updates except a text or two confirming that Charlie was alive and well inside the warehouse.

We had figured out that the warehouse was a dilapidated paper mill right outside the city limits. That location offered ideal seclusion while remaining near a major city. Knowing what I did about this Silas guy, they still needed to move their product, even if they were set on playing games, and being close to a big city like Atlanta provided them the access to an entire network of underground dealers.

We assumed they were using the warehouse to move larger amounts of heroin. Though we had no clue how many total people were inside, we knew there was at least one male and one female. I couldn't imagine two people handling an operation this large, but drug dealers were a crazy bunch of fuckers, defying logical explanation.

I hadn't been blind to the backwoods dealings that Dean had been involved in. I kept my mouth shut, claiming that I loved him and he was just doing what he needed to support us. He had come home blitzed out of his mind enough that I knew the type of crazy we were dealing with.

Even though I had first-hand knowledge of how dangerous these people were, I was about to kick the proverbial hornet's nest.

Terrified was an understatement, and I just hoped that no matter what happened, Max would understand and forgive me after this was all over.

One by one, everyone made moves to leave. There wasn't any use in everyone standing vigil around the big house while we waited for news. Everyone could go back to their comfy beds and rest knowing that the Sheriff had eyes on Charlie.

I had even managed to convince Max that we should get some rest, knowing that as soon as we had word that they had infiltrated the warehouse and gotten Charlie out, we wouldn't be sleeping.

I had to get him to sleep to put my plan in motion, as it was the only logical way to keep him from stopping me. I had been working out details in my mind all afternoon, and knew that if Max caught wind of what I'd planned, he'd insist on doing it himself. I didn't want him in the middle of all of this. It was my battle to fight.

We stood side by side in the bathroom brushing our teeth, the silence oppressive as my heart beat wildly in my chest. I hoped he wouldn't notice my shaking hands as I reached forward and turned on the water to wash my toothpaste down the drain.

As Max leaned over to rinse his mouth, his hand resting on the small of my back—a gesture that usually comforted me

—it instead filled me with a profound and unsettling sense of dread.

Would he hate me after this was all over?

We padded our way to the bed; him pulling back the covers on his side and me on mine. As soon as we both laid our heads down, he wrapped his arms around my waist and pulled me in close.

I snuggled into his embrace, relishing in the warmth of his chest against my back. The feeling of being in his arms was a comfort I couldn't explain. It felt like coming home. I sunk into his warm body, not knowing if this would be the last chance we would have to be together.

I loved him completely and without reservation; there was no question in my mind about the depth and of my affection for this man. He had pulled me from the depths of darkness, showing me what it was like to be loved wholly and without reservation.

Max was one of the good ones.

"Goodnight, Trouble." he yawned, tightening his arm around my waist and tucking his face into the space where my shoulder met the slope of my neck. He pressed a tender kiss right at the juncture, and I sighed in contentedness.

"Goodnight, Cowboy." I whispered back, barely managing to choke back the sobs that threatened to escape my lips.

I wasn't watching the clock, but it didn't take long before his breathing evened out and I could feel his embrace loosen. I waited an extra ten minutes or so before attempting to remove myself from his grasp.

I inched his arm from around my waist, taking extra care not to wake him. Max was a sound sleeper and today had been draining, but I didn't want to chance having to explain where I was heading, or lie to him.

Once I was confident that I could move without waking him up, I padded to the closet. I had shoved a few things in a small duffel bag at the back of the walk-in closet earlier, under the guise of having to use the bathroom. I'd packed a change of clothes for myself, my cell phone, clothes for Charlie, and my wallet.

Tiptoeing back to the bedroom, I attempted to open the bedside table drawer without making a sound. When it slid open silently, I nearly fell to my knees in relief. So far, luck had been on my side and I wasn't about to test its limits.

Reaching in, I wrapped my hand around the smooth barrel of Max's handgun stored at the back.

The first night we had slept in the same room, I had almost peed my pants when he set it in the drawer on his side, fully loaded with the safety off. He had promised that it was okay resting in the drawer and he would put it back in the gun safe in the morning.

He had explained that a gun in the gun safe did nothing in the way of protection, should someone come into the house in the middle of the night. Keeping the gun in the bedside table drawer, loaded and unlocked, gave us a better chance of defense.

I still wasn't comfortable handling a loaded firearm without Max's help, but I didn't want to go into this without some way to protect myself.

I flipped the safety back on as I tucked the gun into a zipper pouch on the outside of my duffle bag so that it was accessible.

Taking one last look around the room, my gaze settled on Max's sleeping form. The furrow that had been between his brows over the last twenty-four hours had softened. He looked so serene and at peace. His chest rose and fell in an even cadence, and his lush lips parted with each exhale.

I set the note I'd scribbled earlier on my bedside table and draped the necklace he'd given me yesterday over it, not wanting anything to happen to it in the shuffle. I sent up a silent prayer to whatever being made universal decisions that he would forgive me after all of this if I made it out.

I left our bedroom, walking as quietly as I could and shut the door with a soft snick. I waited with bated breath to make sure it hadn't woken him before I tip-toed to the front door and repeated the motions.

Once outside, I realized how serene the ranch was at night. A symphony of crickets chirped, their tiny voices blending into a soothing nighttime soundtrack. Though still humid, the air lacked the oppressive weight of the day's heat; a gentle breeze whispered through the trees, calling out a soft whisper of warning.

Across the field, I could see the fireflies dancing through the air, beckoning all lost souls to send their wishes to the moon. As I stepped off the porch, one landed on my sleep shorts. I stopped and tenderly scooped it into my palm, taking great care to cup it softly as I raised it to my eyes.

The tiny bug, a miniature jewel of orange and black, seemed to peer back at me as it stood in silent wait for my plea, its antennae twitching slightly. I cupped my other hand over it and closed my eyes.

"I wish that for once in my life, everything goes right. I wish that Charlie and I make it out safely, that Max doesn't hate me, and we can move on with our lives without fear creeping over our shoulders."

My whispered desire coasted past my lips as I opened my palm and allowed the firefly to fly into the darkness. Its tiny light was a beacon of hope as it soared high into the sky.

I took one last look at the big house, memorizing the gentle sway of Ma's porch swing. I felt a gentle breeze coast across my skin, almost as if a whisper of acknowledgment from her spirit, a mother's knowing approval.

I thought about the many times Max and I had sat just watching Charlie play in the grass from the comfort of the creaky steps. Visions of a future where we sat as a family, watching our future kids make memories from the same rickety porch, clouded my thoughts.

I shook the thoughts from my head, not allowing myself to dwell on the could be's, as I walked to my car, started the engine, and pulled away from the only family I'd allowed myself to know and love unconditionally.

SURPRISINGLY, the drive to Atlanta was uneventful; the highway was smooth, and the only sound was the gentle hum of the tires on the asphalt. The roads were deserted. I wasn't surprised that I'd only passed a handful of cars as I drove out of town, only sensing civilization when I hit the main highway.

It only took about an hour and a half to get to the location of the warehouse. Sheriff Cortez had let slip that there was a change of look-out detail around this time, and I hoped that would provide the momentary distraction I needed to get myself inside.

I cut the lights as I pulled up near the building, noticing two patrol cars parked out back. The officers were standing relaxed against their vehicles, chatting about who knows what, not paying attention to their surroundings. I rolled my eyes and made a mental note to mention it to Emmanuel, should I make it out of here.

Scratch that - when I made it out of here. Not making it out wasn't an option.

I parked the car in a small clearing between the trees, about a hundred yards from the parking lot of the warehouse. I left behind the duffel, but made sure to grab the hand gun and tuck it in the waistband of my shorts. Not comfortable enough in my abilities to not shoot myself in the crotch, I left the safety on. I didn't need to shit to go sideways before I even made it inside the building.

I crept down the road, taking care to stay in the shadows. I was sure that the officers couldn't see me from this far away, but I didn't need to alert them to my presence. Somehow getting close enough without being seen, I started looking for an entrance. I noticed a small loading dock off to the side and what looked like a door propped ajar with a brick. It was out of view of where the officers chatted away.

Upon further inspection, I was right. The door was open. Unease filtered through my veins as everything fell into place. This was all happening so perfectly that I couldn't imagine a scenario in which something wouldn't go wrong.

I crept to the metal door and slowly edged it open. It strained on its hinges, letting out a loud creak into the dark abyss inside. I paused, waiting for shouting to come, but when it didn't, I let loose a sign of relief.

Creeping into the room, I attempted to feel my way through the darkness. I kept my hands in front of me to hopefully catch myself before I slammed into something. Tiptoeing forward, I could see light coming from the hallway ahead and made my way towards it. I heard distant whispers, but wasn't able to make out what they were saying.

Momentarily distracted by the noise ahead, my foot caught on the rough metal of a table leg and I went careening forward, slamming my palms down on its flat surface. I felt the sharp sting on my leg, and I winced as I realized I'd caught the edge and cut open my shin.

"Fuck." I whispered through gritted teeth, fighting through the pain. I'd managed to cut myself pretty good and would probably need a couple of stitches.

The light at the end of the hallway got brighter as someone opened the door. A hulking man the size of an oak tree, took up the majority of the door frame, blocking out the light. I couldn't quite tell, but it looked like he had a gun in his hand and his gaze was trained directly in my direction.

Unsure if he could see me through the oppressive darkness, I held my breath in an attempt to make myself seem small.

"Who's there?" he boomed, raising the weapon and pointing it in my general direction.

I did my best to breathe evenly and quietly, but as he stepped into the room, a feeling of dread washed over me. He stomped towards me, a flashlight held in his meaty fingers. Once he was close enough that the rays of light crested my body, a chill coasted down my spine.

His grin was feral as his lips spread, showcasing a yellowing smile. He cocked his head to the side as he grinned, his greasy black hair falling over one eye.

"Well, hello there, pretty little bitch."

ROLLING OVER ONTO MY SIDE, I reached for Stella's sleeping form. When my hands came up empty, the sleep induced fog receded as panic flooded my veins, shooting me up into the sitting position.

Turning my head, I noticed her side of the bed was empty. I laid my palm on her pillow and was met with a stark coolness.

"Stella?" I called into the dark room, hoping that she'd gotten up to use the bathroom, or maybe even just couldn't sleep and went into the living room.

I reached over and turned on my bedside lamp, illuminating the room in a golden glow. Empty. A gut churning dread filled me as I looked around for a clue as to where she'd gone. Something wasn't right.

Had she gotten up and gone back to sit vigil in Charlie's nursery?

A glitter of something sitting on her nightstand caught my eye, and I lifted the covers to scoot over to her side. Sitting on top of her end table was the necklace I'd given her just the day before.

I didn't remember her taking it off, but she may have removed it before coming to bed. The glittering stones stood contrast against the darkness, a mocking one-finger salute to all the progress we had made.

She had loved the necklace, I was sure of it, so why did she take it off?

I shifted the necklace off what looked like a note scrawled quickly on a bright yellow post-it note and my blood ran cold. In that moment, the silence felt heavy, and I knew, with a certainty that chilled me to the bone, that something was very fucking wrong.

I hesitated, not wanting to know what the words written in Stella's graceful handwriting would tell me. If I didn't acknowledge them, it couldn't be real. Right?

Growing the fortitude to see what she'd written, I unfolded the note with shaky hands, gazing over each graceful loop of her words. I felt tears of rage building as I took in her final plea.

Max,

I love you, with all that I am, and all that I hope to be. But, before you, came a little girl who shares the beat of my heart. I can't sit by and wait to lose her. I hope you understand and can forgive me when all of this is through. I'm going to get our girl.

Love always,
Stella

I reread the note with the hope that this was all a bad dream, clutching onto the final words of the woman I loved so fiercely. She'd sacrificed herself to go after her daughter, our daughter.

I crumpled the note into a ball, throwing it across the room with a frustrated groan.

Stella had spent so long fighting alone that she couldn't sit by and wait for someone else to make something happen. She was used to taking matters into her own hands, even to her detriment.

I wanted to hate her for putting herself in danger. I wanted to rage, throw things, break down doors, and run guns blazing into that warehouse to save them.

But, I couldn't.

I couldn't hate Stella for choosing Charlie. I couldn't hate her for being so jaded that she couldn't sit behind while someone else did the legwork of saving her entire world, our entire world.

I couldn't hate the woman with a single bitter bone in my body, but I refused to let her do this alone.

Snatching my phone off my nightstand, I pressed re-dial on the last number to ring through. A gruff voice croaked with sleep on the other side of the phone.

"Stella's gone. She's gone after Charlie." I managed to grit into the receiver.

"Max, what are you talking about?" Sheriff Cortez asked, clearing the thick haze of exhaustion from his voice. "I've got two officers on detail over there now. They would have alerted me that she was there."

"I don't give a *FUCK* who you have sitting outside of that warehouse. Stella isn't here, and she left a note saying she's going to get Charlie." I spat.

I could hear furious typing on the other end as he attempted to reach the deputies in charge of staking out the building. I'm sure they weren't going to have jobs after all this was through, but to Stella's credit, she was crafty. She knew how to keep a low profile. She'd been dutifully doing it with Dean for years.

"Por el amor de Dios," He grumbled. "Max.."

"She's there, isn't she?"

"Yes." he stated matter-of-factly. "But.."

I could sense he was going to try to talk me out of going after them, but I wasn't going to hear it. Stella has spent too long without someone in her corner. I needed to be there.

I knew Sheriff Cortez was doing all that he could to get Charlie back, but Stella wouldn't trust anyone until she could put her own two eyes on her daughter. She was going to go in there and get herself killed, unless we did something, and fast.

"With all due respect, sir, those two are my entire world. I'm not going to sit by while some crazy fucking drug dealers do God knows what to them." I said, hopping out of the bed and reaching for the side table to grab my firearm.

Sliding the drawer open, I noticed its vast emptiness and sent up a silent thanks Stella had armed herself before heading into the lion's den. Pride echoed through my chest and I fell even more in love with the woman.

"Emmanuel?" I asked, his silence a testament to how I'd stunned him with my admission.

"Yes, Max?"

"You might want to call in a few more deputies to meet you over at that warehouse, because if I go in there, every mother fucker in that building, except my girls, are getting a bullet between the eyes, and I won't think twice about pulling that trigger."

With that, I hung up the phone and slid it into my back pocket. I walked down the hallway and across the other side of the house, banging loudly on Wade's door.

I was going to need reinforcements. As much as I hated dragging him into this, he wouldn't want to be excluded. He loved Stella and Charlie just as much as I did. We were a family.

"Hey fucker, wake up!" I shouted, slamming my fist against the wood.

The heavy beat of my desperation was accented by cursing on the other side of the door. I heard a groan and a thump as Wade rolled out of bed and scurried over to the door.

His eyes were wide, his hair a mess, and his boxers askew. He'd clearly been fighting some demons in his sleep, something I'd make sure to talk to him about later. He rubbed at his eyes to clear the haze and looked up at me with a questioning stare.

"What the.." he started before taking notice of the inherent rage coursing through my face. "What happened?"

"Stella's gone after Charlie. Get dressed and grab a gun. We're going to get my girls."

Quickly, and without question, Wade grabbed jeans, a black tee shirt, tennis shoes, and a belt from near the door. He walked over to his own bedside table and grabbed his firearm.

Thank God Pops had always taught us the importance of protecting yourself and those you loved. We were ready, but prayed we wouldn't have to use it.

"Let's go. I'll call Ray from the car." He snapped, squeezing past me to head towards the front door.

Before he got too far, he stopped and looked me in the

eyes, placing his hand on my shoulder with a tight squeeze. "It's going to be okay. We'll get them back."

I wish I matched his confidence. It would have been a welcome reprieve from the gnawing fear that had taken residence in my gut. Stella and Charlie were my world. Their presence in our lives had made everything brighter. Without them, I'd go back to being a bitter shell of a human, void of any genuine relationships. I wasn't going to let that happen. Come hell or high water, I was bringing my girls home.

IT TOOK Wade and I less than an hour to make it to the warehouse. Neither one of us had uttered a word the entire drive, except for when Wade called Ray to make sure she knew what was going on. She had insisted on meeting us there, but Wade talked her out of it, citing that she needed to stay behind in case someone needed something at the ranch. She'd reluctantly agreed and I could hear the pain in her voice as she told us to be safe.

I wasn't sure if her worry was for me, Stella and Charlie, or Wade, but it was painful to hear the crack in her voice as she said goodbye.

I spent the drive trying to avoid thinking of the worst-case scenario. My mind had spun in circles as images of Stella and Charlie, lifeless and covered in blood, popped in and out.

Instead, I focused on all the things I was going to say and do when we finally reunited.

I focused on visions of Stella walking down a flower draped aisle, wearing a slim fitting white gown. Her hair would be curled, brushing over her bare shoulders, a huge smile on her face as she made her way towards me, forever on our minds.

I imagined Charlie's childhood unfolding at the ranch, where she would learn to ride the horses she'd grown to love. Of course, I'd end up buying her a horse and Stella would shake her head at how wrapped around that little girl's finger I was.

Images of Stella cradling her swollen belly as she grew our first child together. How Charlie would be the best big sister, doting on the new baby with unfiltered love. The joy of holding our newborn and growing our family filled me with warmth.

I wasn't giving up on our happily ever after. If anyone deserved a win in the column of life, it was Stella. She'd given up so much of herself for others, she deserved to get everything she could ever dream of.

The cutting of the engine pulled me from my daydreams of a future with the woman and girl I loved.

We'd pulled up beside the two deputies on duty and I nodded in acknowledgement in their direction. An over-whelming sense of rage filtered through me.

How had they not seen Stella go into the warehouse? They were supposed to be covering all the entry points.

Sheriff Cortez pulled up beside Wade's truck, quickly cutting the engine and stepping out. He looked ever the vision of authority in his tan uniform with a shiny sheriff's badge pinned to his chest.

He didn't look like a man who'd been woken from sleep less than an hour ago to the news that a woman he considered another daughter had put herself in harm's way. The gaze on his face was formidable, and I would hate to be the deputies on the receiving end of his wrath.

"I'll deal with you two later," he spat at the deputies cowering to his right. "For now, give me all the information you have." He commanded, as he spread a map across the hood of his cruiser that detailed the inner blueprints of the building.

Fumbling for their words, the deputies filled us in on how Stella had managed to get inside. They had been in the process of a responsibilities hand over, when she'd skirted around them and entered through a side door on the loading dock.

They didn't know a lot about what was happening inside the building, except that the female seemed in charge of caring for Charlie and there was a male who'd been seen entering the building as well.

"Okay, so game-"

The sound of a gunshot from inside the warehouse cut Sheriff Cortez off. Neither Wade nor I hesitated. We sprinted towards the front door, drawing our own weapons as we ran.

I felt my pulse thrumming in my ears as I sent up a silent prayer. Adrenaline coursing through my veins and fear clogging my senses.

Please God, let them be alright.

stella

THE MAN'S grip was a tight, almost painful pressure on my arm as I followed him, the feel of his strong fingers digging in, causing me to wince. The punishing way he held me left no room for interpretation. Move or be moved.

He pushed me through the maze of hallways, leading to an endless void of darkness. I did my best to catalog our movements, but after the fifteenth turn, I'd lost my way and become disoriented.

A child's soft cry, barely audible, drifted from the end of the hallway, and a sudden chill ran down my spine, catching my breath. I would know that cry anywhere. Charlie was alive. She was upset, but she was very much alive. In a last-ditch attempt, I pulled on my attacker, hoping his heart would soften at the sound of my child's tiny, trembling sobs. I struggled against his hold, tugging him towards where I'd heard the cries.

"Please, just let me see her." I cried, unable to mask my fear that this might be the last time I'd be able to lay eyes on my daughter.

"She's fine." He groused, pushing me towards the other end of the hallway, away from my daughter, and into a small empty room. The air felt damp, the humidity hanging like a thick curtain of despair. There was nothing in the room except for a chair and some rope.

My heart beat wildly in my chest as I cataloged my surroundings. There were no points of entry in the room, save for the door we had just entered from. There were no windows, no decorations, nothing.

I took several deep breaths to calm my racing heart, reminding myself that panicking wouldn't help—a clear head was my only chance of survival. A burning desire to save my girl fueled my every step; I had to escape and return to Max with Charlie safely in my arms. I couldn't let the last words he heard from me be a frantic, scribbled note, as I fled.

My vision blurred with images of Max; his warm eyes, the feel of his hand in mine, bringing tears to my eyes. I wondered what he had felt when he had awoken to the realization that I had left. Had he thought that I didn't love him? I silently hoped he'd read my note, its ink barely dry, and that someday, the weight of my mistakes wouldn't hang heavy over us.

The man pushed me roughly towards the ground, dirt and grime scraping my knees. As I folded in on myself, the cool, smooth metal of Max's gun pressed against my skin, a chilling reminder of its presence tucked into my waistband. I wasn't going down without a fight, but I had to be smart in how all of this played out.

Knowing that I couldn't just reach in my pants and pull out a loaded firearm, flip off the safety, and shoot, I did my best to hide the weapon from his sight, taking great care to lean forward so it didn't dig into my belly. The idiot hadn't bothered to search me, probably thinking that I wasn't smart enough to walk in here armed.

His assumptions might have been right for most women, but I wasn't most women. I was a fighter; I was ruthless. I was determined. And scariest of all, I was a mom whose daughter was crying out in fear in the other room. There is nothing scarier than a mother desperate to keep her child safe.

The man leaned over me menacingly, "Well, well, well, little bitch. I told you I'd catch you," he spat, his rancid breath hot against my cheek as he yanked my hair, forcing my head back to whisper the threat into my ear.

A chill ran down my spine as I felt the cold, hard metal of a weapon dug into my side, and I choked down a whimper. Would I even have a chance to fight my way out of here, or would Max find my lifeless body amongst the wreckage when this was all over?

I imagined him, stricken with grief, as he crouched over my corpse, wondering how all of this had gone so wrong. We needed our chance; we deserved a happily ever after filled with laughter and love. I clung to my feelings for him; he had accepted me, flaws and all, after everything I'd been through, and the thought of letting go was unbearable.

"Now that I've caught you, I get my reward," the man whispered as he gripped my neck with one hand and coasted the tip of his weapon from the fleshy part of my side and up my front, running it along my breast and settling it to rest on my throat.

I bit my lip, clenching my jaw to stifle the whimper that threatened to escape, desperately trying to project an image of strength to mask my overwhelming terror. I had a gut feeling that fear fueled this man, and any sign of weakness from me would only embolden him further; his eyes gleamed with anticipation, his pupils pinpoint with drug induced haze.

Pressing his thick and imposing frame flush with my back, I felt the outline of his erection on my ass. I fought the urge to gag and attempted to shuffle forward, putting some space between us.

Grunting in frustration at my obvious effort to get away, he tugged me back into his body, the stench of his body odor oppressive. The repulsive smell of unwashed flesh and something else, something sickly sweet, wafted from him, and I gasped, sucking in air through my mouth to avoid it. His calloused hand reached around and gripped a hold of my neck, replacing the gun and choking off my attempts at breathing.

Just as he had done in the apartment the night Dean died, he sniffed a line from my collarbone to my ear, the scent of my skin filling his nostrils before he proceeded to lick my earlobe, his thick tongue warm and wet against my skin. I tried to shift my head to the side, but his punishing grip on my throat held me firmly in place. I felt his fingers tighten, pressing against my windpipe, slowly cutting off my oxygen.

Darkness encroached, a black circle swallowing my sight, and the world dissolved into a hazy gray. I felt a cold dread, a palpable sense of death's approach, whispering promises of oblivion from the far distance. I did my best to fight against the inky darkness, knowing that if I allowed this man to kill me, I was leaving behind a family, my daughter, and the man that I loved.

With what little strength I still possessed, I carefully reached into the waistband of my shorts, grasping the butt of the gun. Somehow, by the grace of whatever luck I possessed,

I managed to wrap my fingers around the hilt and draw the weapon.

In a desperate heave, I used all my might to push my attacker away, my head slamming back into his face with a sickening thud.

"YOU BITCH." He screamed, holding his bleeding nose as he attempted to right himself and raise his own weapon in defense. He hadn't even begun to raise his weapon when I moved, lifting my gun with a practiced motion, the safety clicking off with a decisive snap, and firing wildly into the room, the smell of gunpowder instantly filling the air.

Time slowed to a crawl, each second stretching into an eternity as everything happened. The bullet launched from the gun in my hands, a tiny projectile that seemed to hang in the air before speeding toward the man. With a held breath, my gaze remained steady as the bullet ripped through his leg. The smell of blood filled the air as I watched the muscle and sinew tear apart.

I hadn't managed a killing blow, but the bullet found its mark, leaving him writhing on the ground, his pained breaths filling the air. I bolted, a desperate need for escape propelling me out the door and toward the room where I'd heard Charlie's muffled cries, a frantic sound that echoed still in my ears.

Suddenly, a strong arm wrapped tightly around my waist, spinning me around to face a hard, familiar body. My legs and arms flailed, a desperate dance of defiance, as I screamed and fought the secondary attacker with my remaining strength, his words finally piercing the fog of terror.

"Stella, stop!" he commanded.

I immediately stopped fighting, the echo of his words playing on repeat in my fear muddled mind. That voice.. *Max*.

With a gasp of relief, I lifted my gaze to his, the scent of him filling my senses as his arms wrapped around me. He allowed me a second to breathe before holding me at arm's length, his eyes boring into mine.

"Baby, you've got to get out of here," he said sternly, pushing me towards the exit. Digging my feet into the concrete flooring in defiance, I held my ground. I wasn't leaving this place without Charlie; I wouldn't abandon her.

"I'm not leaving without her," I sobbed, the dam of emotions threatening to break.

"I've got her," he promised, looking back at Wade, who I hadn't noticed was standing behind us, and giving him a slight nod. With a brief nod in return, his hand found mine, a reassuring pressure as Max's grip loosened.

I looked back in Max's direction as he rushed forward towards the room to get our daughter, a gun held firmly in his grasp. I sent up a silent prayer, not knowing what was waiting for him on the other side of that door.

THIRTY-THREE

WALKING DOWN THE HALLWAY, I did my best to keep my footsteps light. I didn't bother glancing behind me, too focused on the task ahead to check if Wade had managed to get Stella out as instructed. My sole focus was on reaching Charlie and getting her to safety.

I slunk along the cold, damp brick wall, the weight of my firearm a comforting presence in my hand. Reaching the door at the hallway's end, I heard Charlie's shuddering cries, muffled but urgent, from the other side. A burning rage filled my veins, a fire that threatened to consume me at the thought of someone hurting her.

Before I could think, I rounded in front of the door, using my booted foot to kick it open with a resounding crack. A piercing scream ripped through the air as the woman, her face contorted in horror, stood next to my girl. She attempted to grab Charlie from the ground, but I was quicker on the draw.

My weapon was trained on her center mass as I yelled, *"Don't touch my fucking daughter!"* My heart hammered against my ribs, a frantic drumbeat in the tense silence. I saw the fear ignite in her eyes—a sudden flash of terror—as she held her hands up in a gesture of defeat, her knuckles white.

The pungent smell of urine wafted through the air, and I noticed a dark wetness pooling between the woman's legs. My heart hardened, unable to muster even a sliver of sympathy for the woman who had the audacity to steal another woman's baby. This world was filled with monsters, but the most unforgivable were the ones who targeted children.

I kept my gun trained on the woman's chest as I slowly made my way towards where Charlie was seated on the ground. Upon seeing me, her sobs subsided, but her body trembled as she cowered, eyes wide with terror, a silent whimper escaping her lips. I couldn't imagine the silent battle she'd fought, the loneliness, the confusion; the struggle she'd faced over the last day, separated from her mother and me in a strange, unsettling place, without any idea of what was happening.

"Hey, little one." I cooed, slowly reaching out my hand in offering. A moment of apprehension passed over her features, but upon seeing me, she straightened, and with a rush of relief, embraced me tightly.

"Mass" she sobbed. "Mass da."

The overwhelming urge to cry threatened to consume me, but I held back the tears as I held the little girl, her innocent call of "Dad" echoing in my ears. My gaze remained fixed on the woman across the room, even as I carefully lifted Charlie, the soft weight of her nestled into my chest a comfort to my soul.

Walking backward out of the room, my firearm still

trained on the woman, I carefully made my way toward the exit. I assumed that once we left the building, Sheriff Cortez would immediately dispatch his deputies to apprehend the suspects.

As soon as Charlie and I crested the doorframe to the hallway, a guttural cry, like something strangled and desperate, rang out, and a heavy body slammed into us, knocking us off balance. Stella's sobs were ragged and choked, a desperate sound as she snatched her daughter from my arms and held her so tightly.

A wave of relief washed over her face, visible in the softening of her features as her hand reached for mine, a silent sign of thanks. I squeezed her palm gently, pulling my girls into a hug, feeling their small bodies relax against mine as relief washed over them.

"Thank you," Stella sobbed into my chest. "Thank you, Max."

Speechless, I could only nod, their small bodies trembling slightly as I held them close, feeling the frantic beat of their hearts. I didn't need thanks. Stella and Charlie were my entire life, my entire future, and my entire world. I would have walked through the blazes of hell to reach either of them.

"Bro, we've gotta get out of here." Wade called from the other side of the hallway. I lifted my head, acknowledging him with a slight nod as he turned toward the brightly lit exit.

As he turned to leave, a shadowy figure stumbled from the room Stella had been held in, the sound of flesh dragging across concrete accompanying its unsteady gait. A deafening crack echoed through the silence, turning my blood to ice.

I saw Wade's body crumple as he fell face-first through the doorway, the sickening thud echoing through the hall, a bullet piercing his back. A raw, desperate cry escaped my lips, the sound bouncing off the walls echoing down the vast hallway.

A second gunshot echoed, the sharp report followed by the sickening thud of the man falling backward into the wall, blood blooming on his shirt where the bullet had ripped through his chest.

Emmanuel stood opposite Wade, gun trained on the attacker, his hands steady, a steely gaze reflecting years of police work. Lowering his weapon, the acrid smell of gunpowder still thick in the air, he radioed for a trauma unit, his voice urgent as he described the situation at the warehouse.

Heart pounding, Stella and I scrambled to Wade, and I knelt, taking his hand in mine; the damp concrete was cool against my knees, biting through my jeans.

"Fuck!" He groaned, a low, pained sound escaping his lips.

"Shh, it's okay. We've got paramedics on the way. Don't move," I scolded, my voice sharp, as his labored breathing filled the air and his limbs shook with his failed attempt to sit up.

"Max…" he gritted out, his voice tight with pain.

"No. No, you're not giving me some lame ass speech that I need to take care of things if you die. You're not going to fucking die, do you hear me?" Desperation clawed at me as I begged, my grip on his hand tightening, hot tears streaming down my face.

I was acutely aware of Stella and Charlie standing off to the side; her sobs, an echo of the pain coursing through my heart.

"Fuck…You…" Wade hissed, his teeth grinding together, sweat beading on his forehead from the intense pain.

"It's gonna be okay," I promised. The words hung in the air, a fragile hope against the overwhelming darkness.

"Max… I can't feel my legs," he sobbed, and in that moment, I swear my heart stopped beating.

THIRTY-FOUR

AFTER CAREFULLY LOADING Wade onto a stretcher, the paramedics sped him to the nearest trauma center, lights and sirens wailing.

Concerned about potential injuries, the EMTs insisted that every one of us get checked out. Besides the emotional trauma we anticipated, we'd escaped with only a few scrapes and bruises.

In Max's arms, Charlie's small body had relaxed, her breathing slow and deep, finally asleep. I was sure he wouldn't let either of us out of his sight anytime soon, a comforting thought that filled me with immense gratitude. I felt the weight of an upcoming family therapy session; I could almost smell the tension and hear the strained voices as we worked through the trauma we had endured.

Thankfully, Charlie was only a toddler, and the traumatic events of the last 36 hours would be but a distant, hazy memory. Max and I, on the other hand, would never forget the adrenaline coursing through our veins, the pounding of our hearts a testament to what we experienced.

Once the paramedics had determined we didn't need hospital care, we were released to provide statements; the crisp air of the parking lot felt vastly different to the chaos of the accident. Because of the complexities surrounding Emmanuel's discharge of his firearm during a work-related event, he was immediately put on administrative leave, and his responsibilities were temporarily transferred to his deputy sheriff.

No longer needed, our statements written down and filed away, we crammed into Wade's truck—a cacophony of relieved sighs and slamming doors—and roared off toward the hospital.

None of us were going to sit idly at home, waiting for news; the suspense was too much to bear. Rushing into the sterile-smelling hospital, we immediately saw Hank and Ray anxiously waiting in the emergency department's family waiting room.

Ray's bloodshot, puffy eyes, rimmed with unshed tears, threatened to overflow with each blink. I pulled her into a tight hug, placing my hand on the back of her head in a comforting embrace.

"He's going to be okay," I whispered. "Wade is too damn stubborn to let a little bullet have any impact on how much he annoys all of us."

"They took him back to surgery as soon as they got here," she hiccuped. "they said that the bullet entered through his back and from what they can see, it only grazed his spine. We haven't heard anything else, but the doctor promised to update us as soon as he had more information."

Max came to stand beside me, having set Charlie down in Hank's lap to sleep. The nurse had supplied a scratchy wool blanket and a thin, flat pillow, but I knew none of us were going to be setting her down anytime soon. He offered a comforting hand on Ray's arm, but she couldn't hold back the fresh wave of grief, launching herself against his chest with a shuddering sob.

"Shhh." Max cooed, smoothing his hand down her back in comforting waves. With a solemn sigh, he rested his cheek on her head, the quiet moment filled with unspoken emotions. Ray was like a sister to him, and the quiet strength he showed as he comforted her, his voice a low murmur of support, gave me an added realization of how much family relied on each other in times of need.

With a gentle squeeze of his hand, I carefully made my way to the cold metal chair beside Hank, the silence broken only by the soft padding of my feet. With a sigh, I sank onto the sticky vinyl seat, the day's exhaustion settling over me like a heavy blanket; I could feel the tacky surface clinging to my clothes and it made me shudder.

I barely had a moment to rest before a doctor came in, shedding their blue paper gown and scrub cap in one swift motion, the sound of crinkling paper echoing in the quiet room.

I couldn't quite make out the expression on his face, but it was passive and didn't look overly sympathetic. That gave me the slightest pause of relief. I imagined that if he was coming to give us terrible news, his face would have been etched with worry and his shoulders slumped with grief.

"Are you the Daniels family?" he asked, looking around at each one of us in turn.

Hank stood and extended a hand. "Yes, Hank Daniels, Wade's father." he introduced himself, shaking the doctor's hand in greeting.

"Mister Daniels, Wade is out of surgery. Things went as

expected. We are positive that he will make a decent recovery." He paused, letting the words sink in. The sigh of relief, heavy with the weight of released tension, almost brought me to my knees. "The bullet lodged itself in his spine, but it somehow managed to avoid his spinal cord and any vital organs. To be quite frank, sir, your son is extremely lucky. The paralysis he presented with upon arrival should abate, and he will more than likely regain full use of his legs."

"Oh, that's great news," Hank said, a relieved sigh escaping his lips.

"But, and please hear me when I say this, Wade won't be able to do a lot of things like he did before. His spine is going to be fragile and if he puts too much pressure or strain on his lower lumbar, he could exacerbate the current issue and would end up a paraplegic."

"What are you saying, doc?" Hank asked, his brow furrowed in confusion, not quite grasping the weight of his words.

"I know Wade is an excellent horseman. I had the pleasure of watching him at the NFR the year before he retired. Unfortunately, due to the area of his injury and his prior medical history, getting on a horse again won't be possible. All it would take is one swift jostle in the saddle, and your son won't ever walk again."

A guttural cry escaped Ray's lips, a raw, broken sound as she collapsed against Max, the steady strength of his arms a comforting presence against her trembling body.

Wade wasn't ever going to ride again.

I could feel the bitter taste of regret in my mouth, knowing it was all my fault. If he hadn't been there, risking his life to pull my reckless self out of danger, he would have never been shot.

Sensing my inner turmoil, Max gently guided Ray to a seat, the quiet concern in his eyes palpable, then came back to rest a hand on my lower back, his touch warm and reassuring.

"Let's go for a walk." He whispered, pushing me towards the door. He nodded at Hank, a silent gesture to keep an eye on Charlie and Ray, as he walked me out the doors of the hospital and to a bench located right outside.

He gestured for me to sit, his hand outstretched, but I huffed and plopped down onto the unforgiving concrete, the cold seeping into my thighs in defiance.

"Now, I want you to listen to me," he said, his eyes boring into mine, "and I want you to listen good," the last phrase a low growl. "None of this is your fault."

"But..." I started, the word catching in my throat, as I tried to reason with him. He held up a hand, fingers splayed in protest, and I rolled my eyes, the gesture a physical manifestation of my frustration. Even after all we had endured today, Max still had the ability to remain calm and steady.

"No buts. What happened with Wade was a freak accident. It wasn't anyone's fault, except the fucker who pulled the trigger and met his timely demise at the hand of Sheriff Cortez's wrath. Wade knew what he was getting into going into that building. He came in armed, ready to get you and Charlie to safety. He chose to put himself in danger because you two are important to him, to all of us."

A wave of despair washed over me, and tears flowed from in my eyes, salty and hot against my skin. Max took both of my hands in his, his touch warm and reassuring, and gently squeezed.

"Stella," he said, his voice firm but laced with warmth, "you and Charlie are family, and one thing I hope you've learned is that we will move heaven and earth to protect our family."

He coasted his thumb across my lower lash line, gathering the wetness as he went. My eyes were swollen and burning from all the crying; I was so exhausted. The weight of everything that had transpired over the last thirty-six hours weighed down on my shoulders.

"Baby, look at me," He whispered. "You are safe. It's over. Wade is going to be okay. Sure, he won't be able to ride anymore, but that's not gonna stop that stubborn fucker from finding ways to get himself in trouble. You're okay. We're okay."

"We're okay," I repeated, the steady thump of his heart a comforting rhythm against my ear as I leaned against his chest. He pulled me into a hug, a silent caress that communicated his love more profoundly than words ever could. His lips brushed my hair lightly as he held me close.

It was truly over. *We were safe.*

MAX

SIX MONTHS LATER

THE ORNATE FRAME of the full-length mirror in the groom's suite reflected my anxious face; I tugged at my bow tie, the starched fabric feeling stiff and uncomfortable against my neck. I didn't know why I was nervous. There had been no reservations when I'd proposed to Stella a month after her and Charlie's abduction. So, why was the fact that I was going to be walking down the aisle to my forever, giving me heart palpitations?

I had known, as soon as I had stepped foot out of the hospital the night of their rescue, that I wasn't going to wait to ask her to marry me. I already had the ring hidden in a shoebox at the top of my closet. How Stella had managed to avoid it still baffled me to this day.

I had taken her to the cove on one of our weekly "parents' day out" dates, the ring burning a hole in my pocket the whole way there. Remembering our first trip, Ray and I had carefully packed a picnic basket, the familiar weight of it a comforting echo of the day I'd fallen in love with Stella Jacobsen. Giving in to a wave of nostalgia, I decided on another fondue dessert night, the rich smell of melted chocolate filling the air around us.

Since the weather had cooled significantly, bringing in the brisk evening air of fall, the fireflies weren't as prevalent. I had wanted to wait until the first week of May to bring her here, just like Ma had done for Wade and me, but life was short and we weren't ever promised tomorrow. I couldn't wait one more day to have my ring on Stella's finger and the promise of forever.

After we had eaten, I drew Stella in between my legs, wrapping my arms around her to stave off the cold. As she leaned back into my chest, I crested my lips down the gentle column of her throat, feeling her pulse beat steadily beneath my lips.

"Marry me," I whispered, the words hanging in the air, heavy with unspoken emotion.

"Okay," she replied simply, like I had just asked her to take out the trash or pick something up at the store.

I turned her in my arms, allowing her legs to straddle my thighs, as I reached into my pocket to grab the ring. I held the glittering diamond between us, its facets catching the moonlight, causing it to twinkle and glow, just as the fireflies had once done.

"Marry me," I repeated, holding the ring out for her to take. I was a man of many words, but Stella always rendered me speechless. We didn't need words to express how we felt about each other, we just felt; raw and unfiltered.

"Max..." she whispered, my name barely audible above the sound of her own ragged breathing and the soft sobs escaping her lips. She looked up to meet my gaze, her emerald

eyes meeting mine and reflecting all the love we felt between us.

I placed my hand on her cheek, wiping away the tears that continued to fall. "Marry me, Stella. You and Charlie are my entire world. I can't imagine a future without you in it. I told you once that I want all of you. I want your morning bed head, your mid day laughter, and your night time yawns. I want to watch Charlie grow up, never missing another moment. I want to create a life together, one that may or may not involve miniature versions of us so Charlie can have a sibling.. or three."

She chuckled and wrapped her slender fingers around my wrist, holding my hand to her cheek. The tenderness in her gaze told me everything I needed to know; she was just as lost to me as I was to her.

"What do you say, Trouble? Will you put me out of my misery and marry me?"

"Of course, Cowboy."

We had opted for a small ceremony in town at the Mayfair. Connie had been more than happy to facilitate, even offering up complementary rooms for Stella and me to get ready in. We had opted to sleep separately the night before, leaning in to tradition, though it killed me not to roll over and pull her into my warm embrace in the middle of the night. Our family therapist had said it would be a good test of our healing to sleep apart the night of our wedding, leaning into the strength we both had gained through counseling.

Just as I straightened my bowtie for the fiftieth time, the door to my room burst open and a tiny tornado came rushing in, throwing herself at my legs.

"Dad!!" Charlie yelled, the tulle of her dress surrounding her in a cloud, like a loofa gone awry.

"Hey, little one. Shouldn't you be with Mama, helping her get ready?" I asked as I leaned down to pick her up. Her ringlets were tamed back into a semblance of a bun, a tiny crown of white wildflowers sitting atop her head. She leaned her head onto my shoulder and I did my best to shift as to not mess up her clearly styled updo.

"Mama, SUPISE!" she shouted, throwing her hands in the air as if she'd scored the game-winning touchdown. My brow furrowed in confusion as I tried to put together what she could mean. Before I even had a chance to form the slightest idea, all thoughts flew from my head as Stella rounded the corner.

Her long blonde hair, styled in old Hollywood starlet waves, framed her slender face, cascading around her like a waterfall. Her makeup was simple, a faint tinge of blush, some mascara, and a soft nude lipstick. She had opted for a simple dress, a slim fitting floor-length gown in a soft cream satin, the bust strapless and accenting her perfect breasts.

She held out her hands and did a little twirl, showing off the back of the dress that hugged her hips and full ass, high-lighted by a trail of buttons that acted as a runway to one of my favorite parts of her body.

As I struggled to pick my jaw up off the floor, she came closer, her heels clicking on the hardwood floor. I struggled to find the words to express her ethereal beauty, but fuck, was she beautiful. I couldn't believe that in less than an hour, this woman would be mine forever.

"Cat got your tongue, Cowboy?" she teased, reaching out to straighten the bowtie that I'd been fighting for the last half hour.

I scraped a hand over my freshly shaven face, pretending to wipe drool from the corners of my mouth. "Stella, fuck." I breathed, unable to form a coherent sentence.

"Bad word." Charlie scolded. Her new favorite thing was to call us out on anything and everything, cussing included. Nine times out of ten, a frustrated sigh would precede her little foot stomp and hands-on-hips stance, a clear signal that our lack of compliance was unacceptable. It happened constantly around the house.

Clothing left on the floor? *Charlie foot stomp.*

Forgot to put away the milk? *Charlie foot stomp.*

Didn't get out of bed exactly when she wanted you to? *Charlie foot stomp.*

Half the time, I didn't know whether to laugh or remind her that her mother and I were the parents of the household, but all she had to do was bat her little eyelashes in my direction, and I was a goner.

"Stella, baby, you look…" I took her hand in mine and twirled her out so I could get another good look at her. Charlie clapped from my other arm, enjoying watching her mama twirl around in her princess gown. I pulled Stella in close, my lips just a breath away from her ear, attempting to speak without little ears overhearing.

"You look fucking stunning, Mrs. Daniels." I said, placing a gentle kiss to right below her ear. The catch in her breath was enough to have my dick springing to life.

"Save it for after the ceremony," she scolded, a wicked smile playing on her lips. "But I wanted to give you something before we made things official."

She reached into the clutch she had deposited on the table just inside the door, pulling out a small white envelope. She brought it over to me and held it out between her fingers. Hesitantly, I took the envelope from her hands and ran my finger under the seam, sliding it open. I pulled the piece of paper from its resting place and unfolded it.

For the second time in a matter of minutes, I felt like I couldn't breathe.

I battled to hold back the tears, but the salty flood finally spilled over, tracing a path down my face.

"Are you sure?" I asked, looking up at Stella, who was fighting back tears of her own.

Reaching for my hand and twining our fingers together, she smiled up at me and brushed the tears from my cheeks. "I'd wish on all the fireflies on this green earth. She already calls you Dad. Why don't we make it official?"

I looked down at Charlie and smiled. A judge's gavel would make it official; she would legally be mine, and we'd be a real family, a unit bound by law.

"What do *you* say, little one? Want to be a Daniels?" I asked, lightly tickling her sides. She reached her chubby hands out and placed one on either side of my face, squishing my cheeks together affectionately.

"Lub yew Dad."

THE CEREMONY HAD GONE off without a hitch and Stella and I were officially married. The grin plastered to my face, a ridiculous, ear-to-ear stretch, was offensively large; I knew I had the two best girls on the planet by my side.

I watched from the head table while sipping on a whiskey as Stella and Charlie dominated the dance floor. It was well past Charlie's bedtime; however, this wedding was about her as much as it was about us.

From across the dance hall, I spotted Wade, seated at a table with a clear glass of dark liquor in hand. I raised my glass in a silent salute as he raised his back. It wasn't lost on me that there was a darkness in his gaze that hadn't been present just six months prior. He seemed haunted, hollow, lost.

I knew that he would brush it off as just a long day, but I made a mental note to talk to him about it, or at the very least, talk to Ray to make sure he was coping okay.

Stella, Charlie, and I had all gone through multiple weeks of therapy. Each one of us had demons that needed to be addressed. Thankfully, Charlie was young and wasn't going to have much recollection about the events she'd been forced to play witness to, but Stella and I had a long road ahead to healing. I worried that Wade wasn't coping well, especially since he had refused therapy.

His healing had been extensive, and he was still dealing with some lingering pain. He had spent almost three months in physical therapy, regaining the strength and mobility in his legs. Although his gait had mostly returned to normal, a subtle limp occasionally betrayed his injury, a barely perceptible hitch in his step.

He hadn't so much as tacked up a horse after being told he wasn't going to be able to ride again. I knew that it was a tough pill to swallow. For Wade, riding was more than just a hobby; it was a balm for his soul, the feel of the horse beneath him a comforting presence. Having that stripped away was like taking away one of his limbs.

I hoped he was talking to someone, anyone, even just Ray, to ease the weight of his grief.

A sweaty and panting Stella plopped into the chair beside me, reaching for the beer she had left on the table before dancing the night away. The way her throat bobbed as she swallowed was intoxicating, her delicate movement arousing a storm of lust within me.

Charlie plodded over, the weight of exhaustion hanging heavy over her head. I brushed her sweat slicked hair that had fallen from her bun away from her face and picked her up to settle her on my lap. She nuzzled into my warm embrace, closing her eyes as sleep fought to overtake her. Stella laughed, the sound bubbling up from deep inside, as she rubbed a hand over Charlie's back, offering the gentle, warm comfort only a mother could provide.

"Someone's tired." I said softly, leaning down to kiss Charlie on top of her head. Her breathing had evened out, and she was dead weight in my arms.

Stella leaned over to whisper in my ear, "The night is young, Mr. Daniels. Take us home?" she purred.

I responded by gripping the back of her neck and pulling her to me for a searing kiss. "With pleasure, Mrs. Daniels."

THE END

acknowledgments

Whew. What a ride.

I'm sure when a writer tells you that characters are screaming in their heads, your first inkling is that we've gone crazy. I thought the same thing… until Max and Stella.

When I first dreamed of writing a book, I couldn't ever nail down one specific genre, theme, plot, or characters. These two came barreling into my world like a thunderstorm, and I couldn't get them out once they started feeding me their story.

I'll forever be thankful for these two characters for kicking off my writing career and helping me accomplish a dream that has always been in the back of my mind since the day I picked up my first chapter book in the first grade.

But- without the help of some amazing people in my life, Max and Stella never would have been brought to fruition.

My Husband:

Honestly, without you deploying to the middle of the frozen tundra at the beginning of 2025, I don't think I ever would have written this book. But, before then, I have you to thank for always giving me the green light to follow whatever crazy dream I come up with. You've never once told me no, even when we were crazy teenagers with even crazier schemes. You are my right hand man, my confidante, my (sometimes) better half, and my best friend. I couldn't imagine doing life without you.

To My Parents:

Please don't read this book. But, if you decide you *have to* because you want to be supportive (like you've done my entire life), skip chapters 20,21,23, and 24. Additional but, if you decide you must read them, know it is not indicative of my home life and it is a complete work of fiction… partially.

To My Beta and Alpha Readers:

From the bottom of my heart, I cannot express how much your help with bringing this book to life made a difference. Without your grammar checking, your suggestions, and your hyping me up, this book never would have made it past the confines of a Google Doc. You guys are the real MVPs.

To All The Teachers Who Molded Me:

Jimmy Andrews and Chad Johnson- Thank you for always encouraging me to follow my passion for writing and reading, even if I frustrated the hell out of you both with reading ahead on assignments and spending time writing down short stories instead of notes.

My fourth-grade teacher who said there was no way I was reading a one hundred chapter book by Margaret Mitchell in elementary school… eat my shorts.

To the college professor who said that my work would never be marketable because it was too "mainstream" and "gritty" - kindly, fuck you. I didn't need your crappy creative writing degree to be a writer anyway.

To Teenage Me:

Look at all you've accomplished. You've been through hell and back to get here, but you've made it through. Even if you questioned every single day whether you were making the right choices, they led you to the wonderfully beautiful life you created. From reading fanfics on Wattpad, writing short stories on the Neopets forums, and constantly writing down scenarios and scenes in your note margins. You did it. You truly fucking did it.

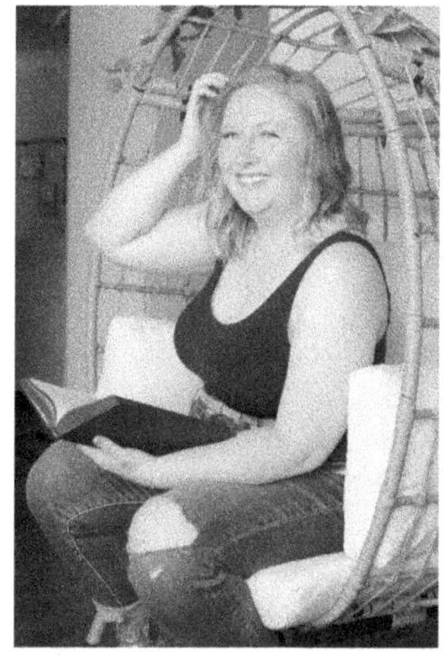

Ashley Templin was born and raised in Fredericksburg, Virginia where she spent the majority of her adult life. Upon marrying her high school sweetheart, Jacob, she relocated to wherever his Army career took them. They have lived in New York, Virginia, and Georgia as of current and can't wait to see where they will end up next. Together, they have a daughter named Mellie, four cats, and a basset hound named Toby. As an avid reader, she found herself constantly bombarded with characters wanting their stories written, hence the dream of being an author. She enjoys a romance novel that brings you to your knees with emotional storylines, spice, and characters that are relatable. In her spare time, she owns a handmade children's clothing boutique, plays Animal Crossing, and spends time finding ways to annoy her husband.

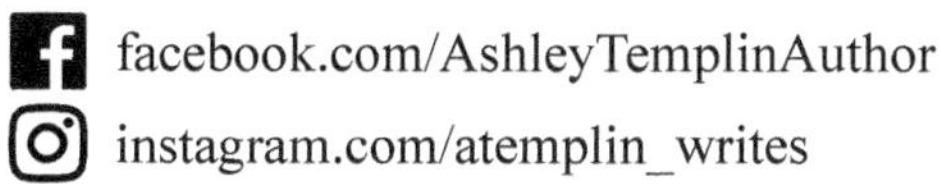

facebook.com/AshleyTemplinAuthor

instagram.com/atemplin_writes